CONTENTS

PAST PLUPERFECT

by Val Whitehouse

Chapter 1

Kate looked at the cream slice and cappuccino that she had pre-ordered for Sally, wondering if she could place the saucer over the coffee to keep it hot, just as her ever-patient mother had done for her bloody father's tea. She decided that the froth would splurge down the side of the cup and the lovely heart shape on the foam would be spoilt. Added to that, it probably wouldn't work. The foam would be a better blanket than a cold china saucer. Her father's tea certainly hadn't benefitted, judging by the way he had swept it angrily off the table, soaking the cloth and her tearful mother's apron. Kate felt the old resentment rising just as Sally arrived to take her mind off it.

"Sorry I'm late. I just had to look at a Facebook thingy whatsit before I came out."

The two friends couldn't have been more different, both physically and in their attitudes to life. Sally was a slim and Nordic blonde while Kate was dark and Celtic; Sally was meticulously careful while Kate treasured a little anarchy in her soul. They had met for their usual Saturday morning indulgence: coffee, pastries and gossip. It was always in the same place, Jo-Jo's; always at the same hour, eleven; always just the two of them, no matter who else they might be having significant relationships with at the time. You could call it a ritual, although that might be endowing it with too much importance. However, if they ever had to miss out on it, they both felt superstitiously anxious about the following week. It was the time when they caught up on all that was happening, and their discussions had often been the basis for major decisions in their lives. So, not just gossip: quality analysis. And fun, of course, allowing them to unwind from stressful jobs and even more stressful social lives.

"What Facebook thingy whatsit was it this time?" asked an amused Kate. Sally's inability to use any I.T. technical term was legendary. She delicately scooped froth into her mouth before replying.

"You know I've been searching for old school friends. Well, this face popped up with one of those do-you-also-know messages."

"I can't believe you're doing this. It seems so unlike you to hark back to people we haven't seen since those halcyon days. I've always assumed that the only people who put themselves up there want to boast about something great that's happened to them, especially if their school days were particularly unsuccessful. You know, 'Ner ner ner- ner ner, I'm better than you-ou' sort of thing," laughed Kate.

"I'm sure there's some of that going on. But I think most people are just curious about what happened to friends they've lost touch with. When you think about it, you and I spent seven years at the same Secondary, yet we've only kept up with one another. Aren't you at all curious about Pru or Cassie or Mary?" asked Sally.

"Or Jo or Jacky or Morgan. Yes, yes, I am now you come to mention it. I mean, I wasn't. I have enough trouble with my own life - and yours, of course - without worrying about how things worked out for anyone else.

But, yes. It would be nice to know if Mary stuck with her boyfriend Gil, and so on. Whatever was Gil short for, by the way?"

"No idea. Anyway, I just thought I'd dabble and see if any of those names came up."

"And?" asked Kate, now beginning to be genuinely interested.

Sally carefully scraped her plate clean, not wishing to waste any morsel of cream slice. She was as meticulous about it as she was about everything. Kate imagined that Sally would be just as conscientious about marking her pupils' essays, and probably just as annoying in her attention to detail!

"Indeed they did, with varying amounts of information. You have to read between the lines with some of them, but others suffer from verbal diarrhea," replied Sally, wiping her neat mouth with her neat napkin.

"No change there, then," said Kate. "Let me guess. Jacky gives half a page and you even find out the colour of her kitchen walls, whereas Lyn's very cagey about everything."

"Lyn's not even up there! But you're right about Jacky. Do you know, she's married to a fantastically successful solicitor, has two amazingly talented children and lives in a spectacular house in Hampstead Garden Suburb!"

"Sounds about right for Jacky. Ever living off the talents of others."

"Oh, Kate, that's a bit harsh. She was just never quite as good at anything as she would like to have been."

"Or as good as the rest of us. We were quite an academic lot, except for Jacky. She must be so pleased to let everyone know what a success she is now!"

"I sometimes think your work at the Unit makes you look at kids with jaundiced eyes!" said Sally, half seriously.

"Not jaundiced, just informed. The Adolescent Unit of a Psychiatric Clinic is a great big mixing bowl. All the ingredients of disturbed lives and character disorders are in there waiting to be watered down to acceptable proportions by an expert chef. Seeing their extremes helps me to recognise traits in ordinary kids. I often think 'There but for the grace of Thingy…' Jacky's a good example. She desperately wanted to be one of the clever kids, but there was no way she was going to be. She might have turned resentful and jealous, and become a bitter woman who constantly said life wasn't fair. But no-one ever made her feel inadequate, either at home or at school, so she happily and confidently tagged along with us and some of our brilliance - ho ho - rubbed off on her. Everyone accepted that she was one of our crowd. Things could have been so much worse for her. Do you see what I'm talking about?" Kate asked.

"I think so. You mean if she'd had a more envious character, or if her parents had been more pushy, or if we'd been spiteful to her, then she might have turned out sort of maladjusted?"

"Exactly. She was lucky. Lots of the kids at my Unit have had a really raw deal. I'm sure I'd have been far worse than they are if I'd had their problems. So Jacky's got a lot to be grateful for."

"Well, she certainly sounded very happy about her life. I must admit to a stab of jealousy, Kate. What wouldn't I give for a nice lawyer and two kids!"

"You realise that I'm recording this conversation under the table and I'm taking it straight round to Mark!" laughed Kate.

Suddenly Sally's face crumpled. Her hand flew to cover her mouth as if she was afraid of what might force its way through her unwilling lips.

"Oh, Lord. Have I put my foot in it? I'm sorry, Sal. Are things difficult with Mark at the moment?" Kate asked, anxious for her friend.

"He's with Jo this weekend. All weekend. He says she's going through a hard time at work right now, so she needs his support," Sally explained quietly.

Kate had never understood Sally's relationship with Mark. He was already married - unhappily, he said, though Kate was unsure about that. She wondered if he wasn't just having his wedding cake and eating it, leading Sally along by the ring in her nose which should have been firmly on her finger by now!

"Bastard! Sorry, sorry. I know it's none of my business. Tell me to bugger off, if you like."

"Bugger off," said Sally half-heartedly.

"Is he ever going to leave Jo properly? I mean, how long have you and he been together?"

"Three years. But it's hard for him, Kate, you must see that," pleaded Sally. "Jo isn't exactly stable, so he's got to choose the right time to tell her he wants a divorce. If she went to pieces and killed herself or something, Mark would feel guilty for the rest of his life. And what chance would our relationship have of surviving if it was built on that sort of foundation?"

"But, Sally, do you really mean to tell me that he's never had a 'right time' in three whole years?"

"It's not really three years, though, is it? I mean, at first it was just a friendship, and even when we became lovers it was just an affair to start with. It's only been about a year since he's been looking for ways of being with me and leaving her."

"Even so. A year's a long time. Surely…"

Sally interrupted, "It's no good going on about it, Kate. I know he'll leave when he can. I must be patient and trust his judgement. There's no panic."

"Oh, really? And who was it last week who was bemoaning the fact that she was 28 and wanting a baby?"

"I was pre-menstrual. You should never take me too seriously about emotional issues when my period's due."

"Feminist alert! You know I don't go along with all that hormonal stuff," said Kate. "It's been thrown at us by men for so long that we've started to believe it!"

"Anyway, that's enough. I'm Mark-less this weekend, and I'm just going to get on with it without any whinges," said Sally decisively. "Now tell me all about your week. Is Robin all right? "

"He's made a miraculous recovery from the heart condition he had last week, and from the probably-severed Achilles tendon the week before. This week it's incipient Alzheimer's, I think," mocked Kate.

Sally laughed. She always laughed when Kate dissected Robin, and she felt grateful to her friend for lightening the atmosphere and trying to take her out of herself. Robin's hypochondria was a constant source of fun.

"Why Alzheimer's?" she asked.

"Oh, he forgot what he'd come into the kitchen for last night, so naturally …"

"How on earth do you keep a straight face?" laughed Sally.

"I often don't. But I try to turn my laughter into something that he can laugh at, too, rather than just ridiculing him. He doesn't react well to ridicule, our Robin."

"Who does? But what do you mean about turning the laughter into…"

"Well, I told him the story of this friend of mine who was always forgetting why he'd gone into a room. He took no notice of it until the day he found himself on the stairs and not only could he not remember where he was going, but he couldn't even remember whether he was going up or down! Robin loved that, and forgot to panic about himself."

"You're awfully good for him. Lots of people would be driven to distraction by him. I mean, he's so unsure of himself."

"Mmmm. Self-centred is more like it, if you ask me. He's so focused on his own physical well-being. Partly that's because his job needs him to be on top of things and alert, I realise that, and he finds physical fitness is all part of it. *Mens sana* and all that. Hence the membership of the gym and his pre-occupation with exercise. I'm not complaining about that, believe me. His torso is something to behold, and I do – as often as I can! And I know that the advertising world can be quite cut-throat. He does need to keep on dazzling clients with clever ideas, so his fitness is of paramount importance."

"He wouldn't ever resort to drugs to give him that extra oomph, would he?" Sally asked.

"Robin? No, never. That's one of the plus sides of his health obsession. He'd never put anything dodgy into his beautiful body. And he's seen so many of the coke-heads go into downward spirals and spin out of control. They lose their accounts as well as their health, so what's the point? No, Robin won't ever go down that path. Thank goodness. Touch wood!"

Both of them tapped the table three times and laughed. It was a habit from school days, when they'd all tried to ward off bad exam questions and acne!

"Are you and Robin up to anything exciting over the weekend?"

"Let me see. We might see a film tonight - but we'll probably end up just having a nice meal out. The trouble with the cinema is that you can't talk."

"That doesn't seem to stop most people. I get so fed up with couples chatting their way through films, as if they were just in their own front rooms," complained Sally.

"Yeah. They can't seem to see the difference. It drives me bonkers, too. But I always tell them to be quiet."

"Oh, I do, too. I just hate having to do it. Anyway, what might you go to see?"

"That's the problem," laughed Kate. "We probably won't agree. He'll want action and special effects, and

I'll want comedy. So we'll end up going for a meal and talking about why we're so incompatible."

"At least you'll be incompatible together," sighed Sally.

"I know. Sorry. What are your plans?"

"I'll keep myself busy, busy, busy. There's an exciting trip to Tesco this afternoon, closely followed by somewhere to buy the paint for the bathroom. Then I'll start decorating if there's nothing on tele tonight - and there usually isn't on a Saturday, for some inexplicable reason. I'll try to finish it all off on Sunday," replied Sally, forcing herself to sound cheerful.

"I thought Mark was supposed to be doing up the bathroom."

"He was. He still would. It's not that he's trying to get out of it. It's just that we have better things to do with our time together than asphyxiate ourselves on the smell of paint. I thought it would be a nice surprise for him when he pops in next Tuesday."

"Well, I'm sorry, Sally, but I don't think you should be knocking yourself out all weekend just to make life nicer for darling Mark. You know how knackered you always get at this stage of the term, and you need all your strength to cope with 9B! Think of those eager faces turning up to you for enlightenment, and all you can manage is a yawn. Why don't you come out with us on Sunday? It's the Antiques Fair at Alexandra Palace," said Kate the temptress.

"Get thee behind me! I ought to do the bathroom..."

"Compromise. Start the bathroom today, but give yourself tomorrow off. You deserve a bit of fun. Oh, I'd love you to come, Sally. You know what Robin will be like. 'I just want to look at these film posters, love. I'll meet you under the big window in an hour.' And of course he'll forget to look at his watch, so I'll have to go hunting for him. But if you're there, I won't go hunting for him because I'll have you to keep me company. And you know how we like to go to that lovely stall that does the Art Nouveau jewellery..."

Sally capitulated at once, as Kate had hoped she would. "O.K. You're on - as long as Robin won't mind my tagging along."

"You know he won't. You're the best thing since sliced whatsit as far as he's concerned. We'll pick you up at ten. All right? "

"Thanks. I must admit I was only tackling the bathroom because I wanted to be fully occupied so I didn't dwell on thoughts of Jo and Mark together. I love Ally Pally. That sounds great."

With that hurried arrangement, the friends decided that the rest of Saturday was becoming an insistent interruption that they could no longer ignore. They both departed for their separate lives with kisses and hugs and promises not to be late on Sunday. Sally decided that she could manage without a supermarket shop over the weekend, accepting the grind of having to buy food on her way home from work on Monday instead. She dashed off to buy paint and cheap paintbrushes, wondering as she did so why anybody spent megapounds on 'good' brushes when it was so easy simply to discard the cheap ones when you finished the job. She had already chosen the colour from an array of cards collected the previous month and, being Sally, she had not wavered from her decision. Turquoise walls would look good with the grey marble tiles and the dark grey towels she already had. She'd get 'bright' without 'garish' and Mark hadn't objected too much. Left to him, everything would be white but he agreed that the final decision had to be hers seeing as it was her flat. "Big of him!" had been muttered by Kate. Kate herself had made her way to Tesco for the weekly shop, cursing that she hadn't got round to doing an on-line order. On the other hand, she thought, it was nice that she could now expand her Sunday evening meal option to include the possibility of Sal joining them. Robin would be fine with that as he felt almost as much concern about Sally as Kate did. They both admired her loyalty to Mark whilst bemoaning the fact that they could see no happy ending to her relationship with him. Since school days, Kate had seen Sally's steadfast attachment to people and jobs as a double-sided coin. It was a source of comfort and stability for Sally but it could also cause her pain when the objects of her affection were not as careful to preserve the bond. Kate knew that Sally had tried to stay in touch with all their school friends but had been disappointed by their dropping out one by one. This possibility of reaching out to them again would, she hoped, build some bridges to give Sally other avenues to walk down instead of sticking to the sole highway that was Mark. It could be rather exciting.

Chapter 2

Kate hurried home, wanting to catch Robin before he left for the gym. As soon as she tried the key in the lock she knew she was too late. The Chubb was on, so Robin must be out. She cursed as she struggled with the door. The wood had warped enough to make the Chubb really difficult to manage. It was a work of art to pull in just the right place whilst turning the key, especially if you were loaded with shopping as she often was. Robin would eventually do something about it if she nagged him enough. But she hated going on about it. It made her feel like a wife, which was something she had long ago decided she would never be. Wifedom equalled slavery to Kate. She knew it was foolish to feel that way in this day and age but the picture of her parents' marriage would come unbidden into her mind. How many times had she come home from school to find her mum in tears over a scorched shirt or a burnt pudding? Kate had vowed that it would never have the slightest chance of happening to her.

She slammed the door behind her, the equivalent of kicking the cat. Her anger over her mother's downtrodden state melded with her exasperation at Robin. "Sod, sod, sod!" seemed to sum it up adequately. She saw a scribbled note on the kitchen table: 'GONE TO GYM.' Kate scoffed. Talk about stating the bleeding obvious! Surely he could have waited for her - she was only fifteen minutes later than she'd said she'd be. However, rational thoughts started to creep into her mind. After all, he wasn't to know how late she'd be. And at least he'd left a note. She sighed as she put the kettle on, and the ritual of tea-making relaxed her tension somewhat. She noted that he'd emptied the dishwasher and wiped down the surfaces. Oh, he wasn't too bad, really. So what if he put his biceps before her; they were lovely biceps! It could be worse, she admitted, and immediately remembered Sally.

Kate took her tea into the lounge and continued her line of thought. She and Sally had been friends right from the first week of secondary school and their friendship had never wavered. When Sally had gone to York University, she'd phoned Kate whenever she felt she could afford to, and had written frequently in between. Kate mused that Sally had probably been the only student who still used pen and paper for communication. Her faithful friendship, even when she was sharing digs with three other girls who had obviously become good mates, had drawn an equivalent response from Kate. Would she have kept up the link without Sally's persistence? She thought so, but she wasn't totally sure. But now, after seventeen years, they were practically joined at the hip, as Robin used to say. The great thing was that he said it without resentment. Robin liked Sally. That was important to Kate. It wasn't a case of 'Love me, love my dog'; it was much more profound than that trite cliché. The thing was, anyone who didn't like Sally would have been exhibiting such poor judgement that Kate couldn't have tolerated them.

It was Robin who had first expressed concern over Sally's relationship with Mark. He didn't make value judgements about the fact that Mark was married: he felt that wasn't his business at all. No, it wasn't that. He just didn't feel comfortable with Mark's continuing to stay with Jo while constantly promising Sally that he was going to leave. Robin had accidentally met Jo while he was being interviewed by a rival advertising agency. She'd been the person assigned to show him round, which had included a quick lunch in the canteen. They'd talked mostly about work and the firm, of course, but some personal things were touched upon. She'd mentioned that her husband Mark was an English teacher, and it suddenly dawned on Robin that she might be the Jo who was supposed to be so unstable and vulnerable that Mark was in fear of upsetting her. This Jo sharing lunch with him was extremely attractive and vivacious and seemed exceedingly well-adjusted and mellow. After all, he reasoned, the ad agency would hardly entrust him to the care of someone who couldn't handle entertaining strangers and presenting an attractive picture of the workplace. Robin didn't exactly probe, but he did manage to ask her what she and her husband were doing the following weekend. He knew Mark had arranged to be with Sally. Jo had grimaced and told him she was visiting her parents because her husband was going to a Teachers' Conference. It all tied in.

He had brought this information home to Kate, showing genuine concern for Sally. He was convinced that there was no evidence for Mark's assertion that Jo was fragile. Although Kate had argued that mental instability was often hidden behind a confident mask, doubts started to creep in. From that time on, Kate and Robin had been wary about Mark and had watched his remarks for inconsistencies. They decided they would not say or do anything to encourage Sally's hopes, but would try to present the voice of caution whenever Sally talked about her future with Mark. They didn't feel they had the right, or the proof, to scupper the relationship; but Kate was open about not particularly liking him. She hoped this wouldn't mar her friendship with Sally but she felt strongly that a true friend couldn't just sit back and not voice an opinion. It was a tricky tightrope to negotiate and Kate sometimes felt close to tumbling.

Thinking about Sally led Kate to remembering their conversation about contacting old friends through Facebook and social media. She decided she'd just take a quick look to see what names she recognised. She went up to the study and logged on. She was surprised to see so many from her years at the school. Yes, there was Jacky, just as Sally had said. Kate couldn't help smiling at the excessive superlatives that dotted Jacky's text. She hoped that Jacky really did live that triumphant life and wasn't hiding disappointment behind a smokescreen of boastful lies. Now, who else was up there? Aha! There was Mary. Kate skimmed through to see if she'd married Gil, her boyfriend for years while they were at school. Yes, she had. But what was this? Oh dear, a divorce after six years. And Mary was bringing up a son on her own now. Suddenly, Kate felt a need to communicate with Mary, whom she had liked a lot. At that moment, the telephone rang. She picked up the study extension and listened to vague crackles until Sally's voice broke through sounding as if she were in a swimming pool. Kate strained to hear.

"Kate? Tricky problem. You ready for this? The colour I chose isn't being produced any more – the colour card I picked up must have been way out of date, which I've already complained about to the supervisor. I don't like any of the equivalent shades. But Fired Earth do a lovely pale aqua - very Arts-and-Craftsy - but it's much more expensive than the own brand equivalent. Decisions, decisions. What to do?"

"Is there a significant difference in colours? Which one do you like best?"

"The Fired Earth one looks just right. But the other one is quite close…"

"And how much paint will you need?"

"Um. About ten litres, I think."

"So how much more will it cost to get the Fired Earth? I mean, are we really talking significant amounts here?"

"I see where you're going. Don't spoil the ship, et cetera. Right. Fired Earth it is. Thanks, Kate. See you tomorrow."

"Hang on, Sally. I thought I might try to reach out to contact Mary. What do you think?"

"Great idea. You're really on board for this now, aren't you?"

"That's a definite maybe. Anyway, see you tomorrow. And no doubt I'll see the colour of the bathroom by looking at your fingernails! Ciao!"

Kate turned back to the computer but was disappointed to see no e-mail address for Mary. She studied the list of names again and realised that Pru had been Mary's closest friend. The information on her showed that she'd turned to writing as a career and had actually been published. It said she was working on a novel. No personal details at all - nothing about a husband, kids. But she did give an e-mail address. Kate thought she'd probably given it so people could contact her about her work, but she had to expect personal stuff, too. Kate quickly tapped out a message: *'Hello, Pru. It's Kate Nelson. Remember me? Sally James (yes, we're still best friends) told me that she thought a lot of our old gang might not mind being contacted on Facebook and such. There's been far too much blood under the bridge to write in detail, but I'd love to catch up on news. Could we meet?'* Kate wondered if she was sending too little information to interest Pru. Would she need something startling to make her curious enough to reply? Well, there was nothing startling in her life! Pru would have to want to get in touch just for the hell of it. She wondered if she should add a question about Mary, but thought it might be a bit insulting to say 'Hi, it's really Mary I wanted to contact.' Not that she'd put it quite as baldly as that! But Pru would read between the lines, which had always been one of her skills. You'd never get anything past Pru. In fact, in one of their end-of-term extravaganzas when they had all written a cod Restoration Comedy, she'd been 'Prudence Perspicacity'. Kate smiled as she recalled those plays and sketches, especially the ones they wrote in the Sixth Form, which were really quite witty (or at least they'd thought they were back then). Maybe if they'd all gone on to Oxbridge they could have become stars of the Footlights or something. Pru had been the driving force behind their writing but all of them had contributed. Kate wondered if Pru now wrote under her real name. If she did, there might be something of hers in the local bookshop. Kate quickly sent off the e-mail and hurried out to Argosy Books.

She loved bookshops. There was something about the smell of them, and the far-away look on people's faces as they read the blurbs and propelled themselves into the world of the book for a few minutes. Kate looked for 'Prudence Fisher' in the Fiction section, hoping but doubting. Nothing. She sighed, disappointed in spite of her assumption that there'd be nothing there. The next step was to find one of the assistants. They were busy, but fortunately the shop took on extra staff on Saturdays so they didn't mind consulting the computer for her.

"Fisher... Fisher... There's nothing under Prudence

Fisher in Fiction. Shall I try Poetry?" asked the ginger-haired girl behind the counter.

"Yes, please," replied Kate, remembering that Pru had written poems at school, even though she'd tended to keep them private.

"Here we are. She's got two anthologies of her own, and she's included in three others. We've got one of them in stock and we can order the others if you want them. One's from a Feminist press, which might take a bit longer."

Kate decided that she'd just go for the one on the shelf and see how she liked it. The girl pointed an ink-stained finger at the Poetry section. "They're in alphabetical order. Will you be all right?"

"I think I can manage that," said Kate acerbically. However, she smiled sweetly at the girl, knowing that so many people nowadays didn't seem capable of tracing their way through their ABC without huge intellectual effort. She made her way to the Poetry section and lifted down the book. It felt strange, holding Pru's words in her hand. She flicked through quickly and gasped at the price for such a slim volume. Twenty-five pages costing as much as a novel! No wonder poetry doesn't sell very well, she thought unkindly. Then she remembered what Sally always said, that poetry was so distilled and required much deeper thought from both writer and reader. Maybe it was still value for money. Pru had always insisted on finding just the right word whenever they wrote their joint plays, driving everyone wild at times.

When Kate got home again, Robin was still out so she decided to try a couple of Pru's poems. She settled herself comfortably on the sofa and opened the book at random.

HISTORY

At school, History was conveniently chopped

Into small, digestible chunks.

Half a term to consume the Elizabethans

(Including their major playwrights, of course.)

Then a gulp of brave, blinded Nelson

With his telescope held to his useless eye.

A few chews to crush the enemies:

Napoleon, Hitler, Stalin - all foreign, you'll note.

Only later did we try to fit individuals,

Ordinary people with ambitions like ours,

Into those clearly defined packets.

How many groundlings had wondered at
Shakespeare?

How many sailors had suffered with Nelson?

How many 'foreigners' had followed their heroes,

Unaware they'd been classified as villains?

Did they know they were part of History?

Ordinary folk don't signify

Except as statistics on a page.

Yet their lives are far more crucial

To the world rolling on

Than the occasional named hero.

Real people, loved or tolerated,

Preserved in the memory

Like flies in amber.

They lived on in fond tales.

Though sepia photographs are only kept now

For their interesting stilted poses,

And no-one remembers the faces let alone the names,

Yet those faces were parents

And their children inherit the earth.

Those names still chime through classroom registers,

Connecting then and now.

History, with all its seeming significance,

Doesn't amount to much.

People are the real history books.

Kate had to smile. The poem was so typically Pru as she remembered her, always politically aware but always with an emphasis on humanity. She had been at the forefront of drives to send money or clothes to war-torn or drought-benighted places. Dear Pru! The thought sent her running to her computer, eager to see if there had been a reply to her e-mail. There hadn't, of course. She realised that Pru would be out and about on a Saturday. She might even be away for the weekend.

Kate returned to the book and was about to start another poem when she heard Robin's key in the door. He erupted into the room and launched himself onto the sofa, hugging her extravagantly. He smelt of antiseptic shampoo, which he always used to combat the dandruff he was constantly expecting to get. Showered, shaved and pleasantly tired, he was content to snuggle.

"Did you have a good chin-wag with Sally? How are things between her and the Tide Mark?"

"He's a mixture of that and the Water Mark this weekend - dirty scum and gone away!" Kate relayed bitterly. "He's decided that Jo is particularly fragile and needs his supportive presence right now."

"You mean they've probably got a good party to go to. Bastard!"

"My feelings exactly. So Sally was going to spend all her precious time painting the bathroom so it would look nice for Mark when he deigned to see her next."

"That's a bit abject, isn't it? Is she turning into a doormat?" asked Robin.

"I've persuaded her to come to Ally Pally with us tomorrow. Is that O.K?"

"Of course. Maybe she'd like to come round tonight as well."

"Robin, you're an angel. But I think that would be over-doing the protection, don't you? Sally's a strong woman. She needs to keep her independent streak polished and ready for action, just in case she really needs it."

"You think he's going to ditch her and stick with the luscious Jo?"

"In a way, I wish he would. But I think he'll carry on this little game for as long as he can. After all, he gets the best of both of them, doesn't he?"

"I couldn't hack it. The tension would drive me insane. I'd be forever worrying that my fibs would be found out and that I'd end up with neither woman."

"I'm glad to hear it. And you're right, too. You'd never manage a double life."

"Why try? I'm very happy with the single one I've got. Not that it's exactly single. I mean, we're not married but we are a pair, aren't we? Aren't we?" urged Robin.

Kate laughed. Her reluctance to make their union official made Robin ever-so-slightly insecure, and she loved it. She kissed his nose. "Who'd like a nice cup of tea?"

"Great. And then we can decide which film we're not going to see."

Chapter 3

The queue for the Antiques Fair wound round the building. Kate, Sally and Robin joined it resignedly and waited to shuffle forward as the front people started to go in. Once it started moving, it really didn't take long.

"Is it all right if I go off in search of film stuff?" asked Robin predictably. He knew that Kate liked to go round in tandem so she could share her discoveries and discuss possible purchases, and he was on to a good thing with Sally there to keep Kate company.

"Go on then. Try not to buy anything too huge, though. We're running out of wall space."

"There's still loads of room in the lounge," said Robin, ducking to avoid the swinging arm that he knew would be thrown his way.

"No, no, a thousand times no," squealed Kate. "I put up with 'Goodfellas' and 'Angel Heart' in the hall, I tolerate

'Chinatown' in the bedroom, I accept 'Once Upon a Time in America' in the study. I even quite like all the lobby cards dotted around. But the lounge is sacrosanct."

"Suppose I were to find 'Breakfast at Tiffany's'…."

"Oh sure. You're likely to find one here at an affordable price!" scoffed Kate.

"I can dream. There it will be, tucked behind 'Red Arrow', where nobody's noticed it because it's in a bag marked 'Tiff' and nobody's heard of a film called 'Tiff'. I carry it away in triumph, beating my chest like Tarzan, offering it to my Jane…"

"Yeah, yeah. Tell you what, if you find it I'll be happy to hang it. Now off you go and search, boy!"

Robin scampered off, leaving the women to browse more languidly. They decided to start at the opposite side of the hall to the entrance, hoping to beat the crowd a bit. Sally was looking for another Minton Secessionist plate to add to her collection, and Kate wanted to look at the Charles Horner enamel pendants at a jewellery stall.

They loved going shopping together when they were really in the market for buying because they encouraged each other to spoil themselves and be extravagant. But if ever their hearts weren't in it or they were in dire financial straits, they contrived to go shopping with different people. They didn't exactly decide to do that, but it had evolved over the years. It was subliminal somehow.

"I love this plate," exclaimed Sally. "The colours are just right to tone in with the new bathroom."

"Show me your fingernails," ordered Kate. "Yes, you're right. The paint lodged under there looks wonderful with the plate! But are you sure about putting an expensive Minton in the humble old bathroom?"

"Why not? Everyone sits in there contemplating the walls, so let's give them something to admire."

They continued browsing and buying, buying and browsing for about an hour ending up with the Minton plate and a silver and enamel pendant along with a silver letter opener and a wooden duck. Then they turned to the coffee bar with smug smiles of complete satisfaction on their faces. They queued for tea and bacon butties, vying with each other as to who should pay for them. Sally won. They looked for somewhere to sit and were lucky to find a space, claiming the chairs before they could be nabbed by someone else.

"How did the painting go?" asked Kate, opening her mouth wider than seemed physically possible to accommodate the food.

"Ceiling done, and the walls painted with the first coat. So I'm pleased with it. It did me good, too. There's nothing like physical work to take your mind off things."

"Things being Mark, I take it?"

"Absence makes my heart grow fonder, cliché though that might be."

"I think you'll find that that's 'absinthe makes the heart grow fonder'," interrupted Kate.

"When he's away, I just can't help thinking about him and what it would be like if he were there. Making a meal, watching a film, they're just completely different activities without him."

"Course they are. But you're a very self-sufficient woman. You may miss him but you're not going to fall apart when he's not around. I mean, look at you, clutching a new plate and tucking into brunch like a good 'un. We're having a good time, aren't we?"

"Yes, sure. I'll enjoy the day wandering around here, especially as it's with you. But I can't help wishing Mark would be at home tonight so I could share the things I've bought with him. It's no reflection on you, Kate. You'd be the same about Robin. Remember when he had to go off to his Gran's funeral last summer leaving you at home? You went all wimpy. Tears were shed, I seem to recall!"

"That was different!" Kate insisted. "He was upset about his Gran and I wanted to be around to comfort him. I was crying for his sake, not mine."

"Maybe. But methinks the lady doth protest too much. There was rather a large element of Poor Kate Alone about it. Don't worry, I won't tell him you missed him more than you ever let on. Though why you should want to hide it from him, I'll never understand."

"Independence, my dear Shrink!"

Sally laughed. "You haven't called me your Shrink for ages. I was beginning to wonder if I'd lost my role in life. Figuring out your deep, dark secrets has always been so satisfying!"

"Sally, this is not the time to start delving into how my parents interacted. Just accept my plea for independence at face value. And stop deflecting the conversation from an examination of your feelings, you worm."

Sally's face became serious, which was quite a feat given the bacon fat dribbling gently down her chin. She looked into Kate's eyes. "My feelings are obvious and unchangeable, Kate. Please don't try to turn me away from Mark. It's just not possible, and you'll hurt me so much in the attempt. I know you don't like him much. And I understand that the dislike is based on fears for me. I'm truly grateful for your concern and for your love, believe me. But there's nothing I can do about my feelings for Mark. It's as if I don't have any choice in the matter. It's written on tablets of stone."

"Pardon me if I keep looking for a sharp chisel."

"Kate! Enough!"

"All right, all right. Let's drop it for now and enjoy the day. Where next?"

They ambled through the gathering crowds towards the furniture at the end of the hall. Sally had furnished her flat with old stuff, lovingly polishing the wood until it glowed. Kate was much more of a modernist, but she loved to look at some of the really good antique pieces that neither of them could afford. They were drawn to a gorgeous oak wardrobe which had copper art nouveau insets on each side of the mirror.

"I could fit my whole bedroom into that," laughed Kate.

"But isn't it lovely?" insisted Sally. "I'd love to furnish a house like this. When Mark and I finally get together, we're going to get a place with b-i-g rooms so we can indulge in furniture like this."

Kate bit back an 'oink oink flap flap' and ran her fingers appreciatively over the patina of the wood. Sally had moved on to a mahogany sideboard, opening one of its cupboards to reveal square compartments for bottles. The woman in charge of the stall walked towards Sally, her antennae picking up the vibrations of serious interest. Kate held herself at the ready to extricate Sally from any hard selling, knowing how susceptible Sally was to beautiful things for her home. Sometimes, it seemed to Kate, Sally would buy extravagantly at times when Mark was at his most unreliable, as if she were furnishing a nest that he wouldn't be able to resist flying home to.

Meanwhile, Robin was enjoying himself. He hadn't really thought that he'd find a 'Breakfast at Tiffany's' poster. It was shorthand for him, and now for Kate as well, for the dream outcome, the crock of gold, the Holy Grail. It kept him going even when the materials he was flicking through were mundane. Tacky reproductions or rodent-munched disasters were the foothills you had to toil through in order to have a chance of attaining the summit. And the summit for him was Audrey Hepburn with her long cigarette holder, looking unbelievably svelte, a mixture of sex and innocence. This time, Robin was pleased to see a set of lobby cards for The Rocky Horror Picture Show. He smiled at raunchy Tim Curry as Frankenfurter, comparing this young image with the rather chunky figure he cut in later films. Tempus fugit, thought Robin wryly, determining to do double time at the gym next week. He was tempted to buy, but decided to ask Kate first just to prove how egalitarian their relationship was. Sometimes he got tired of showing her how much he was unlike her father. Kate was so touchy whenever he verged on having too much to drink or when he raised his voice. Robin always stayed deliberately calm and quiet when they argued, but once she'd accused him of threatening her even then, saying that her dad had always been at his most dangerous when he was quiet. When Robin had pointed out that he just couldn't win, that modulation was considered just as bad as shouting, she had at least been able to laugh with him about her inconsistency. But the comparison with her father was always there underneath the surface. Robin resolved to discuss it all again with her soon. He really wanted to make their relationship more secure, which to him meant old-fashioned marriage, and he was tired of fighting against Kate's prejudices. 'The sins of the fathers' was certainly apt in their case. Robin shook off the gloom that always accompanied such thoughts. He decided to look for Kate and Sally so he could broach the subject of the lobby cards.

He tried the S row first, which was usually Kate's starting point, and then headed for the furniture section. What he saw stopped him in his tracks. Surely that was Mark, with the not-so-delicate Jo. Bloody Hell, he'd better find Kate double-quick to warn her to keep her eyes open and be ready to steer Sally away from danger. He took a moment to absorb the picture: Mark's arm round Jo's waist, Jo smiling up at him adoringly. It was an intimate scene and Robin felt that his suspicions about Mark were completely justified. This was surely not the picture of a marriage heading for divorce. He then observed that they were buying something: a huge wardrobe. Would they be doing that if Mark were contemplating moving out? Robin turned away, ready to scour the hall for Kate and Sally. He practically knocked them over. They were right behind him. His first reaction was to attempt to manoeuvre them back the way they'd come, but one look at their faces revealed unequivocally that they had already seen Mark. Sally's face was a kaleidoscope incorporating shards of incomprehension, disbelief, realisation, dismay and pain. The pattern shifted, but always with the same final view. Kate's arm went protectively round her stricken friend's shoulder and Robin stepped in front of her to block out the torture. Sally's eyes filled with tears, Kate's with contempt. Robin feared that some of the contempt might be aimed at him simply for his sharing the same gender as Mark. He felt that he might be challenged to prove his love, as if he were in the middle of 'Much Ado About Nothing', and this was a "Kill Claudio!" situation. What was he supposed to do? Run Mark through with his trusty sword?

Sally's legs sagged and Robin moved quickly to her side to shore her up. She recovered straight away but he and Kate continued to hold her tightly between them. All three of them watched helplessly as Mark and Jo laughingly shook hands with the dealer and Mark took out his cheque book. It was as he turned to use a nearby table to write on that he looked up and saw Sally. Every spark of animation left his face and he stared bleakly at her. Then, like a robot, he turned his attention back to the table and rigidly began to write. Jo and the dealer continued to chat pleasantly, unaware of the drama. Robin was the first to break the spell that seemed to bind them. He looked across Sally to Kate and said urgently, "Let's get out of here." Kate hesitated momentarily, glancing back at Mark with murderous intent. Her instinct was to confront the bastard and make Jo aware of the worthlessness of her husband. But her affection for Sally took control. It was better to protect Sally than to attack Mark. They turned Sally round and propelled her stumbling figure gently towards the exit.

Chapter 4

They sat Sally down on the sofa with a blanket wrapped around her shivering body. They'd decided without actually discussing it that Sally's own home was the wrong place for her to be, faced with a half-painted bathroom and all the reminders of Mark's absence around her. Robin made tea and put extra sugar in Sally's, obeying the dictum about treating shock. Normally, Sally would have hated it. Now, she clutched the hot mug as if it were a life raft. It took several minutes before her teeth stopped chattering. Then she had to dash to the loo. But at least she was calmer when she returned. They still hadn't spoken, apart from the cooing and hushing sounds that had emitted from Kate all through the journey home. Now seemed the right time to broach the unmentionable.

"How are you feeling, lambkin?" asked Kate.

"I think I might have a touch of 'flu coming on," replied

Sally.

Robin couldn't stop his hand from clutching his throat in hypochondriacal panic but Kate's glare soon sobered him. He realised that Sally was apologising for her shivering and making an excuse for it.

"You've had a shock. It's nothing to do with 'flu," said Kate, unwilling to let the truth be evaded so cravenly. "You've just seen your partner looking perfectly happily married when he'd told you he was trapped in a miserable relationship."

"It may not have been what it looked like. I mean, we know he has to keep Jo's spirits up. She's very fragile, you know."

Kate scoffed; she couldn't help herself. Robin just looked sad.

"No, really," insisted Sally. "If you're working hard to keep someone from harming themselves in a deep depression, you'd do anything, wouldn't you? You'd have to make it seem to them that you were happy to be with them, wouldn't you? Otherwise, you'd be doing more harm than good."

"Sally, they were buying a huge wardrobe together. You don't do that if you're planning to leave," urged Kate.

"But suppose she really wanted it. What could you do? You'd hardly say, 'No, don't let's buy it because it will soon only have to house your clothes as mine will be gone.' You'd have to go along with it."

Robin cleared his throat. "Actually, Sal, I think I'd say something like 'It's a big decision. I think we ought to mull it over for a bit.' I'd get out of it somehow without being too hurtful."

"Then they'd risk losing it and think how devastated Jo would be. So I think it was brave and generous of Mark to see it through and not risk damaging her," said Sally defensively. "If anything, he's gone up in my estimation. I admit I was deeply shocked at the time, and you two were so obviously condemning him that I was carried along by your opinion of what was happening. But now I've thought about it, I can see how it must have been entirely innocent. Poor Mark, how awful for him. He must be so worried now, thinking that I'm doubting him."

Kate could hardly believe her ears. She glanced over at Robin, who was looking equally uncomprehending. She managed to indicate the kitchen with her eyes, and Robin got up saying he was in need of more tea. Kate said she'd help him so that Sally could just sit comfortably for a few minutes.

"I'll just telephone to see if I've got any messages on my answer machine," said Sally. "I expect Mark will have phoned through to explain."

In the kitchen, Kate fell into Robin's willing arms and hugged him tightly. He reached out and switched on the kettle before stroking her hair. They both sighed.

"Unbelievable," whispered Kate. "How can she do this to herself?"

"She's in denial. She's making all sorts of excuses for him because she doesn't want to face up to the alternative."

"Which is that he's a lying bastard!" hissed Kate.

Robin smiled and tipped her nose with his finger. "My little vixen, defending her young!"

"Well, don't you feel the same?"

"Yes. I'd like to punch him on the nose, to be quite honest. And I'm not the aggressive type usually. The problem is: do we let her go on with this charade and find out the truth gradually in her own time? Wait for the scales to fall from her eyes naturally? Or do we push her to face up to it now while we're still with her to catch her when she crashes?" pondered Robin.

Kate made a fresh pot of tea and got fresh mugs from the cupboard. She added biscuits to the tray, thinking they could all do with a bit of comforting sustenance.

"He won't have telephoned. That will probably make a difference to her attitude. Let's go back in there and play it by ear," she said, lifting the tray while Robin opened the door.

When they went back into the room, Sally was sitting staring at her mobile. She looked up, dazed.

"No message, I suppose," concluded Kate.

"Yes. I mean, no. I mean, yes there was a message."

Kate and Robin sat down, one on each side of Sally, fearing the worst. Robin poured tea while Kate took Sally's hand and asked her what the message said.

"He said he was sorry. He'd been trying to tell me all week but hadn't been able to bring himself to do it." She paused. "Jo is pregnant."

Kate gasped. Robin spilt tea over the tray. Neither of them knew what to say. After what seemed like an eternity, Robin ventured, "I take it that it's Mark's baby."

That was the moment of true recognition for Sally. That Mark had been staying on with Jo was one thing; but that he had still been making love to her was an entirely different situation, and one she could not bear. Her tears shuddered out, racking her body. Her grief was violent and noisy. All her friends could do was to wait until it was spent, and then comfort her physically with hugs and strokes. The fact that they were right about Mark gave them no pleasure whatsoever.

"How could he? He said they had separate rooms. He said they were talking about the future and that he always intimated to her that their paths were going to be separate. He said she was gradually coming round to it, learning to treat him just as a friend. He wanted them to stay friends, you see. He said it would be awful if all their time together went for nothing and they couldn't be amicable towards each other. He even hoped that one day he'd be able to introduce me to her. He made it all seem so cosy in the future - no wrenching pain for anyone; no bitter rejection; just happy ever after. How could he?"

"Well, he could hardly tell you the truth, could he?" whispered Kate.

"What is the truth? We'll never really know, I suppose," said Sally.

"He was obviously hoping to keep both of you happy," said Robin. "I mean, you were happy, weren't you? You believed what he said and looked forward to the future. He must have hoped that it would just go on like that."

Kate couldn't help interrupting: "But it couldn't go on like that, could it? Sally was only happy because she thought the future was going to be different, not go on in the same way. Sally's not the kind of woman to have a part-time lover for the rest of her life."

Sally concurred. "I was beginning to push him to make the promised break. Perhaps it was that that tipped the balance in Jo's favour. Oh God, I couldn't bear it if it was that that made him go back to her bed..." She began to cry again, but quietly this time, with a kind of dull misery.

"For heaven's sake, Sal. He never left Jo's bed. You didn't drive him back, he never stopped being there. It's called having your cake and eating it. He obviously got off on having two women. I wouldn't put it past him to have asked you all to move in together so that he could have a genuine *menage a trois*, his own personal harem." Kate couldn't keep the disgust out of her voice. "He's contemptible."

"No, Kate. He loved me. I know he did. You can't pretend something like that. When he was with me, we were genuinely happy. Really. He concentrated completely on me. Honestly, there was never any indication that he was watching the clock or wishing he were somewhere else, or with someone else. You can't fake something like that. Can you, Robin?"

Robin was taken aback by the direct question. "Um. Well … I suppose what you're asking is, can a man love two women at the same time? Can he have genuine feelings for both of them?"

"Typical man!" scoffed Kate. "All he was doing was getting as much sex and cosseting as possible without too much commitment on his part. Love doesn't come into it."

"I asked Robin."

"It's a difficult question," began Robin.

"No it bloody isn't," cut in Kate. "You can't _love_ two women at once. Love between partners is exclusive."

"Perhaps we're not talking about love exactly. But

genuine fondness, genuine attraction - surely that can go to more than one person?" said Robin.

"Are you defending the bastard?"

"No. All I'm saying is that it isn't quite as clear-cut as you're making it. I mean, I love you; but I'm also deeply fond of Sally; and I can appreciate that Jo is a very attractive woman. That doesn't make me a heel, does it? That's the way most people experience life."

"But that's not what Mark's done, is it? He hasn't just been deeply fond of someone else, he hasn't just found another woman attractive. He's slept with two women and told them both that they're his one and only. That's why he's a bastard."

Robin thought about what she'd said and conceded: "Yes, you're right. It's the doing something about it that makes all the difference. I read somewhere that men think about sex every few minutes. I don't think it's true, actually - or at least not once you're past being a teenager. But I'll accept frequently. The thing is, nothing comes of the vast majority of those frequent thoughts. Otherwise, Kate would never leave the bedroom!"

"Robin, for goodness sake! Men and their tacky mental interiors aren't the point here…"

"My thoughts towards you are anything but tacky. All I'm trying to say is that men do have thoughts of sex in their heads quite a lot, but it's like wallpaper. It's like background music."

"Not for Mark, though. That's what you mean, isn't it?" asked Sally.

"I'm afraid so," said Robin apologetically. "He seems to have done more than just think about it. Maybe he's more highly-sexed than most, or…"

"Or maybe he's just a selfish sod," finished Kate. "I'd like to cut his balls off. To me, he's just short of a rapist in the male pecker order."

"Don't you mean 'pecking order'?"

"I know what I mean!"

"I know you're angry for my sake, Kate. But I can't let

you get away with that. Rape is a crime of violence, not sex. And Mark was never anything but gentle. He's not a rapist, whatever else he may be."

"All right. I'm sorry. He can keep his balls intact. But I still feel I want to punish him. How dare he do this to you? How dare he?"

Robin got up decisively. "What we all need is a bit of the old creature comforts. I'm going to raid our wine cellar, otherwise known as the cupboard under the stairs. Kate, why don't you get us some bread and something?"

It seemed a good idea. They busied themselves while Sally washed her face upstairs. When she came down, they tucked in to whatever could be scavenged from the fridge. Most of the 'tucking in' was done by Kate and Robin, with Sally pushing some bread and cheese around her plate half-heartedly. However, she did manage some swallowing to please Kate, who was watching her intake like a mother hen. The wine was ingested much more willingly and gradually the alcohol and the emotional exhaustion took their toll on Sally. She intimated that she could hardly stay awake, so Kate helped her up to the spare room and put her to bed.

When she came down again, Robin had opened another bottle of Rioja. Kate collapsed on the sofa next to him and they hugged silently for a while.

"God, we're lucky," said Robin.

"We are. I promise never to take you for granted again."

"That's probably going too far," laughed Robin. "But I like the sentiments. Here, let me refill your glass while we try to work out where to go from here. I mean, with Sally."

"She's really been floored by this. That bastard!"

"We need to do something practical. Should she move in here?"

"I think so. For a while, anyway, until she can face an empty flat. Oh Lord, the bathroom's half painted. It's going to remind her every time she goes in it..."

"I'll finish it off for her. It won't take long."

"Bless you. That would be nice. But what can we interest her in? What will take her mind off Murk?"

"Don't you mean 'Mark'?" asked Robin, feeding her the line. They both chorused: "I know what I mean!"

"I've got it! Our old school chums!" cried Kate.

"What?"

"Sally put me on to it yesterday. I've already tried to get in touch with one of the girls we used to go to school with. I'll try to get Sally interested in having a reunion, getting some of the old gang together. She'll have to get involved if I send out feelers signed from both of us. What do you think?"

"It's an old trick, but it might just work! Yes, why not. Give it a try."

"There may even be a reply up there from my first venture already. I'm too tired to look now, but tomorrow..."

"Tomorrow is another day, tra la."

Chapter 5

The household limped into action at 6.30 in the morning. Actually, Kate and Sally limped; Robin ran, or jogged, as was his usual routine. It didn't take Kate long to see that Sally would be unable to function at school. She persuaded Sal to telephone in sick and then she did the same herself. She felt rather guilty about it but one look at Sally's face convinced her that she was right to do so. She managed to force some corn flakes into both of them before Robin erupted back into the house. After showering, he joined them at the table and proceeded to devour all before him. Sally couldn't help smiling at his energetic appetite even though it had the effect of completely killing hers.

"I've got a half day today," he managed between gulps, "so I thought I'd pop round to your flat and finish your bathroom. Is everything there? And in obvious places?"

"Oh, Robin. You don't have to do that. I like

decorating. I can easily do it myself," protested Sally.

"Yes, but you're going to be staying here for a while," said Kate.

"Am I?"

"Of course. I mean, if you want to. I think you need a bit of support and company for a few days, don't you? Just till you're back on your feet again."

"Is that O.K. with you, Robin?" asked Sally.

"You know it is. I need some support myself. Kate's never quite so horrible to me when you're around!"

"Oh well, in that case I'd better stay. Just to be your buffer. Anything to help out a friend."

Sally's voice wobbled slightly and they all knew that she was very close to tears again.

As if obeying the conductor's baton, they rose and started to busy themselves with clearing the table. Sally started to wash up until Kate reminded her that they had a dishwasher, thus changing her washing into mere rinsing. Kate put Robin's painting clothes into a plastic bag and sorted out a key to Sally's flat so that he could go straight there from work. He reminded her that he would need a dust mask as well, causing Kate to ask after his incipient emphysema with a snigger. By the time she'd kissed him goodbye, Sally was sitting at the table again looking rather lost.

"Kate, do you think I should phone Mark so that we can really talk it through?"

"What's there to talk about, Sal?"

"Well, I'd like to know more about the baby. I mean, was it an accident? Did Jo trick him into it? When's it due? Things like that."

Kate sighed, seeing that there was more work to be done than she had thought. Sally was not reconciled to Mark's being a shit of the first order yet. She took a deep breath, both to calm herself and to clear her mind of anything extraneous or over-emotional. She took Sally's hand before she spoke.

"Sal, it doesn't really matter how it happened, or why, or when. The over-riding fact is that Mark is going to be a father. There's going to be a baby, whose welfare has got to come first on everyone's agenda. Mark is going to be staying with Jo, the mother of his child. They're going to be a family."

"And I've got to stay out of it. That's what you're saying, isn't it?"

"You know you've got to do that. You can't go on seeing Mark. I don't even think you should be talking to him anymore. He's made his bed. Oh dear, not the happiest of phrases under the circumstances…"

"Actually, it's probably the most appropriate phrase there is. That's exactly what he's done. But I still can't believe that he was sleeping with us both deliberately, Kate. I can't believe it. Jo must have fooled him into…"

"Into what? Sally, listen to yourself. Men don't make love to women by mistake - 'oh, whoops, I didn't realise you were Jo!' Men don't wander into another bedroom and have sex in their sleep."

"No, but she might have blackmailed him into it."

"How?"

"She was unstable. She might have threatened to harm herself unless Mark showed some affection."

"Showing affection doesn't have to lead to full-blown sex, not unless he wanted it to. And we only have his word for Jo's instability. For all we know, they had a perfectly normal loving relationship with Jo entirely ignorant of Mark's extra-marital affair. No plans for a divorce. She may well be thrilled to be pregnant. She might have been trying for a baby for some time."

"That's going too far, Kate. That really is into the realms of fantasy. You really don't have a good word for Mark, do you? You're determined to see him as the villain, twirling his moustache evilly. Can't you see that he might have been duped, drawn in against his will, trying desperately not to hurt a woman who's been his wife for years?"

"All I'm asking you to do, Sally, is to look at it dispassionately, as if it was someone else's problem.

What's the most likely scenario?"

"I can't say. There are so many possibilities," Sally said stubbornly.

Kate sighed. She was getting nowhere. Sally was still hoping that Mark had been honourable. She may even have been hoping that there was still a future for them. Kate felt that she had to get Sally to see the impossibility of that, at least. She tried again: "O.K. Let's just accept that Mark may have been an innocent in this. Maybe he's just as shocked as we are. Maybe he's desperate to explain to you. But that doesn't alter the fact that there's a baby coming. You can't carry on the way you were. It has to stop now that Mark and Jo are going to have a child. You must see that."

Sally's eyes filled with tears. "I know. I know. But, oh, Kate, what am I going to do? How am I going to bear it?"

"You're going to take your mind off it completely. You're going to help me with a project. It was you who gave me the idea in the first place, so it's only fair that you should help."

"What are you talking about?"

"I want to arrange to meet as many of the old gang at school as I can get hold of, just to see how their lives have gone. Maybe we could arrange a grand reunion - you know, like the Americans do. 'Class of 2006'. That sort of thing. Or maybe that's too ambitious. We could just have coffee with a few of them. What do you think?"

Kate sounded so enthusiastic that Sally couldn't help smiling. "I could certainly do with something to take my thoughts off my own situation. Yes, it would be nice to see what's happened to some of them. We were all so full of ambition and hope, weren't we? Wonder if we still are."

"So what do you think?"

"All right. We might as well. What else am I going to do today?"

They went up to the study, with Kate tugging Sally behind her like a recalcitrant child. Kate desperately hoped that there would be a message from Pru so that her plan to immerse Sally in something other than her own misery could get started. Kate's fingers felt like the straw-filled gloves she used on her Guy Fawkes when she was a child as she struggled to key in the relevant information. Her clumsy efforts were rewarded, however, as she saw a message from Pru awaiting her: *'Super to hear from you, Kate. Why don't we meet and chat? Any evening this week would suit me except Wed. I live near the British Museum. There's a good Pizza place in Coptic St. Would that suit? Let me know.'*

"Don't you just love this technological age? Here we are, finding an old friend and arranging to meet without any detective efforts at all. Eat your heart out, Sherlock!" whooped Kate.

"It would be lovely to meet Pru again. Let's do it."

"Right. Which day?"

"Strike while the iron's lukewarm! What about

tomorrow?"

"Let's see if Pru really is free at short notice. I'll send off to her straight away."

Kate was delighted that Sally seemed to be throwing herself into the venture. She offered Pru either Tuesday or Thursday at 8 o'clock and settled back to wait for a confirmation. It came through within minutes.

"Wow! She must be sitting at her pooter right now," said Kate. "Of course, she's a writer. So she's actually working. Not like us wicked shirkers."

"There we are, we're all set for Tuesday. Tomorrow! Great. It will do me good to have a focus. Thanks, Kate. I'm sorry if I sounded less than grateful earlier. I know your criticism of Mark is probably right and I sound like a mindless wimp to keep trying to justify his actions, but my heart won't let me accept him as a bastard without a struggle. I have to think the best of him until it's proved otherwise, do you see?"

"I do understand. I just don't want you to have to go through another let-down when…"

"Let's just see what happens," pleaded Sally.

"All right. And I'll really try hard not to say 'I told you so'. Now, what would you like to do for the rest of the day? Your choice."

"You're going to hate me for saying this, but I really must do some school work. I'm determined to go back tomorrow and I want to be really on top of the work so that nothing can rock me. I mustn't break down at school, and you know how kids always seem to have a sixth sense when it comes to teachers' moods. If you're fragile, they seem to know it. Not that I think my little lovies would take advantage. In fact, they'd probably be upset to see me upset. But that would be just as disconcerting. I need to have complete control over myself and the lessons. So - forward planning!"

"I can't believe you haven't already planned your whole term's work! I know you."

"Of course I have. But I want it to be water-tight. So I want to go over it all. Is that all right?" apologised Sally.

"You do that while I go down and make us a nourishing

soup. Oh, my mother would be proud of me. She used to call chicken soup 'Jewish penicillin' and for years I didn't know it was a joke. I'll chop up lots of vegetables into a chicken stock from the freezer. Delicious!" said Kate.

Sally got out one of Kate's notepads and stared at it. She half-heartedly picked up a pen and did nothing but doodle for five minutes. She bemoaned the fact that all her school notes were at her flat and that she would have to start from square one here. Then she felt absurdly glad that she would have to start over again as it would take up more of her time to do so, and time was unfortunately what she felt she had too much of today. She started: "Period 1, Year 8. Reading Chapter 7 of 'Lord of the Flies.'" And so she continued through the morning until Kate called her down for lunch.

"How are you getting on?" asked Kate, taking toast from the toaster with exaggerated gestures of saving her fingers from third degree burns. "Down to Period 7 yet?"

"I've just finished Period 6, and luckily the last lesson is a silent reading session with my darling Year 7 class. So I've finished. I'm all yours this afternoon."

They slurped soup for a while, with Sally trying very hard to eat far more than she wanted because Kate had gone to such trouble to prepare it.

"What would you like to do this afternoon?" asked Kate.

"Honestly, I just want to burrow down under a duvet. Not very exciting for you."

"Why don't we burrow down together on the sofa and watch an old black and white movie? Real self-indulgence," suggested Kate.

"I feel so guilty. I'm sure I could be at school. What will they all think of me when I go back tomorrow?"

At the thought of that, Sally felt the tears pricking her eyes again. She tried to breathe deeply. Kate, of course, noticed her difficulty.

"Oh, sure. You're just fine. No problems at all. Those

tears welling up in your eyes are just because of the pepper in the soup, I suppose?"

Sally acknowledged that Kate had a point. They continued consuming the penicillin for a few more spoonsful before Sally blurted: "I wonder what Mark's doing now?"

"Choking over his school dinner, I hope," snarled Kate. "It's a good job you don't both work at the same school, isn't it? Just think how awkward that would be."

"You mean I'd have to make a quick decision as to whether to slap him on the back or let him choke?"

"Good girl! A returning sense of humour! That's a great sign."

"But really I do wonder what he's doing. Today must have been hard for him, too," said Sally.

"Poor thing. My heart bleeds for him."

"Oh, Kate. I can't just switch off. I'm so used to having him in my head twenty-four hours a day."

"Let's go and watch a film, something to fill your head

with something else. What shall it be?"

"How about 'Casablanca'?" suggested Sally.

"I hardly think a story about a husband and wife staying together in spite of one of them being in love with someone else is a good idea! How about 'His Girl Friday'?"

"Same thing, surely? Cary Grant persuades his wife to stay with him rather than go off with someone else, doesn't he?"

"You're right. I'd forgotten the story underneath those wonderful one-liners. Well, what about 'Singing in the Rain'? That's inoffensive, isn't it? And we can admire Gene Kelly's bum together."

"O.K. That's the one."

When Robin came home at five, they were still there, in front of the television under a duvet and fast asleep. If he'd known that, he would have crept in. But as he was in blissful ignorance, he slammed the front door and burst into the room with a triumphant "Tra la!" The friends woke up with a start and Sally started to make excuses for their napping.

"Aha!" crowed Robin. "Caught in a somnolent posture!"

Kate laughed. "We were just testing the duvet's Tog rating. You're back early."

"One bathroom repainted and looking extremely smart! It only took a couple of hours," boasted Robin.

"In that case, why weren't you home before now?"

"I can't win, can I?" asked Robin.

"No. Don't even try."

"Have you really finished it all off? That's brilliant, Robin. Thanks so much. You're a brick," said Sally.

"Don't you mean 'prick'?" teased Kate.

"I know what I mean," they all chorused.

"I just need to have a quick bath. O.K? Won't be long. Then I'm taking you two lovely goils to the cinema. They're showing 'The Four Hundred Blows'. One of the best films ever made. How about it?" enquired Robin.

"Well, I'm not too sure. We could just stay in…." ventured Sally.

"No, I won't hear of it. It will do us all good to get out. What do you think, Kate?"

"Sure. Come on, Sal. You clear up the kitchen while Robin and I share the bathroom, then we'll let you in for a splash. We could fit in a pizza or something first."

"We're pizza-ing tomorrow with Pru. So we should have something else tonight, shouldn't we?"

"Good thinking. How about Mexican? I could murder a Margherita."

With that decided upon, Kate and Robin went upstairs. When Robin had shut the door, he took Kate into his arms and whispered, "Don't say anything yet. I'll just turn on the shower to cover our voices."

"Makes me feel like I'm in a James Bond movie! Go on then. What's so secret?" laughed Kate.

"Guess who I met at the flat?"

"Oh no. Not Him with a capital H?"

"The very same. He breezed in as if he owned the place just as I was washing the roller. He stopped short when he saw me, I can tell you."

"What did he say?"

"He had the nerve to ask me what I was doing there. I said I was painting deadly poison on his razor just in case he had the effrontery to come back."

"Good for you! What did he say to that?"

"He started to pretend that he didn't know what I was talking about, till I came straight out and told him that Sally was staying with us for a while after his rather devastating news about the baby. He was a bit deflated by that. I don't think he'd expected Sal to tell us. He started to say that it was all a mess but that it would all sort itself out as soon as he talked to Sally. I told him that Sally didn't want to speak to him, and that we certainly intended to support her desire to separate herself from him for good."

"Actually, she was saying today that she wanted to talk to him. But I agree with you. I don't think it's a good idea at all. What was Mark's reaction?"

"He said it was all a misunderstanding. So I said, 'You mean Jo isn't pregnant?' and he had to admit that she was. So I asked him exactly what the misunderstanding was."

"And?"

"Look, we're supposed to be washing. Let's get under the shower and I'll carry on telling you about Shitty McShitface in there."

They stripped off with alacrity, throwing clothes into the washbasket with gay abandon. Their washing was perfunctory to say the least, but the main object was to impart as much information as possible quickly without alerting Sally.

"So what was this misunderstanding?" asked Kate, soaping Robin's chest.

"He blustered a lot and said that it only affected Sally so he didn't see why he should talk to me about something so personal. 'Sally will understand how difficult it was for me' was what he ended up with."

"The awful thing is that he's probably right. Sal's desperate to think the best of him and I'll bet he'll wind her round his little finger if we let him have the chance. Did he really suppose that she'd be there at the flat, just waiting for him? Arrogant bastard!"

"I suggested he take the opportunity to collect the things he needed and asked him to let me have his key to return to Sally. He really looked narked at that. Asked me what business it was of mine. I just dried my hands and rolled my sleeves further up so that he could see my biceps…"

"Show-off!" interposed Kate delightedly.

"Then I started to walk towards him meaningfully. He backed off, threw the keys on the table and left, swearing. It felt really good, I'm rather ashamed to say. I don't usually flaunt the results of my gym training, do I? But it came in useful today!"

"Good for you. I'm really proud of you. If we weren't in

such a hurry, I'd smother you with gratitude! And you know how smothering I can be when aroused!"

"Get thee behind me, or we'll be making Sally uncomfortable with the noises emanating from the shower."

"Right. Let's get out of here and dry off. We'll need to talk later on about what we tell Sally, and how we handle it. But we'd better get on with making this evening as pleasant as possible for her, hadn't we?"

"Can you just look at my hand before you go? I got a splinter in Sal's bathroom and I don't think I got it out."

With a sigh, Kate looked at Robin's finger. "It looks all right to me."

"Are you sure? It's quite painful."

"For God's sake, Robin, it's only a splinter!"

"These things can go septic."

"Don't you mean sceptic?" laughed Kate.

"I know what I mean."

Chapter 6

The next day started in similar vein to the previous one,
except that all three of them had to leave the house. They
were all exaggeratedly polite about sharing the bathroom
and enquiring about who wanted what for breakfast.
They managed to close the front door without any loss of
temper, which made Robin thank Sally for being there.
When Sally looked nonplussed, he explained that hardly
a day went by usually without some major disturbance in
the morning. Sally hugged them both and set off for the
bus stop. When she'd phoned in that morning to say that
she was returning, she had detected quite a lot of
inquisitive interest from Mandy, the Senior Teacher in
charge of cover. She knew she'd have to give some sort
of explanation but she determined that the only person
who would know the real reason for her absence would
be Fran, her Head of Department. Fran knew about her
situation and she even knew Mark, having worked with

him in another school. Sally had never felt that Fran liked Mark much, but she'd told her all about it anyway because Fran was such an understanding and non-judgemental person, and because she felt she ought to be absolutely honest with her HoD.

Sally arrived in the Department early and was pleased to see that Fran was the only one in the office. Fran took off her glasses and swivelled her chair round. Her face was full of concern as she asked how the invalid was.

"Oh, Fran. I feel rather a fraud. I wasn't actually ill. I just had a bit of a shock on Sunday and I didn't think I'd be able to face work until I'd pulled myself together."

"Not bad news, I hope?"

"No. Well, yes. I mean, no-one's dead or anything. But I'm grieving all the same."

"Do you want to tell me about it?" enquired Fran, puzzled but tactful.

"It's Mark," said Sally, drawing a chair up to Fran's. "It

looks as though he won't be leaving his wife after all. She's pregnant."

Fran took a moment to absorb what had been said.

"Oh, Sally, I'm so sorry. I really thought Mark had changed this time…" Fran broke off as she saw the look on Sally's face. "I mean, I thought things were going to work out for you…"

"Wait a minute. What did you mean about Mark 'changing'?"

"Forget it. I just meant, well, I just hoped that things would go well for you," mumbled Fran inadequately.

"Fran, tell me what you meant!"

Fran moved papers about on her desk, put down her pen, picked it up again and sighed deeply. "Oh, hell. I never meant to say anything to you about knowing Mark before. I mean, you know we worked at the same school but I never ever said anything about him, did I?"

"No," replied Sally, hardly daring to breathe. "But you're going to tell me now, aren't you?"

"It seems I'll have to after putting my big foot in it. Well, here goes. Mark had an affair. She was an Australian teacher, over here for a year and then moving on to see a bit more of the world before eventually going home. We all thought at the time that they both knew it would end when she had to leave so there was no real harm in it. The whole Department knew, and we all connived at not letting Jo catch on to it. It made us feel very uncomfortable, actually. No-one wanted to moralise, and it was none of our business – at least, that's what we kept telling ourselves. Unfortunately, the girl got too involved and asked if she could stay on for the following year. That didn't suit Mark's plans at all. He had obviously liked the idea of the affair having a finite life without any future. He got pretty nasty to the girl when he realised that she wanted more. It ended messily, with her leaving before the end of term because she couldn't face being in the room with Mark."

Sally's hands felt arctically cold and she rubbed them together to bring life back into them. Fran continued: "The Head found out about it and suggested to Mark that he might like to find another post. It was all very tactful and quiet, but there was no doubt that the Head wanted him gone. That's why he left and took a job at his present school. When you told me you'd fallen in love with a teacher called Mark, it didn't occur to me at first that it could be the same one. You were so happy and full of such high hopes. Then you mentioned his full name one day, and I knew. But what could I say? It wasn't for me to act as police person. He might well be truly in love with you - you certainly made it sound as if it was so. I just waited to see what would happen, hoping desperately that he was sincere this time. I'm so sorry."

Sally felt as if she was in the middle of a tunnel inexplicably full of cotton wool. All her normal senses were muffled. She knew she had to walk on to the end and climb out into the real world but she felt safe in her swaddled surroundings. Slowly, she put one mental foot in front of the other and reached the unpleasant noise of life.

"I'm really sorry, Sally. Are you all right?" asked Fran in that guilt-ridden tone that only women can fully appreciate.

"It's O.K. It's one of those 'I didn't know I knew that' moments. But I did know. Obviously, I wasn't the first affair he'd ever had. He's a serial adulterer, isn't he? I knew, but I didn't want to know."

"And I'd bet you anything that Jo is exactly the same. Somewhere underneath the exterior she presents to the world there lies a woman in full possession of the pin that could puncture her own lifebelt. She won't acknowledge it until someone makes her." Fran paused. "Are you going to be that person?"

"What? You mean tell her about her husband's infidelity when she's just found out she's pregnant? God, Fran, what do you take me for?"

"No, of course you wouldn't. Sorry I even thought it. It's just that people hit out when they're hurting, and Jo would be an easy target."

"I could really work off my pain by stamping around in her blood, couldn't I? Don't think I haven't considered it. I almost justified it to myself by saying that I'd actually be damaging Mark, which might be a really comforting thing to do. Let him feel what it's like to be rejected. He'd be kicked out by Jo and then he'd come running back to me, and I'd take huge pleasure in rejecting him, too. He'd end up with neither of us and it would serve him right. But there's no way of doing that without really damaging Jo, and she doesn't deserve that. It's not her fault, any of it."

"And it's not your fault, either," insisted Fran.

"Up till now, I've been sort of denying that the situation is as serious as it is. I was telling Kate that I needed to give Mark the chance to explain, that there must be an explanation. But I knew really that this is the end. There's no way back. He's a shit, isn't he? And I've been a bloody fool!"

"There you go, blaming yourself. You mustn't do that. Mark is handsome, charming and intelligent. He's in the same job as you, so you've got lots to talk about. He made you believe he loved you and that he was going to make a future for you both. All the blame is his," insisted Fran.

"And what about the fact that I was quite willing to break up another woman's marriage? I can't absolve myself from all blame, Franny."

"Life can be a messy business. There's no way of walking the path without stepping on things. You didn't set out deliberately to squash a butterfly on the way, but perhaps if you hadn't done that you would have fallen over a crack and broken your neck. Who knows?"

The door opened and a frantic figure wrapped in an over-large coat erupted into the room. "Where the Diana Dors are my Sixth Form essays?" James, for it was he underneath the tweed, hated to use swear words, blaming his Catholic upbringing. Instead, he replaced them with alternatives that gave him the satisfaction of swearing without the guilt. On learning that Diana Dors' real name was Fluck, he revelled in using it to disguise his verbal intent. Sally smiled in spite of herself, having a soft spot for James's creative use of language.

"Don't tell me you promised the students that you'd have

marked them by now?" said Fran with true Head of Department raised eyebrows. James flung his coat over the coat hooks and dived for his desk, which was piled high with papers. "Oh, damn! I mean, Busters! Where are they?"

"Can I help?" asked Sally, moving across to his desk and quickly removing two half-empty mugs of mould-encrusted coffee before James's panic sent them flying.

"Thanks. They're on the character of Iago. I was sure they were in my bag, until I settled down with a large whisky and a nice sharp pencil last night. And, yes, Fran dearest, I did promise them back today. The best laid schemes and all that. Oh well, no doubt they'll forgive me, especially when I remind them that the next essay was due last week and they've only given in two so far." James continued to shuffle things until he found them. Then he collapsed into his cushioned chair and sighed plaintively. "Any chance that I'll get them done by Period 3?"

"Depends how thoroughly you're going to mark them. You could just do Impression Notes for this one, couldn't you?" suggested Fran.

"No, I don't think so. This is the only essay I'm planning on Iago, so it's an important one. I owe it to them to make this an in-depth crit. I'm just going to have to confess. They'll forgive me because they love it when we do something human, don't they? It gives them the chance to feel superior."

"I'm feeling all-too-human today," sighed Sally.

"Sorry, Vol. How are you? Missed you yesterday."

James had started calling her Sal Volatile from the first time they were introduced, and this had been shortened to the affectionate 'Vol' soon after. Sally loved it. Somehow it made her feel special and different. She liked James, with his careless way of throwing clothes on as if he didn't notice what he wore which always turned out artistically eccentric and attractive. Pity he was gay, she'd often thought.

"I'm wading through custard, but at least I'm moving forward," she replied. She glanced at the clock and saw that it was only twenty minutes to Registration. She wondered how she was going to get through the day, but knowing there was no alternative she took a deep breath and plunged into her own piles of student papers on her own desk. Actually, she was well up on her marking because she always set herself the task of correcting work until 6 o'clock every day so that she could then go home unencumbered. Gradually, the office filled up with teachers in various stages of preparation and panic as the day neared its ritual opening. Most of the Department remembered to ask how she was but were satisfied with a perfunctory answer. They didn't really want to know details, and that pleased Sally, who definitely didn't want to give them. When the pips sounded for Registration, James did his usual rallying cry: "Grid your lions everyone!" This had arisen from a felicitous mistake by one of his dyslexic students who had meant to write 'gird your loins' and it had so amused James that he took it into his vocabulary with alacrity. Sally thought she had a lot of gridding to do on this particular morning!

Kate, meanwhile, was feeling snowed under because of the pile-up of the previous day's work. Part of her job was to process the recorded notes of each therapist after their session with a patient. This being a unit solely for adolescents, some of the interviews were lengthy and garrulous. The senior psychiatrist, Dr Tailor, always reported his sessions in great detail, insisting that even the seemingly irrelevant could prove to be of crucial significance in the development of the young mind. So Kate was slightly dismayed to see two of his tapes on her desk ready for transcription. With a resigned sigh, Kate set to work straight away, promising herself an hour's transcription before making a coffee and going through the post, which would have arrived by then. Fortunately, her fingers flew expertly over the keys today. She had discovered that there were certain days when her fingers were like sausages and even the simplest of jobs took twice as long. She was loathe to name 'time of the month' as the culprit because she always fought against what she felt was a mere excuse for shoddy or thoughtless work.

Dr Tailor wafted into the room. His tall, angular form seemed surprisingly insubstantial and Kate had often been startled by his presence, which she had taken for a mere shadow at first. The nobility of his appearance was accentuated by his hawk-like nose and watery blue eyes, which were turned enquiringly on her as he took off his cashmere overcoat.

"Good morning, my dear. I do hope your friend is feeling better today?"

Kate stopped her machine, whipping off her ear-phones. His voice was so quiet and well-modulated that she had not heard his question and had to ask him to repeat himself. He displayed such genuine concern and sensitivity to Sally's predicament that Kate found herself telling him all about it while he made them both a coffee. She thought what an absolute darling he was as she watched him remembering that she took one sugar without having to ask. He did not feel demeaned by the act of coffee-making for his secretary. His bony, elegant hands stirred carefully and placed the mug gently and precisely on her coaster. Then he sat opposite her and cradled his own mug while he listened to her. She knew why he was such a successful therapist, because she felt herself telling him all her feelings about Sally and Mark, fully confident that he would understand. She dreaded the day, quite soon, when he would be retiring and his second-in-command, the dynamic and exhausting Dr Moran, would take over.

"Your friendship with Sally is obviously very important to both of you. She must be relying on you tremendously at the moment. If you need to take any more time off to care for her, I'm sure we could arrange to send tapes home to you and let Miss Troop manage the office routine in your absence."

His kindness overwhelmed her, but she did wonder if she had exaggerated Sally's grief, making him think there might be a possibility of Sally harming herself. Then it occurred to her that perhaps there was indeed such a possibility. Was Sally in danger? Did Dr Tailor's experience of potential suicides make him more aware of the truth than she was?

"I can see that you're worrying about her safety, my dear.

I don't think you need to. From what I've heard, and from what I gleaned from meeting Sally last Christmas, I think she will cope with the upset caused by her lover's desertion. Support her affectionately, as I know you will, and try to involve her in other things, and I feel sure she will come through it."

"That's just what I'm trying to do!" Kate replied triumphantly. "We're meeting up with an old school friend tonight and I'm going to arrange for a reunion of some of our old mates whom we haven't seen since we left school. It's quite a project to find out where they are now, so we're using the Internet to trace them."

"Excellent. We all share nostalgia for the past. It will be an absorbing interest to get the group together and to find out about their lives since school. With any luck, some of them will have greater problems than Sally is coping with. I know that sounds unfeeling, hoping that people will be less than happy with their lot in life, but there's nothing like other people's misery to make us appreciate the many aspects of our own lives that are worthwhile."

Kate felt soothed by the warmth of his smile. Talking to

him had been just what she needed and she was doubly glad to have seen him first in the morning. Then she heard Dr Moran's loud voice and tread on the stairs. His bulk filled the doorway and his personality filled the room. Kate withdrew back into herself and Dr Tailor stood up, holding his mug like a votive offering.

"Ralph," boomed Dr Moran, failing yet again to pronounce the name properly as 'Rafe', as Dr Tailor preferred. Everyone had given up correcting him, assuming that the mispronunciation was a deliberate slight against the older and less assertive man. "Promoted you to coffee-wallah, have they?"

"Might I make you a cup?" asked Dr Tailor with a slight incline of his head.

"Please let me do that," said Kate quickly. She hated to see the supercilious look on Moran's face as he ridiculed the old-fashioned courtesy of his senior.

"Don't bother, Kate. I popped into *Pret* on my way in, picked up a cappuccino. I just wanted to tell you to send the Old Trooper into my office when she arrives. I've got another book chapter to dictate to her. All right?"

With that, he swept out, waving his cappuccino flamboyantly. Kate noticed that he didn't bother to ask about her absence the day before – probably hadn't even noticed it, unless it had impinged on his own comfort. She knew his energy was admirable and that he was a highly successful author as well as a well-respected practitioner, but she could never quite like him. He swept all before him but often didn't notice that he was running over people's feelings in the process. Dr Tailor was constantly being semi-ridiculed for his lack of drive, as Moran saw it; but Kate would rather work for someone courteous than for someone as rudely pushy as Moran. She was glad that the bulk of his work fell on the twitchy shoulders of her part-time workmate, Betty Troop.

"My first patient is at ten, I believe," said Dr Tailor when the whirlwind of Dr Moran's presence had subsided. "I don't expect him to arrive until about quarter past. He has to show me that he's reluctant to come and doesn't really need me, you see," Dr Tailor smiled. "It's just possible that he'll ring and cancel, but I don't think so."

Kate returned to her work and was half way through the second tape when Betty arrived with the post in her hand. Betty wore her usual mournful colours, which accentuated the pallor of her skin. Although she was an excellent administrator, much better than Kate, she had no ambition to be other than a part-time secretary. Part of the reason for that was her slightly unhealthy infatuation with Moran, whose secretary she had been for years. He only required part-time servicing while he was not the Head of the Unit; but soon he would take over the admin tasks that Dr Tailor shouldered when he stepped into the older man's shoes. He should then inherit the Unit's senior secretary, Kate. However, Kate had no desire to work for him, whereas Betty desperately wanted to remain with him. They were all treading on eggshells, trying not to offend one another while negotiating the future staffing.

"Nice to see you back, little colleague," said Betty. She never liked using anyone's first name, which was just one of her slightly strange idiosyncracies. "Has your friend got over the worst of her illness?"

"She's getting on fine, thanks. Sorry to let you down at such short notice yesterday. Was everything as crazy as usual, or more so without me?"

"Probably more so, but nothing to worry about. Dr Moran wanted to dictate some more *magnum opus* to me, but I had to decline so that I could stay in the office."

"Oh yes. He wants you to go straight in to him."

Betty became a little flustered at the thought of immediate contact with Moran. She took off her coat quickly and arranged her unremarkable brown hair. A quick polish of her glasses, and she was ready to pick up pad and pencil in the service of her hero. Kate always thought of medieval courtly love whenever she watched Betty. She worshipped Moran from afar, as it were, and would have been shocked if he had ever made an assault on her virginity. It was enough for her to curtsey and flatter and work her fingers to the bone for him. He knew it, of course, and threw just enough civility her way to keep her adoration. But one of the things that Kate most disliked about him was the way he talked about Betty behind her back, calling her The Old Trooper and making fun of her twitches and verbal circumlocutions. One of the games he played was to try to make Betty use someone's first name in conversation, and Kate watched with sympathy for Betty and anger at Moran whenever he embarked on one of his teasing sessions.

"I'll go straight in, then, shall I?" asked Betty. "There isn't anything that needs to be done first, is there?"

Her need to be with him was palpable, so Kate oiled the way for her, even though she would have liked to have had a run-down of the previous day's events in case there was anything that she needed to follow up.

"Off you go. I'll hold the fort here. Shall I bring a coffee in to you?"

"Oh, no. I expect he'll be dictating so fast that I wouldn't be able to drink it anyway. See you later."

When she scurried out and along the corridor, Kate

returned to her tapes until Dr Tailor's first patient was due. At ten, she pushed aside her computer and settled to opening the post until the young client arrived. As predicted, he was late and walked in with a casual insouciance that belied his need. Kate took him straight in to Dr Tailor. Kate liked the atmosphere of the office when everyone else was fully occupied in their own domains, so she was able to glide through the routine of the day without too much effort. She wanted to reserve enough energy for the evening, when she and Sally were meeting Pru.

Chapter 7

As they walked towards the pizzeria, Sally linked arms with Kate and asked, "Are you sure we'll recognise Pru after all this time?"

"No! But it'll be fun trying, won't it? I was just wondering how much we've changed and whether we'd be recognisable if you only had a school photo to go on. My hair's a different colour, and yours is swept up off your face, but I don't think that would put anyone off. I mean, it is faces that stay in your mind, not hair."

They went in and started studying faces straight away. A waitress approached them, smiling invitingly. "Table for two?" she asked.

"Actually, we're meeting a friend here. Could we just have a quick look round in case she's here already?"

"Of course. If you don't find her, I'll pop you onto a table near the door so you can watch for her coming in."

Kate and Sally set off through the restaurant, looking at

all the women sitting alone, which didn't take long as most people were in groups or couples. Having failed in their search, they sat where the waitress put them, near the door and next to the window where they could watch the street as well as the entrance. It wasn't long before a woman arrived, conspicuously carrying a poetry book with the name 'Pru Fisher' on the cover. She looked slightly anxious, peering through Harry Potter glasses. When she saw Kate waving, she hurried over with relief. Kate realised that she would have recognised Pru with no trouble at all. Even though her hair was much more spikey, even though the colours of her clothes were more muted shades of olive and purple instead of the oranges and yellows she used to wear, still it was unmistakably Pru. They all hugged like the long-lost friends that they were, and made those strange bird-like whoops that reunions always seem to elicit. When they had shared the usual greetings, they sat down and were quiet for a minute or so, just taking in what was different about one another.

"God, we all look so grown up!" said Pru, which made them all giggle like schoolgirls. This brought the waitress hurrying over with menus, a smile on her face as she anticipated a happy meal instead of the angst-ridden conversations she had to work through quite frequently. They quickly chose their food. The only debate was the wine. Judging by the well-washed and mended state of Pru's clothes, Sally had the feeling that Pru wasn't exactly well off, so she steered Kate away from the Prosecco and agreed with Pru's tentative suggestion that house wine was usually fine. Having despatched the waitress, they settled back in their seats to look at one another again.

"I thought I'd better bring a banner with my name on it," said Pru, indicating her book, "just in case. But I'd have known you both. Sally looks much more elegant and ice-maidenish, but those blue eyes are just the same. All-seeing eyes! There was never any possibility of telling fibs to Sal. She could see straight through any deception."

Sally sighed and fiddled with her napkin. "Then I must have changed enormously," she said sadly.

"Lawks-a-mercy! I've said something wrong already, haven't I?" asked a mortified Pru.

Kate didn't know whether to leap in to defend anyone or not, and was glad when Sally followed her remark with an explanation. She watched Pru's face carefully for her reaction.

"It's just that I've been completely taken in by someone and I'm just trying to come to terms with my own stupidity and inability to see what everyone else thought was obvious," said Sally.

"A man, I take it? Well, that's altogether different. They're such practised liars, aren't they?" Pru shrugged. "Been there, done that! I was talking about when we were girls. You always used to see through us; but men are an entirely different species."

"Not all of them," said Sally. "Kate's found herself a gem. He's kind and funny – and he thinks the sun shines from her every orifice!"

"Shouldn't Kate be the one telling me this?" asked Pru astutely.

"Oh, she doesn't know what she's got. Not yet," replied Sally.

"Then we'd better tell her loads of stories about unhappy relationships so that the veil will fall from her eyes. I could contribute a few, I can tell you. But I don't want to dull the brightness of our reunion with predictable tales of male infidelity. Here comes the wine, so let's toast happiness in being together again."

After a few slurps, they started again on a more enjoyable topic as Kate indicated the book lying on the table. "You made it into print, then? I always knew you would. All those class plays! It's ages ago, but I can still remember some of the lines. That sketch about Adam and Eve, where I played Eve and had to talk about Adam's digging up the sods of Eden with his ho, ho, ho! Remember?"

"With that cloth stretched across the stage so only legs and heads were showing, to get over the need for nakedness! And Morgan drawing great black hairs on her legs to make her into Adam! Oh, yes!" whooped

Sally.

"I'm not sure I ever got any better than that," laughed Pru. "I've certainly never played to a larger audience."

"Poetry's not a great seller, then?" asked Kate, already knowing the answer.

"That's why I'm trying a novel now. But I can't get out of the habit of weighing every word when I'm writing - unlike my foot-in-mouth method of talking - so it takes me all day to write a page. At this rate, I shan't publish until I'm fifty."

"Well, it worked for Mary Wesley."

"I'm afraid my bank manager hasn't got that much faith in me. He seems to want me to be a credit to him right now. I'll probably have to go out and get a 'proper job', as my mum says. 'All that education, Prudence, and you haven't even got a proper job to show for it! I thought at least you'd be a teacher.'"

"Don't!" shouted Sally. "Anything but that. I've never been so completely exhausted, even when I was studying for four A Levels or reading for my finals."

"So you're a teacher, are you? That makes sense. I bet you're a really good one. Conscientious. Caring. You were the one we all came to when we were in trouble. We knew you'd always listen and not be sarcastic or clever-clever."

"Not like me, you mean?" interposed Kate.

"Katy, you were always so immersed in your own family atmosphere. You only just coped yourself so someone else's burdens would have floored you. How are your parents, by the way? Are you still feuding with your father?" asked Pru.

"Things are slightly different now. Mother's not quite as abject as she was. I suppose someone seeing them together now would even think they were relatively happy. It's easier to rub along together when there aren't any children to make demands on your time and your income. But I can't forgive him for the way he treated us when I was a kid, no matter how he tries to win me over. I still hate going over to see them. Most of our communication is done over the phone so that I don't have to look at him trying to ingratiate himself with me when I'm in the room, then hear him sniping at her when I'm outside the door."

"You never could take hypocrisy," said Pru. "It was one of the many things I admired about you, your ability to cut through the crap. It meant you always said what you thought, and I appreciated that. You were the best critic of those adolescent sketches. I bet you'd take one look at my novel and tell me exactly what was wrong with it."

"Or what was right with it," said Sally.

The pizzas arrived and were duly sprinkled with black pepper, stopping their conversation momentarily.

"Anyway, let's go back to the point when we left school, full of notions that we would shine our little lights into the darkness of the adult world," said Pru. "What did you do after that, Sally?"

"Well, you already know. I went to York, read English, then took teacher training. Been a teacher ever since."

"Husband? Kids?"

"Neither." She took a deep breath. "My partner is already married. He's a teacher, too – that's where we met. We'd planned to marry when he divorced his wife and I wanted to have children soon after that. I thought he did, too. Well, I suppose he's getting them, but not with me."

"I don't think I'm quite following this," said Pru.

"What she means is that he's staying married to Wifey Number One because she's pregnant. We only learnt about this at the weekend so it's all a bit raw."

"Sorry. It's probably a bit too soon to talk about that. Let's move hastily on. What about you, Kate?"

"Me? Oh, I seem to have fulfilled all my early lack of promise! I refused to go to University, as you probably remember. Went and did a secretarial course instead."

"Not just a secretarial course, Kate," interposed Sally. "It was pretty high-class. You did all sorts of exams in Economics and Accountancy and stuff, didn't you?"

"Yes. Chartered Institute of Secretaries. Flying colours."

"As usual. Your A Level grades were better than anyone else's, weren't they?"

"Much good it did me. Anyway, when I left college, I went to work in an advertising agency. I had this vision of being a high-powered account executive. They gave me this lovely guy to work with as his P.A. An Oxford graduate. Very clever. Do you know, we spent hours one day thinking up a new name for a scouring powder. I got home that night and I knew I couldn't go on with it. It was all such a waste of talent. His, I mean. But mine, too, I suppose. I handed in my notice and started looking for a job in a more 'caring' environment. I ended up working in a Psychiatric Clinic specialising in the treatment of youngsters. I'm only the Administrator, but it's a good place."

"Trying to ensure that today's adolescents don't get screwed up by their parents' feuding, is it?" asked Pru, with a twinkle in her eye.

"So nobody needs to get as messed up as I did, yes!" laughed Kate.

"And you, Pru. What happened to you after school?" asked Sally.

"I loved Uni. Not that I did much work! All my time was spent writing."

"And that isn't work?"

"It never felt like work. It came so easily then. Ideas and words just seemed to ooze from my pen. Not any more. But back then … oh, it was glorious. I flunked out with a poor degree, but immediately a publisher who'd seen some of my work in the college magazine contacted me with the idea of my contributing to an anthology. I really thought that that was it, that I was set for life as an author. But nobody ever tells you how little money poets make. It just isn't enough to live on, unless you really make it big. I guess Seamus Heaney did quite well eventually. But he was a genius, of course. And I'm just a fairly ordinary jobbing poet who does a few poetry festivals and tutors a few writing courses."

"But you're happy?" asked Sally.

"I am when I'm writing. I'm in another world. I become

completely unaware of my surroundings. It makes me a difficult person to live with. I suppose. Which is one of the reasons why I don't. Live with anyone, I mean."

The staccato quality of Pru's reply alerted Sally to an awkwardness that Kate didn't seem to be aware of. She caught Pru's eye, and Pru immediately snorted with laughter. "There you go! What did I say? Good old Sally has seen right through my subterfuge!"

"What?" Kate asked.

"I'm currently living alone, as I said. But it's because I've just split up, yet again, from my partner. There is an element of truth in what I said, that it's hard to live with a writer who's constantly living in her head. But the main reason for the split is that I won't have children and Sebastian can't handle that. We're the opposite of the stereotype, really. Seb's longing to be a father, whereas I just know that I won't be able to concentrate on my writing if there's a baby demanding constant attention."

"Baby's do go to sleep, you know. Can't you see yourself beavering away while infant slumbers?" asked

Kate.

"That could be Seb talking! That's just what he says. But I've seen the mind-death that seems to afflict young mothers. They can't remember the name of the milkman, let alone work in rhyming couplets. No, I know what would happen and I'm not willing to let it. That means, according to Seb, that I love my writing more than I love him. And I do, when it comes down to it. You know that game we used to play? 'If the house was burning down, what would you rescue?' For me it would be my writing. Not Seb. Not a baby. Definitely my writing."

"I don't think it would, you know," said Sally. "Human beings would always come before abstract things. At the back of your mind, you'd know you could re-write something. But you could never replace a person."

"The voice of conscience pricks the selfish bubble of my imaginings! Well, you're probably right in a real life situation. But in my mind it's a different matter. In a way, I don't want to have people intruding into my pecking order of importance. To be a really good writer, you have to be totally focussed. And I want to be a good writer, more than anything else."

"I really liked the poems I read," said Kate. "I have to admit that I only bought a book of yours when I tried to contact you on the Net. But I'm so glad I did."

"Thank you kindly, ma'am."

"I feel awful!" said Sally. "I haven't read anything of yours since school."

"Here. Take this one. Tell me what you think next time we meet up."

Pru slid the book across to Sally, who put it gratefully into her bag. The waitress cleared their plates and the dead bottle of wine, asking if they wanted more. They were all tempted, but empathy with Pru's impecunious situation prompted Kate and Sally to urge refusal on the spurious grounds of needing to lose weight. They settled on coffee instead.

"Do you keep in touch with anyone else?" asked Kate.

"I still see a lot of Mary. Even more so since she and Gil divorced and she's struggling to bring up Conrad on her own. Looking at her is the main motivation for my reluctance to be a mother, actually. She's finding it very tough. Fortunately, she has a good job as a Lecturer. She earns a reasonable amount and she has time off in the holidays. But the emotional strain of being a single parent is enormous. Mind you, she's doing a great job. Conrad is a very interesting kid."

"How old is he?" asked Sally.

"He's eight."

"What? He can't be!" exclaimed Kate.

"It doesn't seem possible, does it? But I assure you it's true. Mary became pregnant while she was at Uni. She and Gil got married, and the University were adamant that she could only complete her course as long as the baby didn't interfere with her attendance at lectures and all the rest of it. I have to admit that Gil was marvellous about looking after the baby so that Mary could carry on with her studies. He was always very aware that she was the bright one and that he would never match her academically."

"He was a plumber, wasn't he?" asked Sally.

"Electrician. Runs his own firm now. He's very capable in his own field, but he was never interested in the exam treadmill. He reads voraciously and could hold his own in any intellectual environment, but he's never seen the need to prove his intelligence by amassing qualifications. At least, that's his story."

"I remember people dismissing him because he left school at sixteen. No-one thought Mary would go on seeing him. She was such a high-flyer, wasn't she? Sally and I had a bet that she'd drop him as soon as she was at college and could compare him with her fellow intellectuals."

"Maybe we over-estimated the calibre of most students! Anyway, she obviously stuck with Gil," said Sally.

"I used to think that he had made her pregnant on purpose, so that she wouldn't leave him," continued Pru, "but I think it was a genuine accident. Anyway, he did 'the right thing', as my mother said with great satisfaction. Of course, she was astounded that Mary carried on with her career. As far as she was concerned, a mother's place was in the home! Poor mum, she despairs of our generation. Especially me!"

"What caused them to split? You'd have thought that they had survived the hardest part when they juggled studying and baby care, wouldn't you?" asked Sally.

"True. I'm not exactly sure what went wrong. There was never a particular incident, like one of them being unfaithful or anything. I think it was just that they found themselves following divergent paths in life. Gil remained very attached to his working class roots and loved working with his hands. He began to look on Mary's colleagues as – what did he call them? - 'Ponces' - that was it. He saw them all as a bit removed from the real world. They could talk *ad nauseam* about the political situation and how they disapproved of everything, but they never got their hands dirty to really help anyone. Gil used to give his time free to the local Old People's Home, doing odd jobs and reading to the oldies. When he suggested that Mary and her fellow lecturers could form a rota with him to read to the old people and write their letters for them, no-one actually volunteered. He was very bitter about it, and he directed a lot of the bile onto Mary. The sad thing was that she agreed with him to a certain extent, but she also saw the other side of the coin, that the lecturers had enough of the reading and writing thing all day long in their jobs. The last thing they wanted to do was more of it in their spare time. But Gil refused to see that there was anything but hypocrisy behind it. Every time any of them came round, he'd absent himself, getting in a good few sneering comments before going. It wore them out in the end. Funnily enough, they seem to get on much better now they're divorced. Gil still has regular contact with Conrad and whenever he goes to collect his son he stays for hours chatting to Mary. I predict that one day they'll just get together again. But they'll never re-marry, I'm sure of that."

"Do we know anyone who's happily married?" wailed Sally.

"Well, there's Jacky, if you can believe her glowing reports," said Kate. "Do you still have any contact with her, Pru?"

"No. We really should all get together, shouldn't we? You two, me, Mary and Jacky. Anyone else?"

"Perhaps we should just get that lot together first, and then perhaps more contacts could be made from there. It might be too overwhelming to have more than that to begin with, don't you think?" said Sally.

"That's too cautious," said Kate. "Let's go for a few more, at least. Who would we really like to see again?"

"Well, I've always wondered what happened to Cassie. She was always on the verge of disasters, getting involved with drugs through her father's trendy friends, remember? She always felt so much more mature and sophisticated than the rest of us, but she was often out of her depth really. And then there was her pregnancy scare which turned out to be nothing but a late period. She always seemed so laid-back about everything. Nothing ever seemed to faze her. I'd love to know where she is now," mused Pru.

"See if you can trace her, then. Anyone else?"

"I think Michelle married one of Jacky's cousins. Do you remember how Michelle used to stay with Jacky whenever her parents had to remain in Paris? Her father was the director of one of those French cosmetic firms, wasn't he? Michelle always seemed to have expensive perfumes and stuff. Well, I think she knew Jacky's family quite well because of the frequent stop-overs, and she met and married one of the cousins."

"I'll contact Jacky, then, and get her to invite Michelle as well," offered Sally.

Kate was pleased that Sally was offering to do something to further the plan. It meant that she was engaged, that she was willing to focus on Life Without Mark. She found herself wanting to get home so that she could tell Robin all about it, and boast about the success of the plan to distract Sally.

"When shall we three meet again?" quoted Pru. "With as many of the others as we can get hold of, of course."

"Shall we give ourselves a week? Is that enough time?" suggested Kate.

"Let's go for it. Same time next week. Here again?" asked Pru.

"It might be nicer in someone's house next time when there are more of us. We could make it my place, if you like. Sally's there anyway, and the main room is large enough for a small party. Robin won't mind. Could you get to Archway fairly easily, Pru?" asked Kate.

"That would be fine for me. Wine and nibbles? With everyone bringing a contribution?"

"Great. I'll provide bread and cheese so there'll be enough sustenance even if everyone else brings totally unsuitable things! Oh, I feel really excited about this!" exclaimed Kate.

Chapter 8

Robin listened indulgently as the two friends shared their evening with him. He had seldom seen Kate so enthusiastic, and he realised that some of it was manufactured for Sally's benefit, trying to raise her level of interest. It seemed to be working. Sally was consistently smiling instead of looking blank. Her body language was much more positive. She even volunteered to compose an e-mail to Jacky before going to bed. When Sally had gone up to the study, Robin drew Kate to the sofa and sat her down.

"I don't want to put a damper on all this. It's wonderful to see Sally so involved and I'm sure you're right in trying to take her mind off things. But reality intrudes a bit, I'm afraid. I called in to her flat today to pick up her mail and make sure all was well. There was a hand-delivered letter for her. I'm sure it was from Mark: I recognised the writing. I made an executive decision not to give it to her tonight. I can always pretend I didn't call in today and say I picked it up tomorrow. I just couldn't bear to bring her down with a crash when you'd done such a great job of lifting her up."

"Good thinking, Batman. Whatever he says, it's bound to upset her. I wish there was some way we could know what the bastard's written."

"You could always steam it open over the kettle," laughed Robin. "No, no, I didn't really mean that. Take that look off your face!"

"I'm just wondering if we could! No, you're right. That would be really obnoxious, wouldn't it?"

"It would. But I think you should plan to be around when she opens it tomorrow. She'll need your support."

"Oh, damn. She was talking about calling into her flat after school tomorrow to pick up some more clothes. If she does that, she'll be there before you, and she'll know there wasn't a letter. Perhaps we'll have to give it to her tonight. Or maybe tomorrow morning? What do you think?"

"Morning wouldn't be good, would it? If she gets really upset, she's got to go straight in to work without time to get herself over it. Maybe I could take the letter back tomorrow morning so she finds it herself after school."

"Oh no, Robin. That would mean she'd be on her own when she read it. You said yourself that she'll need my support. God, I feel like a cantilevered bra!" said Kate.

"Interesting image! Then it's got to be tonight."

At that very moment, they heard Sally's light tread on the stair. Robin crossed to his jacket, draped over the back of a chair, and took the envelope out of his pocket.

"I've done it and sent it off into the ether," said Sally happily. "Anyone for a cuppa?"

"I'll make it," said Robin quickly. "There's a letter for you. I picked it up from the flat this evening."

Immediately, Sally's expression changed. Gone were the bright eyes, gone the open smile. A bleak quality crept into her face, as if an icy wind had replaced the sunshine. She took the letter from Robin's outstretched hand and glanced at the writing.

"Come and sit down, Sal," urged Kate.

Sally sat on the sofa and took a deep breath before tearing open the envelope. She read it silently before she passed it to Kate, who concentrated on not showing too much emotion as she read it.

'My darling Sally,

I beg you not to tear up this letter, at least not until you've read it. I know how upset you must be, with all our dreams seemingly in the dust. But please let me explain how this has happened.

You know how unstable Jo is. She's up and down like a yoyo. A little while ago she was going through a particularly bad patch. I got home one evening to find her lining up the pills and threatening suicide. She needed comfort and I gave her what I could. What else could I do? You, of all people, would not have had me walk away at that moment and risk her life. I was manipulated, I admit it. But the fact that it led to pregnancy was a huge shock, to both of us.

I know you are thinking that you must never see me again. I know you so well, my darling. You could never contemplate your own happiness if it meant misery for another. But all is not lost for us. Nor is the future decided. Jo is seeing the doctor next week for advice about a possible termination. She doesn't think that her mental state could cope with a pregnancy, let alone a baby. If her doctor supports her, and I'm sure he will because he's been treating her depression for years now, then it won't be long before we can have a future together again, you and me. You see, once she accepts that she can't cope, she'll be well into the support system. If they can get her into a clinic to stabilise her, then there's no reason any more for me to tread on eggshells around her. I'll be able to make a new life for us. Do you see? It really might be that this disastrous news is actually for the best and can lead to our happiness.

Will you wait for me? Can I count on your love and support at this difficult time? Everything should be decided over the next few weeks. Hang on, darling, please.

Can we meet and talk about our future? It's so hard in a letter to tell you all that I'm feeling. I miss you so dreadfully. I can be free this weekend – could we be together? Ring me on my mobile.

Kate also read the letter in silence. Her first reaction was that Mark was still the puppeteer, yanking Sally's strings unmercifully. One glance at Sally's face made her realise with horror that the letter had opened up a tiny chink of light for the hopeful Sally.

"Sally, surely you don't believe him?"

"I don't know. I want to. I want to so much. I know you think he's a total shit. And Robin agrees with you. But I don't want you to be right. I want him to be honourable and in love with me still."

"I understand. Of course you do. So let's try to think about it coolly, as if it were happening to someone else. In fact, let's try it out on Robin."

Robin was entering with a tray of tea and heard his name. "What?"

"We just want your gut reaction. Mark has written to Sally saying that the pregnancy was a mistake and that neither he nor Jo wants the baby. Jo will probably go for a termination. That will compel the N.H.S. to give more help for her clinical depression. If Mark waits till then, he'll be able to leave her while she's being cared for. So he won't be risking her suicide. What do you think?" asked Kate.

Robin put the tray carefully down on the coffee table and gave the women his full thoughtful attention. "My first concern would be about the so-called mistake of the pregnancy. I mean, I don't want to embarrass you, Sally, but pregnancy does require sex as an antecedent, and I thought you said they had separate rooms and all that."

"Apparently, she was suicidal," explained Sally. "She

blackmailed him into having sex. It was the only way to comfort her."

"But blackmailing him into sex must mean that she wanted sex with him. So as far as she's concerned, the relationship isn't over. Is it? She still wants him," continued Robin.

"That's no surprise. We know that. That's the reason why he couldn't just leave her," said Sally.

"But if she still wants him, maybe the pregnancy wasn't accidental. It could be that it was exactly the opposite."

"What do you mean?" Sally interrupted.

"Well, if she's trying to blackmail him into staying with her, then having a baby would be the best move she could make. It would really tie him to her, for years."

"That isn't what he says in the letter. He says she was shocked at the news," insisted Sally.

"But if it truly was an accident, and she has a termination, then her depression is going to be astronomically worse after it. If he couldn't bring himself to leave her before, how could he contemplate it when she's in a worse state?"

"He explained that. He said she'd be in the hands of the doctors."

"But she's already in the hands of the doctors," said Kate. "She's already being treated for depression. Has been for years – he said so."

Robin stroked his chin, contemplating the situation as if he were a fictional detective. "If Mark just wanted to make sure she was being watched over, he could have done that ages ago. He could have gone to their G.P. and explained that he was going to leave. The doc could have taken precautions. Come to think of it, why didn't he do that?" asked Robin.

"I feel thoroughly confused about everything. I could ask him about all this if I see him this weekend," said Sally, holding her breath for Robin's reaction.

"Hang on a minute. What's this about seeing him?" he asked.

"He says he can get away to be with Sally this weekend,"

explained Kate.

"You mean he's so concerned for Jo's fragile state that he's proposing leaving her on her own? At a time when she's trying to decide whether to have an abortion or not? That doesn't make sense. It isn't hanging together, Sal. What's he up to?"

"He gets another free weekend with his adoring lover, doesn't he?" said Kate bitterly. "Oh, I'm sorry, Sally. But surely you can see that Robin's right over that? He can't leave Jo alone this weekend, can he? Not if he's as caring as he says he is."

"I don't think it would be right for us to be together this weekend, under the circumstances," said Sally with dignity. "But that doesn't mean that a termination wouldn't completely alter things. This letter has put a new slant on the situation. Possibly."

"Let's see what happens, eh? Take it one week at a time. Don't see him until the pregnancy situation is resolved. Be strong," urged Kate.

"That would seem to be the right thing to do. I'll phone

him and explain…"

"It would be better just to leave a message at his school. You know how hard it would be for you to refuse him once he's talking to you."

"You make me sound such a pushover. So weak. Am I really so abject?"

"You're a lovely, gentle person who doesn't want to cause pain, especially to someone you still love," said Robin, taking Sally's hand. "It isn't weakness. It's one of your strengths, your consideration for others. But Mark would take advantage of it, Sally. And that would make it worse for you, because you'd then be riddled with guilt. Don't talk to him until it's all resolved. Then, if the outcome is happy for you, you'll only have missed a few weeks of seeing him. If things don't turn out as you would like them to, then at least you'll have had more time to distance yourself from him. It makes sense."

"I know. You're right. Of course you are. I'll just leave a message with the school secretary. I'll say something that sounds bland to anyone else, but conveys my meaning to him. Oh dear, what can I say?"

"How about: 'The meeting this weekend has been cancelled.' That should make it clear," suggested Kate. "I'll do it for you, if you like."

"Would you mind? That would help me tremendously. I wouldn't be tempted to talk to him, then. Thanks, Kate."

"Off to bed, then. Let's all try to get a good night's sleep!" concluded Robin.

Of course, that was impossible for all of them. Sally took the letter up with her and re-read it, trying to fathom the truth behind the words. If she believed Mark, then she could see that he had been put into an almost impossible situation by his needy wife. She didn't relish the idea of his making love to Jo, but if it was instigated by compassion, then she could understand and even forgive. She could imagine how it could happen, and her heart filled with pity. Yet she couldn't help thinking that a man with that much selfless compassion for a sick wife wouldn't suggest leaving her alone at a time of her having to make a momentous decision about the baby. Robin's instinct about that sounded right. Then she had a thought which made her sit up in bed with eyes wide open. Of course, he could leave her at the weekend if she wasn't actually going to be alone! She might be seeing her parents, or a close friend, staying over the weekend and talking through the problem with them. That would give him the opportunity to see his True Love to make plans with her for their future together. Sally was so excited by that idea that she nearly rushed into Kate and Robin's bedroom to tell them about it. Something – perhaps embarrassment – stopped her. However, she heard sounds in the bathroom, so she opened her bedroom door to see if it was Kate. Had it been Robin, she would have crept back to bed. But Fate decreed that Kate's teeth were the last to be cleaned that night. Sally beckoned her into the room.

"Kate. I've just realised that Jo must be going away herself for the weekend, probably to talk things over with her parents. Of course Mark wouldn't leave her alone. Don't you see? You've been so anxious to condemn him that you've overlooked the obvious explanation."

Kate sat down heavily on the bed. She frowned as she thought about it. Had she been too keen to see Mark as the villain of the piece?

"That's possible, I suppose." She paused, thinking. "But wait a minute. If you were contemplating an abortion, would you discuss it with your parents? They'd be the last people I'd want to talk to. In fact, I'd want them positively not to know about it. Their generation tends to be much more pro life, doesn't it? So if your decision went the way of abortion, as seems to be the foregone conclusion in this case, you wouldn't want parents to know anything, would you?"

"Well, a close friend, then. She might want to discuss it with a close friend," insisted Sally.

"But what is there to discuss? She's shocked by the news. She knows she can't cope with a child in her depressed state. She's already made the appointment to see the doctor. What is there to talk about?"

"I'd want to talk to you," said Sally.

"Yes, but would you want to stay for the whole weekend?"

"That might depend on where her friend lived."

"Yes, I suppose so. But people don't tend to have best friends who live miles away, do they? I mean, you may be friends with women who don't live in London, but real intimacy is usually reserved for those you see quite frequently, isn't it?" Kate said reasonably.

"Maybe. I could just phone Mark tomorrow and find out, couldn't I? And if she's not going away, then I could tell him I couldn't see him till it was all decided and tied up with a bow."

"But you'd be giving him the idea, wouldn't you? 'I'll only see you if Jo is going away for the weekend' would lead him quite naturally to assure you that she was."

"I'm sure I could approach it a bit more obliquely than that! Give me some credit for intelligence, please," said Sally.

Sally's tone of voice warned Kate not to push too hard. Her friend was hurting and in turmoil; she needed to be protected and not offended.

"Look, Sally, I know how much you want Mark to be absolved of guilt and you want to see him. But we did agree that hanging back this weekend would be the right thing, didn't we? Suppose Jo needs him for something, or she wants to talk to him on the telephone if she's away from home, wouldn't it be right that she should be able to contact him? If he's with you, he's completely inaccessible to her. She's the one who needs our compassion this weekend. Isn't she?"

Sally dissolved into tears. "You're right, of course. Of course. I'm being really selfish and thoughtless. We'll stick to Plan A and you can phone tomorrow to say I'm not available over the weekend. When it's all over, we'll be able to look back on this with a good conscience."

"That's my girl! It isn't easy, I know. But we'll have lots to do to keep you occupied. Just think of all those friends we're about to be reunited with!"

Chapter **9**

After school the following day, Sally was doggedly marking work in the Department office. She and James were the only ones left at six o'clock, sharing hot drinks and exchanging howlers and apposite phrases from their classes' work.

"Did you know that Shakespeare was 'The Bird of Avon'?" asked James, snorting into his coffee.

"That must be why we talk about the wings of poetry," replied Sally. "I hope that's not from one of your Sixth Formers."

"Fortunately not. I'd give up if it were. No, it's one of my Year Nines preparing for dear old SATs. I'm really enjoying this essay, but for all the wrong reasons! Listen to this: 'Romeo belonged to a gang called The Jets and Juliet was a shark. They lived in Italy but fought in New York. That's because they was all immigrants. Romeo's friend Mercuntio – I kid you not! – caused all the trouble.

Romeo and Juliet fell in love but they shouldn't. When Romeo got shot, it brought the gangs together and they all got on again. Except for the dead ones.'"

"That'll teach you to show them 'West Side Story' too soon," laughed Sally.

"I have a feeling that this little chap missed most of the play, even when he was in the room. However, I do recall him shedding a clandestine tear at the end of the film, so all is not lost educationally. How's your set?" asked James.

"I'm marking my A Level attempts at understanding King Lear. 'Howl, howl, howl, howl, howl,' seems to sum it up quite nicely! Mind you, it's a welcome relief from star-crossed lovers and messages going astray."

"Talking of which, did you get that message I put on your desk at lunchtime?"

Sally froze. It was odd how things could seem so normal one minute, and then be blurred at the edges next minute. She started lifting papers and books as she searched for the missing missive.

"I put it under your mug. I thought you'd be bound to see it there. Sorry, I should have mentioned it, but I completely forgot."

Sally moved her dirty lunchtime mug and revealed a note in James's untidy writing. As she both hoped and feared, it was from Mark, urging her to telephone him about 'the cancelled weekend meeting.'

"Disappointing news?" asked James, aware of the effect that the note was having.

"I'm trying to distance myself from ... my boyfriend. Just for a trial period. To see how we feel about each other," she explained.

As far as she knew, James was not aware who her 'boyfriend' was. She wanted to keep it that way. English teachers formed a small fraternity in their local area and Sally knew how gossip penetrated every chance meeting or organised conference. She did not want to be pitied or condemned by people she had to work with on a daily basis. She was glad that she had confided in her Head of Department, Fran, and she felt sure that Fran was not a gossip. But James? Sally wasn't sure whether he could bridle his chattering tongue.

"He's married, isn't he?" said James, and it wasn't really a question.

"Does anything stay private around here?" asked Sally with some anger.

"It's common knowledge, Vol. You know how it is. I mean, you didn't need to be told that I was gay. It's fairly obvious. Well, it's just as obvious that your fella needs a screen around him because you're always so careful how you talk about him. You never bring him to Department parties, either. So it's clear that he's married. Q.E.D."

"Quite Easily Destroyed! I suppose you also know who it is," she said, hoping that it was not so.

"No, I don't. Frankly, Scarlet, I don't give a damn. Your life is yours, to muck up how you like. I cling to the right to muck up mine, so why shouldn't I allow you the same privilege?"

"I didn't think it was going to be quite so bad a mess as

it's turned out to be. That's why I'm calling for a cooling off period."

"That sounds eminently sensible. Actually, I'm going through a similar briar-patch myself. It's all very prickly and uncomfortable."

"But you've been with Lloyd for yonks! I'm so sorry. At your birthday bash last year, I spent a lot of time with Lloyd. I really liked him. I remember that we talked for ages about Virginia and the Bloomsbury set. He was directing a production of 'Vita and Virginia' and you were planning to go to Sissinghurst to see Vita's white garden. I almost invited myself along, he made it sound so beautiful and exciting."

"He can make the telephone directory sound like that. Unfortunately, he has that mesmerising effect on everyone he meets and so lots of people find themselves in love with him. It's hard for me to believe that I'm the only one whose love he reciprocates," sighed James.

"You mean your briar patch is just about worries rather than Lloyd actually straying from the path?"

"I just can't believe that he still loves only me...."

"And that matters, does it? Exclusivity?" asked Sally.

"How do you feel about it? Is it all right that you're singing a duet with His wife?"

Sally laughed. "There's not much singing going on, I can assure you. Not at the moment."

"Just an interval? Or has the curtain come down?"

"I don't know. I can't hear any applause. But that could just mean that it was a lousy performance," said Sally.

"Oh, we English teachers are a peculiar bunch. Here we are, talking about life and death, and we can't stop ourselves from using the odd metaphor! I suppose it makes it hurt less."

"But it does still hurt, doesn't it? What do you think will happen to you and Lloyd?"

"I've either got to believe his protestations of faithfulness, or I've got to make up my mind that it doesn't matter if I'm not the only one. Rather like you, I suspect. Isn't that your situation?"

"Not quite," said Sally. She took a deep breath, and decided to tell James a little more. After all, she reasoned, he had bared some of his soul to her. "You see, there are reasons why he hasn't been able to leave his wife even though he's wanted to."

"There always are," sighed James.

"Don't be cynical until you know the whole story," admonished Sally.

"Sorry, Vol. You're right. Just because it's a stereotypical situation doesn't mean that it's not different this time. I think this is turning into a two-mug problem. I shall replenish the kettle, rinse the mugs and administer to your caffeine requirements. See how domesticated I am?"

He busied himself with the coffees while Sally contemplated just how much to tell him. It was a long and complicated tale, but she used the time to pare it down to its bare essentials.

"Here we are," said James, struggling to find a space for

the mugs on their crowded desks. "Off you go again. Reveal the particulars that make your situation so particular."

"Well, now there's an additional problem. She needs an abortion."

"You don't do things by halves, do you? I can see how that could alter the situation. However, they're easily obtained, from what I've heard. Or is the problem the fact that she got pregnant in the first place? Is her new boyfriend wanting to back away from the new responsibility?"

"There's no new boyfriend," stated Sally bleakly.

James looked steadily at her, letting the silence expand between them. Eventually, Sally felt she had to speak.

"Yes, it's his baby. No-one else is involved."

"That would cause you some dismay. It's the same faithfulness problem that I'm trying to deal with, isn't it? Do you need exclusivity or can you go on sharing?"

"I can't share. We planned it to be divorce followed by

marriage. Old-fashioned, I know. But there have been all sorts of obstacles to the divorce, let alone the marriage. She doesn't know about me, you see."

"You Jezebel, you! You surprise me. More than that, frankly, you shock me. Not that I find the situation shocking. It's the fact that you are one of the protagonists. Vol, it's so out of character."

"I know. I feel awful about it. As soon as I found out he was married…"

"He didn't tell you?"

"Not exactly," she faltered. "I found out, and later that day he told me. I don't know if he told me because he found out that I'd found out. If you follow. Anyway, as soon as I knew, I wanted to end it all. Then he told me that he and his wife were deeply unhappy and that he was only staying with her because she was depressed. He was looking for a way to tell her when this bombshell about the pregnancy fell on us."

"How long has it been going on?"

"Coming up to two years."

"And he's been looking for a way to tell her all that time?"

"Don't sound so incredulous. It's a very complex situation, James."

"So you don't want me to question how she came to be expecting if their marriage was over in all but name?"

At that moment, the outside line registered an incoming call. An answer machine was left on every evening so that the English staff could leave full details of their cover work without having to rely on the school office to pass it on wrongly. James and Sally stopped talking and listened in to see which colleague had succumbed to the latest bug. When she heard Mark's voice, Sally went to pick up the phone, but James held her arm gently and shook his head. She relaxed and sat down, listening to the message.

"This is a message for Sally James. Could you tell her that the weekend meeting is imperative and that she must ring to confirm. She knows the number. Thanks."

"Sounds like one of you isn't convinced of the need to cool off for a while," remarked James. "I take it you're the one who's holding off till the abortion is over and the wife is back on her feet."

"That seems to be the only right thing to do. I'm not very good at this hole-in-corner stuff. There's been enough secrecy and betrayal to last me a lifetime, thank you very much. I just want a normal relationship with a man who loves me as much as I love him."

"Hear, hear to that! Me, too!"

"So, much as I want to contact Mark and see him this weekend, I'm not going to," she said firmly.

"Mark? You said 'Mark', didn't you?"

"Damn! It just slipped out …"

"A common problem with men of a certain age. Sorry. No time for humour. Er, would the Mark in question be Mark Jennings, by any remote chance?"

"Why?" asked Sally. She wondered if James had also heard about the affair with the Australian girl that Fran had told her about.

"Oh, no reason. He's just the only Mark I can think of who's a teacher. I'm assuming that Loverboy is a teacher?"

"He is. But I'm not going to identify him more than that, if you don't mind. I really didn't mean to talk to anyone about all this. Perhaps I shouldn't have."

"I shan't say anything, Vol. You know me better than that. Oh, I know I'm a motor-mouth sometimes, but only as a social lubricant. I'm great to have around at parties – I can talk *ad infinitum* about any old rubbish. But I keep my friends close."

"Thanks. Fran knows about it, but that's all. My best friend, Kate – you've met her and her partner, Robin – is the only one who knows absolutely all my murky secrets. I'm staying with them at the moment. I can't face my flat. Not until the future becomes a little clearer. Hopefully, that won't take long. As soon as Mark can extricate himself and see his wife taken care of, we won't have to keep in the shadows any more. Everything can be out in the open and normal. I can't tell you how much I'm longing for that."

"Of course," said James.

"Thanks for listening, James. I shouldn't have burdened you with it, but I'm glad I did. Now, I'm going back to Kate's and I'll try to forget everything but Shakespeare!"

When Sally had gone, taking the rest of her King Lear essays with her, James allowed himself to utter the misgivings he had been concealing since he'd heard the name 'Mark' escaping from Sally's lips. "Dors! Dors! Dors! Please don't let it be him!"

Sally called in at her flat on her way back, planning to pick up enough clothes to last for a couple of weeks. The new key was stiff in the lock so that it felt as if she were entering a different place instead of her much-loved home. It smelt of new paint, which added to the air of unfamiliarity. Picking up the day's mail, mostly junk, she headed for the answer machine. As she suspected, there were several from Mark, in ascending tones of frustration. She replayed the final one: 'Sally? I know you're staying with Kate and that moron she lives with. How dare he stop me coming into my own home by changing the lock? Because that's how I think of it, darling – the place I share with you is my home. Sweetheart, I could spend all weekend with you. We could even choose the honeymoon destination, if you like. How's that for commitment? Jo's seeing Dr Shah next week and it all should be over soon. Please phone me. Use the mobile number. I'm waiting for your call. Darling. Please.'

Sally erased the messages, partly as a way of scotching the temptation to ring Mark immediately. She then busied herself, recycling the junk mail and putting the other envelopes into her bag. When she inspected the bathroom, she was pleased to see that dear old Robin had done a good job and had even cleaned up after himself, which was something that always delighted her about him. She wondered if Kate realised how messy most men were. While she was packing a suitcase, kidding herself that she was merely going on holiday to make it less of a chore, she started thinking about Mark's phone message. If Jo's appointment with the doctor was early in the week rather than later, things could resolve themselves quite quickly. After all, everyone would want the termination to take place as soon as possible. Sally found herself desperately wondering when the appointment was and whether she could find out. A plan formed in her mind. What if she phoned Jo, pretending to be the surgery confirming her appointment? If Mark answered, she could just hang up. As she selected her less-grey underwear, promising herself some new lingerie, she made up her mind that no harm could come of this plan of hers. It would help her to survive the waiting if she knew some definite timing. She fastened the case and picked up the bedroom extension, keying in Mark's home number with care, as it wasn't the one she was used to ringing when she contacted him. The phone was answered straight away, by a woman.

"Is that Mrs Jennings? This is the doctor's surgery here," said Sally, disguising her voice by flattening her vowels.

"Yes, it is."

"I'm just phoning to confirm your appointment with Dr Shah next week."

"I don't have an appointment next week. My next appointment is at the hospital for the scan."

"Oh, I'm so sorry. I was looking at the wrong week. Silly me! You've already seen the doctor, haven't you?"

"Yes. To confirm the pregnancy," said the woman happily.

"Sorry to disturb you. My mistake. And congratulations!" Sally choked out.

"Thanks so much."

Somehow, Sally managed to replace the receiver. She didn't know how she'd kept up the conversation or the disguised voice after the word 'scan' came like a bullet to her heart. Pain and confusion were like body blows, driving the air from her lungs and leaving her breathless on the bed. Jo was having a scan, not a termination. She sounded happy to be pregnant, had accepted the congratulations warmly. So what was Mark up to? What was he trying to do? Sally's first reaction was to need to talk to Kate, as always when she was in trouble or misery. And she was in both right now. She lifted the receiver again and keyed Kate's number like an automaton, hoping that she'd be home.

"Kate Nelson speaking."

"Oh, thank goodness. Kate, oh Kate. Oh, Kate."

It was all she could say, and she didn't even say that, but sobbed it.

"Are you at the flat? Don't move. I'm coming straight round in the car," said Kate, and hung up.

Sally's sobs, once unleashed, became howls. Yet even as she felt herself overwhelmed by emotion, a small corner of her mind told her that King Lear must have sounded just like this. She even had the presence to wonder how the brain could do that, how it could keep a thread of sensible thought clinging on through the deluge of tears. By the time Kate arrived, Sally had calmed down sufficiently to let her in with no more than a sniffle.

"What's wrong? Are you all right?" said a breathless Kate, hugging Sally to her and leading her to the sofa.

"It's O.K. I was in a panic, but I'm much better now. I just had a shock, that's all. It was a message on the machine…"

"Nothing's happened to your parents, has it?" was Kate's first thought.

"No, no. Nothing like that. Let me play it for you."

Sally went to the phone and then realised that she'd erased the messages. Her forgetting that she'd done that made her collapse in tears again, cursing her own stupidity.

"Hey, come on now. Sit down again and start at the beginning. You got home and played the answer machine. There was a message. Go on from there."

"There were several messages from Mark, all asking to meet at the weekend. The last one said that Jo had an appointment with the doctor next week. I suddenly felt I wanted to know when it was. I know it was paranoid of me, but I just had to find out. I phoned Jo."

"You did what?" Kate exploded.

"Not as me. I said I was the doctor's receptionist confirming her appointment. I thought I could get her to tell me when it was, you see. And she wouldn't think anything of it. But she denied that she had one. Then she said her next appointment was for a scan at the hospital. Oh, Kate, she was obviously overjoyed to be pregnant, you could hear it in her voice. She doesn't want an abortion at all."

"So that bastard is telling you more lies," hissed Kate through clenched teeth.

"But why? Why is he telling me that Jo's unhappy when she's not?"

"I can only surmise that he wants to go on seeing you and that he'll go on lying about the termination until he can't anymore and then he'll invent some reason why Jo's keeping the baby. All this time, he's drawing you deeper into the relationship. Maybe he'll come up with a story that they're going to have the baby adopted and <u>then</u> they'll divorce. More time to go on stringing you along. And it will never happen, Sally. He'll never leave her, and he'll always have reasonable-sounding excuses for not doing so. And he'll hope that you'll eventually just get used to being his part-time partner. I'm sorry to sound so hard, but I'm pretty certain that's what's in his mind."

Sally looked devastated but the grounded part of her brain had to agree with Kate's response. Misery flooded through her, filling every crevice of her body with the chill cold of unwanted knowledge. She just sat there on the bed, unable to speak or move. Kate went into the kitchen and made a hot drink, which had to be black coffee because of the lack of milk. When she took it into Sally, she could see that Sally was beginning to thaw out. The coffee helped, too. Soon Sally was able to conduct a conversation.

"I just don't understand how he can carry on this charade, Kate. I don't understand him at all. I want to fall back on the old prejudices and say that all men are bastards given half a chance, but I know that's not true. I mean, look at Robin. I can't imagine him doing anything like this," said Sally quietly.

"You know that book? 'Men are from Mars, Women are from Venus'? They're a different species."

"I remember when I was doing teacher training, we had this lecturer who'd done some research on the old nature versus nurture question. She'd helped to pioneer some anti-sexist education in schools. You know, boys being given dolls to care for instead of guns to play with in Primary schools in order to help to change their perception of men's role in life. She ignored the fact that, deprived of toy guns, they just picked up sticks and said 'Bang, bang.' But we all made up such fun lessons, reversing the sexes in traditional fairy tales so that it was the girl who rescued the Prince from the fire-breathing dragon and so on. I was a real convert, proselytising to the more world-weary members of staff. And I know it really made a difference. We were able to change prejudices and perceptions. The boys I taught did learn to be moved by sadness, they did allow themselves to write poetry without thinking of themselves as wet. And the girls became much more confident. In fact, some of them became so bolshy that we sometimes regretted they weren't docile and quiet. But deep down, underneath all the change, there were still fundamental differences. They'll never be eradicated, because they're there in the genes. Men and women are different. That doesn't mean that we mustn't encourage women to be in charge of their lives, pursuing careers and all the rest of it. But we should also acknowledge that they'll never be the same as men."

"Heck, we don't want to be! So many men are emotional cripples…"

"And some of that is because of the way they were brought up…"

"But not all of it. Some of it is because men simply don't deal with emotion in the same way as women do. Robin's pretty good, you're right. He cries at sad films along with me, and I love that. But even he has difficult times dealing with love and responsibility. And the only other man in my life was my bastard father. And, as you know, he was unable to cope with it at all. He didn't know how to talk to my mother or to me. Whenever they started a discussion, it would lead into a quarrel. And the end of the quarrel was physical violence. He couldn't follow an argument through, couldn't deal with my mother getting emotional and upset. It led to my mother withdrawing into herself and never saying a word eventually."

"At least Mark wasn't aggressive," sighed Sally.

"Wasn't he?" challenged Kate. "Maybe he never hit you or Jo, but I'd say his manipulation of you both was pretty cruel. Isn't that a form of aggression?"

"Maybe," sighed Sally tiredly.

"It certainly shows a need to be in control," Kate continued. "I think he gets a kick out of juggling two women, keeping them both in ignorance while he's the only one who knows all the facts."

"He does like to organise everyone," said Sally, sipping her coffee. "That was one of the things I liked about him, actually. It was nice to relax and let him take over my life. After organising lessons all week, I loved being taken out and never having to book tickets or reserve tables. Does that mean he's a control freak?"

"If he was obsessive about it, then yes. Was he?" asked Kate.

Sally reflected for a minute or two. "Looking back with that wonderful 20/20 vision called hindsight, I think he was. I used to try to arrange surprises for him when we first went out together. I thought he'd like it just as much as I did. You know, both having the same sort of things to do in our jobs, I guessed he might like just to relax and let me take over sometimes. But he was always rather stiff about it. He made me feel that he'd already arranged something that was going to have to be cancelled because I'd done something without consulting him first. So I stopped doing it. I let myself lie back and be steered wherever he chose. Maybe that was obsessive."

"Well, I think that's a form of aggression. He was forcing you to do everything he wanted, taking away your freedom. It's just like my dad, really, keeping the little woman in the home, making her conform to what he wanted. Seeing my mum become a doormat made me vow that I would never be one. And I hate the thought that you might have turned into one if you'd stayed with Mark."

"I don't think that would have happened. I'm not doormat material. Am I?"

"You're far too nice for your own safety! You'd go along with something rather than hurt another's feelings. You've always been like that."

"Only in small things," defended Sally. "Not if it was something important. I wouldn't give up my principles. Letting someone else organise your social life isn't the same as allowing them to make you do something you disapprove of."

Kate wanted to argue that that was exactly what Mark had done in persuading Sally to have an affair while he was still married. She bit back the words, but she couldn't help the expression on her face telling Sally what she was thinking. Sally took the criticism in silence but she was hurt by it; she determined that she would try to think the whole thing through unemotionally when she was alone later, but she realised that that was a pretty tall order. How can you be logical when your emotions are insistent on being the centre of your attention?

Chapter 10

The phone call from Jacky that night was a welcome relief to them all. They were sitting together, all three of them trying to concentrate on the television programme they'd chosen as being the least obnoxious, but their heads were filled with separate and separating thoughts. So the sudden ringing urged them back into the real world. Robin answered it, confused at first as to who was calling until he realised that the prattling voice must be the first of the old school friends to have been contacted. As he passed the phone over to Kate, he felt a definite sense of relief that the evening would have some sort of focus now.

"Jacky? How good of you to reply to the e-mail so quickly," laughed Kate. "Actually it was Sally who sent it. She's staying with me at the moment. Hang on, I'll put the phone onto conference and we can all talk at once. Well, not at once exactly! You know what I mean!"

Sally scooted across next to Kate while Robin turned the television off. He picked up the newspaper and opened it at the crossword, though he had every intention of listening in to the conversation.

"It was great to hear from you," said Jacky. She sounded breathless and excited. "I've been thinking about you a lot recently, I don't know why. How about you?"

"Kate and I meet up every Saturday for coffee and even cakes sometimes. No, let me re-phrase that: for cakes and sometimes coffee. Cakes are obligatory. Actually, I'm staying here at the moment. Just for a week or two. But it was at one of those coffee mornings that we had the idea of a reunion."

Kate felt the need to rescue her from too much explanation and guessed the best way of doing that was to turn the spotlight back onto Jacky.

"You seem to be a very happy pixie," she said. "Life sounds good."

"Absolutely. I'm sitting here in my little study with my kiddies playing with their Daddyman just before they get tucked up in bed, and I couldn't be happier."

Kate mouthed 'Daddyman?' incredulously. Even Robin lowered his newspaper and raised his eyebrows.

"Tell us about 'Daddyman' first," said Sally, stifling a giggle.

"His name's David. He's a solicitor. Well, a partner, actually. He specialises in Divorce. I think that makes him really value a happy home life because he sees so many ghastly relationships and such unhappiness, especially when kidlets are involved. Whenever we have a little tiffette, he remembers his latest client and takes a deep breath. Not that we quarrel much at all."

"Lucky you!" laughed Kate, putting her tongue out playfully to Robin, who responded in kind. "And your kids?" she asked, just stopping herself from enunciating 'kidlets' instead.

"Isaac is three and Rachel's six. They're gorgeous poppets, of course,"

171

"Of course. What else could they be?"

"David's already planning their careers! He says they're the brightest children he's ever met, you know!"

"Do they leave you much time for doing anything for yourself?" enquired Sally.

"Not really. I'm very happy at home, though. I don't miss the whole career bit. I'll do it one day, when the children are older. There's plenty of time. And fortunately David earns enough to … well, you know. He'll support me in whatever. I can stay at home if I want to make a career out of that. It's becoming acceptable again, isn't it? I mean, being a homemaker." She sounded breathless again, as if she were apologising.

"Whatever makes you happy," agreed Sally, kicking the grimacing Kate.

"That's what my hubby says. I do lots of creative things anyway. I took a course on Paint Effects and I've rejuvenated every single room in the house."

It was Kate's turn to kick Sally, as she stuffed her fist into her mouth to silence her laughter. "Rejuvenated?"

she managed to squeak.

"Yes, well, the house is old-fashioned. It needed a bit of a face-lift. We live in Hampstead Garden Suburb," she said, as if that explained all.

"One of those lovely Arts and Crafts houses?" asked Sally, whose expression was changing from mockery to outrage as she envisioned Jacky's flippant hands ruining the period features.

"Oh, it's a gorgeous house. Well, it is now. You must come over. David has quite a lot of meetings so I have plenty of time to see friends on my own."

"Well, our first meeting's going to be here. Can you come next Tuesday?" asked Kate.

"Try to keep me away! I'm so excited!" enthused Jacky.

"We were hoping you might be able to contact Michelle. Didn't she marry one of your cousins or something?" asked Sally.

"How did you know that? Yes, she did. They live in Holland Park, in quite a nice house."

"Do you think she'd come?" asked Kate quickly, anxious to head Jacky off from a blow-by-blow account of the probably inferior state of Michelle's abode.

"Tricky. I think she's over in Paris at the moment. Her father's just died and her mother's falling apart. But I'll phone and make sure." At that moment, a muffled wail travelled down the line. "Whoops! I think Daddyman might need some help. He does tend to get them a bit over-excited at bedtime and then he wonders why they don't just fall straight off to sleep. Mummy to the rescue! Must go. See you both next Tuesday!"

All three of them burst out laughing. Robin was first to recover. "I was half expecting her to call herself Mummywoman. Whatever happened to suffragettes and the Women's Movement? I think your school history lessons must have been sorely lacking by the sound of it. She even called him 'hubby' at one point, didn't she?"

"She certainly seems to have moulded herself into the perfect Stepford Wife image. Too much Mills and Boon,

I suspect," laughed Kate.

"And can't you just imagine what she's done to that lovely Arts and Crafts house? It doesn't bear thinking about!" said Sally, half mocking and half offended.

"Stencilled vine leaves in the dining room. Clowns dancing around the walls of the nursery. Rag rolling in every conceivable space," agreed Kate.

"I expect even the insides of the cupboards have benefited from her improvements," agreed Robin.

"And the children, too. Gilded, no doubt!" added Sally.

"Oh, surely they need no embellishment? Doesn't Daddyman think they're perfect already? Oh, Lordy, can you believe 'Daddyman'? Priceless!" chortled Robin.

They all subsided into smugness about their own lives, until Sally said plaintively, "Still, there she is, happiness personified, in a big house with a wealthy 'hubby' and two kids. And where am I? In a mess!"

"But gamely independent. Not reliant on the crumbs that a supercilious husband deigns to let fall from his table," said Robin.

"Oh, come on, Robin. We don't know anything about –
what's his name? David?" said Sally. "He may be
perfectly nice and devoted."

"Perhaps. But my experience is that men don't much
value wives who are as abject as she sounded."

"And did you notice how she let slip that he was often
out?" agreed Kate.

"Did she?"

"Yes. She said something about 'leaving her lots of time
for meeting friends'."

"I think there might be a little more unhappiness behind
that bright chatter than we're being led to believe,"
opined Robin sagely.

"Jacky was always running behind trying to catch us up.
It may just be that she wants us to know that she's
probably overtaken most of us now, in terms of wealth
anyway."

"Also in terms of marital status and children, in her

opinion anyway."

"We'll see. I wonder if Michelle will be able to come. Shame about her Dad popping his clogs," said Kate.

"Didn't she have a rather difficult relationship with her father?" asked Sally. "I seem to recall her ranting about him a lot."

"Yes, you're right. Was it to do with his having to go back to Paris a lot for his job? Leaving her to stay at Jacky's house?"

"In which case," Robin joined in, "the ranting would have been because she missed him – loved him – rather than that she quarrelled with him. Wouldn't it?"

"Could be," agreed Kate. "Kids are never all that aware about what's happening around them, are they? It came across as anger but it may well have been a sort of grief at his absence. We thought we were so sophisticated and understood it all, but we didn't really. Anyway, I do hope Michelle will come. I liked her."

"You liked all the free cosmetics she gave us, you mean!" laughed Sally.

"What?" asked Robin.

"Oh, her father worked for some chi-chi French firm and she used to get oodles of freebies. We had great sleepovers trying out all the newest shades of eye-shadows and lipstick. It was an adolescent paradise. We must have looked rather like Ziggy Stardust, but we thought we were at the cutting edge of fashion."

"Don't knock Ziggy!" objected Robin. "He was before my time but he was my total hero. I think I fell in love with the image of Bowie long before I noticed the charms of the female of the species."

Kate laughed. "Robin, you're encourageable!"

"Don't you mean 'incorrigible'?"

"I know what I mean!"

The telephone rang again and Kate picked it up mid-laugh. The jollity ebbed from her face and she cleared her throat noisily. "No, I'm afraid you can't. It's not possible and it's not a good idea either, is it?"

Sally tensed and Robin's eyes flickered between the faces of the two women, alert to the possible need to support one or both of them. It was obvious that it was Mark on the other end.

"No. She doesn't want to talk to you. Interfering? I'm not interfering, Mark, I'm just relaying the wishes of my best friend. She has nothing to say to you at the moment."

Sally hung her head dejectedly. Robin was afraid that she might be on the verge of taking the phone from Kate's hand and he felt that that would be a mistake. He got up and led Sally away from temptation, towards the table where the still half-full bottle of wine sat invitingly. This allowed Kate to dispose of Mark with more confidence.

"Mark, please understand. I am not preventing Sally from seeing you. She's a grown-up and she has decided that there is no point in your seeing each other at the moment. No, there isn't anything that needs explaining. It's all very plain. Babies take precedence over everything, don't they?"

Sally's hand shook as she clutched the glass that Robin had carefully poured for her.

"Please don't shout at me, Mark. And please don't try to contact Sally here again. She does not wish to talk to you."

Kate hung up decisively and looked up. She took in Sally's mood at a glance. "If he phones again, will you take it, Robin? He was getting very abusive at the end."

"Of course I will." He turned to Sally. "That is what you want, isn't it?"

"It's what must be," she replied. "There seem to be so many lies and deceptions in the way Mark is handling this situation. I don't know what to believe any more. I want to trust him, but every additional piece of evidence seems to confirm his … perfidy. What a lovely old-fashioned word that is; it just sums up so perfectly what I think of Mark at the moment. I feel like one of those mediaeval princesses shut up in a tower, betrayed by the perfidious one I thought I could trust. Which makes you two my knights in shining armour, I suppose."

"Hey, I like that," said Kate. "A female knight in shining whatsit. Yes. And never fear, fair maiden, we shall protect thee against all the wicked stratagems of the enemy!"

"I think 'enemy' might be going a little too far," said Sally defensively.

"We shall see. Every opportunity will be given him to retrieve his honour, short of entering thy presence."

Robin chuckled at this exchange. "I suppose you're pledging my rusty sword, too!"

"Don't you mean 'trusty'?" laughed Kate.

"I know what I mean," they all replied.

Chapter 11

Somehow, Sally stumbled her way to Friday. There were several messages from Mark about the weekend 'meeting', which she studiously ignored. Her Department showed signs of curiosity, but Fran and James shielded her by inventing a boring computer nerd called Adrian who had made unwanted overtures to her and who wouldn't take no for an answer. Thus, the whole Department united to build a wall round Sally, never allowing her to answer the phone or be hassled by messages through the office. Sally was touched by their loyalty and care, and decided that teachers were the most compassionate and sensitive people in the entire world. The usual routine on a Friday was for all those who could manage it to go to the local pub for a wind-down drink after school. Sally felt it would be churlish for her not to accompany them this week when they had all been so supportive. It was a jolly hour, with everyone vying to tell the best amusing story about the week's teaching.

"Right," said James, bringing them all to order round the pub table. "I'll start off with the best spelling errors of the week. I had a beauty from 7R. I'd asked them to write a story for homework, about anything at all. Let their little imaginations flare and flourish, I thought."

"You mean you couldn't think what to set them!"

"Oh ye of little faith! Anyway, Jimmy Laing chose to write 'A Day in the Life of a Penny'. I rather think the idea may have come from his father. I seem to remember being set something very similar when I was at school all those centuries ago."

There were murmurs and groans of recognition round the table. James waited for them to subside before continuing. "The problem for poor old Jimmy was that the plural of penny eluded him. So we had him walking down the road with his 'penis' in his hand, wondering what to do. Every sentence after that compounded the error. He took his penis out of his pocket, he threw his penis from hand to hand, and he gave his penis in exchange for a bar of chocolate. The decadence of the unfortunate boy knew no limits! Finally, the much-handled penis ended up snapped shut in the till. My eyes watered in sympathy, I can tell you."

"My best story of the week came from a cover lesson," said Fran. "This Year 7 class were doing history projects. One lad was researching the Great Fire of London and he was in the library surfing the net for info. He was coming up with lots of written stuff but he was desperate for a picture – they take up lots of space, he said, so your folder looks big! 'Miss, why can't I get any video stuff on the Fire of London?' Bless him! I said, 'Think about it' and he really concentrated hard for a minute or two. 'Oh, of course!' he said. Light had dawned, I thought. 'They would all have burned in the fire, wouldn't they?' he said."

"Your turn, Vol," said James.

"Not much to report this week, I'm afraid. I suppose the best was someone mentioning the Magna Carta and asserting that it was in the Louvre. I was rather puzzled, and it was only when they talked about its enigmatic smile that I realised what they meant."

"Priceless," said Iris, their youngest recruit. "I haven't got any bloomers this week."

"Brazen hussy," interrupted James. "Knickerless in Gaza!"

"But I did overhear some lasses in the playground talking about their fantasy boyfriends. They all agreed that a sense of humour was really important and they liked boys who could tell a good joke. One of the girls confessed that she was hopeless at jokes because she always messed up the punchline. She said she even got 'Knock, knock' jokes wrong, which was why her last boyfriend had dumped her. She'd said 'Knock, knock', so he'd responded with the expected 'Who's there?' She'd said 'Damian', so he'd asked 'Damian who?' She should have replied 'Dame Ian McKellen' so they could have had an uproarously funny anti-gay laugh. However, she'd forgotten the name and had said 'Dame Ian Rush' – she had no idea where that name had come from. Of course, she also had no idea that he was a hero footballer if you were a Liverpool fan, which the boyfriend was. The lad was furious, apparently."

"Of course, it's all right to have a good laugh at gay actors, but heaven forfend that we should ridicule sainted footballers," groaned James.

"Well, we all know that footballers are never homosexual, don't we?" laughed Iris.

"Anyone for another round?" asked Fran.

There was some discussion about time and the possibilities of being later home, but in the end all but James and Sally departed. Sally wanted to say a special thank you for James's exceptional care over the week and she wanted to be alone with him when she said it.

"You've been an angel this week," she ventured.

"Moi? Well, perhaps just a bit of a winged guardian," he acknowledged. "But here we are, duly arrived at the weekend without your being waylaid by... "

He broke off abruptly, his eyes glued to the pub door. Then suddenly he wrapped Sally in his arms as if they were lovers, and whispered urgently in her ear, "Pretend you're enjoying it. Yon doorway seems to be full of an ex of yours."

She stiffened momentarily before concentrating all her

energy on relaxing. "Is it Mark?" she asked unnecessarily.

"In the flesh. Mmmm. Your hair smells gorgeous. Watch out, here he comes."

"What's going on? Sal? Sal, what are you doing?" asked an outraged voice which they both worked hard to pretend had taken them by surprise.

"What business is it of yours? Who are you?" asked James with seeming bafflement.

Mark stretched himself to his not-inconsiderable height and puffed out his chest like a pouter pigeon. His dark eyes flashed disbelief, staring at Sally relentlessly. He took in her flushed and panic-stricken look and he mistakenly saw it as one of guilty embarrassment.

"Ask her who I am if you really don't know," he rasped.

"Oh, I can take a pretty good guess. You're late, as in Sally's late boyfriend," responded James.

Sally struggled, both physically and emotionally. She knew James's embrace had been a ploy to protect her from the persuasive arguments that would certainly have come her way from Mark. But was it what she wanted? Did she really want Mark to think their relationship was so over that she was already in the arms of the next lover? She opened her mouth to speak, but was unable to think of anything at all to say. It was James who leapt in again to continue the charade.

"It's time we were leaving, darling. Say goodnight to your erstwhile friend," he said.

"Just a minute," interrupted Mark. "Sally and I have some unfinished business, if you don't mind."

"Well, I do, actually. I believe she's asked you for Time Out, and I'm assisting her to banish misery from her mind, transitorily or otherwise. We're *carp*ing a few *diem*s, at least until you're a bit more sorted out, sunshine. So please don't try to impede our egress or you might just find yourself taking a Luciferian fall."

James gathered up a rather limp Sally and strode with her from the pub without as much as a backward glance. Mark was left gaping in disbelief and annoyance.

Once outside, James grabbed Sally's hand and started to run towards his car. He managed to manhandle her into the passenger seat and himself into driving mode before Mark's irate form emerged from the doorway. James drove off round the corner and down the road before re-parking the car, confident that they would not be followed.

"Sorry about the liberties taken, Vol, but it seemed expedient at the time. Anything to get you out of harm's way."

"What must he have thought?" asked a shaken Sally.

"That he isn't the only chocky in the box, which might be extremely good for him. Let him absorb the possibility that you aren't totally dependent on his amorous advances. I must say, I rather enjoyed the role of macho lover. Did I do it well?"

"To the manner born, dear heart. But did I want him to think that about me?"

"Why wouldn't you?"

"Suppose there really is some way out of his marriage. Suppose we were meant for each other after all," Sally said.

"Come on, Vol, get real. Give it some time, by all means, but don't beguile the shining hour with porkies."

"How did you know it was Mark in the doorway, anyway?" asked Sally, suddenly alert to the fact that she had never given Mark's full identity away to James, nor described him adequately enough to be recognised.

"Ah. It's a fair cop. I had a feeling in my water that Mark Jennings might be the chap. So when I saw him I jumped to fairly obvious conclusions."

"Why did you think it was him?" persisted Sally. She was beginning to feel something cold and uncomfortable in the pit of her stomach, a foreboding taking shape in her reluctant mind.

James sighed and took her hand. "He does have a wee bit of a reputation, you know. You do know that, don't you?"

Sally breathed in as deeply as she dared. "I knew I

wasn't the first. Fran told me about the Australian girl at his last school."

"And did she tell you about any of the others?"

"Others?" Sally's voice seemed to come from far away.

"Vol, there've been quite a few. Some no more than one-night-stands at conferences, it's true, but there have been several more serious sorties into the realms of amorous shenanigans."

Sally was shocked and wondered what other secrets were hidden in Mark's closet.

"Why didn't anyone warn me?"

"Probably no-one knew you were involved with him. Or if they did, they didn't want to face the fate of bearers of bad tidings. Usually, these things have a habit of not lasting long and blowing over. You must have been the exception who stuck in there longer than expected."

"Sally the limpet, that's me," she sighed bitterly.

"What I can't understand is why he's hanging on so tenaciously."

"Thank you very much!"

"No, don't misunderstand me. I mean, I think the man's always been a gadfly. He'd settle for a wee while but he'd soon want to be off again to fresh woods and pastures new. The flight was part of the fun. But you say you've been with him for two years. That is a serious settle. You must have proved to be as interesting as you are gorgeous!"

"La, sir! You flatter me!"

"Perhaps his feelings are genuine, after all. Now that would be a turn up for the folio. The biter bit. Broody hill, but that would be something!"

"Poor Mark."

"What?! Come on, Vol. If there's a 'poor' to be attached to anyone, it's got to be to you or Jo. In fact, primarily it's got to be Jo's undeserved epithet."

"Why 'undeserved'?"

"I don't suppose you've ever met her, have you?" asked James circumspectly. "From what I hear, she's a genuinely nice woman. As are you. He certainly knows how to pick them. Though what either of you sees in him, I shall never understand. I suppose he has symmetrical features and all his own teeth, but he isn't exactly a matinee idol. I love that term, don't you? It always puts me in mind of film stars like Cary Grant – whom I adore unreservedly, by the way. Mark can be quite interesting, I suppose, but no more so than any teacher who has a passion for his subject. His bodywork has so far escaped rust and accidental damage, though there are likely to be quite a few husbands out there who would gladly cause a few irreparable dents. But on the whole, a fairly ordinary example of his species, I'd have thought. Perhaps there's something hidden from my homosexual eyes. Oh well, heigh ho. It's time to get you back to your own car, I think."

"Do you think the coast's clear? I'd hate to run into Mark again without your all-encompassing presence."

"I'll drive you round there and make sure all's well before I depart."

As they buckled up and made themselves ready to re-join the world, Sally was anxious to talk about something else, anything that would steer James from his analysis of Mark.

"How are things with you? Is home life any less prickly?" asked Sally.

"Funnily enough, taking an interest in your difficulties seems to have alleviated mine somewhat. Maybe it's given me an awareness of how lucky I am really. Just having him, I mean. If he says he loves me above all others, why should I doubt it? Why cause myself more angst than lovers usually do?"

"Good for you. Enjoy what you have, believe what you can. There's no evidence that you're being lied to, is there? I mean, the anxiety you're feeling isn't based on proof of deceit?"

"I think it's all in my own befuddled brain. I couldn't bear to lose him, you see, so I dread it and see it in every gesture and sentence, daft rugger that I am!"

"If you've been watching that carefully, I'm sure you'd

have seen some evidence by now, had there been any. I have a good feeling about your future, James."

"I'm taking it day by day. Sufficient unto the thingy, and all that."

They drew up alongside Sally's car and scoured the road for signs of Mark. When they were both satisfied that he had departed, Sally kissed James fondly and chastely on the cheek.

"I could get used to this!" he said. "Safe journey home, petal. Have a good weekend. And don't forget that that 'meeting' was cancelled for a good reason. No going back on it."

"Scout's honour. Thanks for everything. See you next week."

Sally drove off, locking the car doors from the inside. She had a vague vision in her head of a scene in a film, she knew not which one, where a woman who was stopped at traffic lights had her car invaded by a murderer. She acknowledged that Mark was no killer, but what she had heard from James had certainly put him in the criminal category. Feelings of disbelief had given way to excessive anger, most of which was foolishly directed at the people around her who had known about his reputation and not warned her. How could they have allowed her to become ever-more-deeply mired without throwing her a reality lifeline? Gradually, she realised that she had told no-one about her affair with Mark, so how could they have warned her? Eventually, the irrational ire abated and she concentrated on the legitimate anger she felt towards Mark. How could such a pleasant exterior hide so base a nature? Images from Jacobean dramas filled her mind. Smiling men in doublet and hose leered their perfidy, leading innocent maidens to their doom. She almost laughed at her own dramatic rendering, but the realisation of the true nature of her lover brought her back to the hideous tragedy in which she was playing her part. The streets that she drove along looked drab and depressing, reflecting her mood. They were the same streets that she and Mark had inhabited, but their sheen had disappeared. She noticed all the deficiencies: the street lights that weren't working, the dog shit that had been tramped in by numerous careless feet, the tattered curtains hanging in dirty windows. Where were the laughing children, the shiny painted front doors, the brightly-lit homes? They seemed only to exist when Mark was there with her, and she dreaded a vista of depression stretching into her future in which she would walk alone and unloved.

"Stop that, at once!" she told herself. "No more of this. The future holds incandescent friendship and humour, if only you'll let yourself see it!"

She determined that she would turn herself round, with a little help from her friends, and the reunion with old school buddies would be her first step along the way.

Chapter 12

By the night of the reunion, they had managed to contact six of their old classmates. Poetic Pru was coming, of course, as was her best friend Mary; Jacky had managed to persuade 'hubby' David to babysit and had also been able to contact Michelle, who was back in England after her father's funeral and who would probably be able to join the party; Cassie (she of the famous father) would deign to come; and surprisingly bringing up the rear would be the mysterious Lyn. So, a party of eight old school friends would be chasing cock Robin from his home, poor thing. He wasn't too bothered, though.

The moving and re-moving of the furniture, the shopping and the food preparation had required all their concentrated effort over the weekend. This was a godsend for Sally, whose mind kept veering off to Mark whenever she relaxed her grip. Then on Monday evening, Kate had insisted that they go shopping for something new for Sal to wear. It was another activity to lose herself in, and Sally found that she had thoroughly enjoyed trying on lots of floaty things in Monsoon. Kate couldn't keep her hands off something purple and elegant, so both of them returned home with satisfied smiles on their faces. By seven o'clock on Tuesday, they were ready and waiting.

"God, this reminds me of going to parties as a teenager! Trying desperately not to crease the new togs before anyone had seen how chic you looked. So you had to sit in weird positions to stay wrinkle-free. It was even worse if you were going anywhere by car. Seat belts may save lives, but they bloody well ruin the just-ironed look. Remember?" asked Kate.

"My worst memory was my 15th birthday do, when I spilt a glass of tomato juice down myself just as the doorbell rang with the first guest. Ghastly! I was convinced that some wayward spirit had it in for me. It was a sign, I told myself. Everything was going to go wrong from then on."

"It was me at the door, and I had to mop up the juice as well as the tears before anyone else came. But after that, the party went really well, didn't it? You made a big impression on – oh, what was his name? He had blond hair, blue eyes, nice hands."

"Benjamin," supplied Sally, smiling. "You're right. Apart from the hands, which were a bit too exploratory. But all my prognostications about impending disaster came to nothing."

"As usual."

"Probably because I was careful only to step on the black squares on the kitchen lino!" laughed Sally.

"Those superstitions! 'If the first bus that comes along is mine, I'll get a good mark in Latin.'"

"'If a red car passes me, we won't have hockey today.' The frightening thing is, I find myself still doing it, especially if I'm going through a bad patch or if there's some big decision to be made," sighed Sally. "Like now. I've been saying to myself, 'If Jacky's the first to arrive, it will all go well tonight.' Pathetic, isn't it?"

"I've been doing just the same. I chose Jacky, too, because I thought she'd be so keen that she probably would be first to get here," laughed Kate.

The doorbell rang. Kate jumped up and ran to the door, admitting Jacky with more laughter than her arrival warranted, and catching Sally's eye with a knowing wink.

"I expect I'm first, aren't I? I always am. It drives David mad, but I can't help it. I have this fear of being late. It's so rude, isn't it? Oh Sally. You're here already. So I'm not first. Oh, silly me, you're staying here, aren't you? So I am first."

Jacky hardly stopped for breath, but managed to slip out of her coat and pose in her sparkling pink confection. Every appendage seemed to be heavy with gold – ears, fingers, wrists. Kate's face registered the surprise she felt at seeing someone of her own age looking more like a dowager duchess. Fortunately, Jacky thought the expression was caused by admiration.

"You don't think I'm over-dressed, do you?" she cooed, pirouetting.

"Um, just a bit. But it's fine, don't worry," said Kate, though worry was obviously far from Jacky's mind.

"I brought some shampoo," Jacky chirped, reaching down for her Harrods coolbag carrier.

Sally wondered fleetingly why Jacky would want to wash her hair, then realised that she had been treated to another of Jacky's verbal flutters.

"Let's open it quickly," laughed Kate, "so we can get a few glasses in before anyone else arrives!"

"Do you have any flutes?" asked Jacky.

Once again, Sally found herself momentarily bewildered by Jacky's terpsichorean enquiry, until she realised that glasses were being described.

"Champagne can be drunk from an old shoe and still taste good, so I'm sure it can cope with my Ikea cheapies," reassured Kate as she frothed fizz into three glasses.

"Cheers! Here's to us!" toasted Sally as they clinked and sipped appreciatively. "Come and sit down, Jacky. Tell us all about life in the wilds of suburbia."

"It isn't wild or suburban, actually. It's just nice. I really love it. Not being compelled to work is very liberating. My hubby likes me to be there for him and the kiddies."

Kate looked appalled and opened her mouth to make some waspish comment. Sally leapt in to prevent a lifestyle disagreement so early on in the evening, asking Jacky about her husband.

"Oh, he's a pussycat, really. Sometimes he growls a bit, but I know how to handle him. A whiskey and soda, a gentle foot-rub, and I'll have him purring."

"Presumably you don't wear that rig-out to massage the lord-and-master's tootsies," said Kate, caught between disdain and laughter. It was probably fortunate that the bell sounded at that moment, marking the end of round one. Kate hurried out with relief. When she opened the door, she wasn't entirely sure who was standing there and was grateful that Michelle introduced herself straight away. She should have known, she told herself: no-one else would arrive looking quite so chic. Michelle's matching coat and dress in dark chocolate silk, the outlandish height of her heels which would have had anyone else tottering uncomfortably, the gentle waft of perfume that was both understated yet terribly expensive, all this summed up Kate's idea of the stylish French woman that Michelle personified.

"Cherie, how are you?"

"My name's Kate. How forgetful of you!"

"Ever the comedienne," laughed Michelle.

"More to the point, how are you? We were so sorry to hear about your father," said Kate.

"Jacky told you? Yes, of course she did. I'm fine, I'm coping. It's my mother who's coming apart at the seams. That's why I've been over in Paris. I'm trying to persuade her to come over here and stay with us for a while, just until she can grasp the fact that she can actually live a good life without him. Do I hear Jacky? I should have known she'd be here first!"

Michelle walked into the room and greeted Jacky and Sally with the three cheek kisses that seemed *de rigeur*. There was laughter and comments about 'little cauliflowers' before they all settled back down with their drinks. Both Kate and Sally were struck by the contrast between their two old friends. Though related by marriage now, they were far apart stylistically. Michelle's chic made Jacky's ostentatious glitter look frumpish and ageing. Sally suddenly felt sorry for Jacky, who had no idea how to dress even with the advantage of her money. She could imagine every member of their family coming to the same conclusion when they saw them together. Poor Jacky. She wondered if 'hubby' David was blind to the comparison. Perhaps Jacky was dressing to please his taste, though. She hoped so. Certainly, Jacky seemed totally confident about her appearance. She tuned in to Jacky's sincerity in asking about Michelle's mother, and she felt glad that there was obviously a firm bond between the two women.

"I was just mentioning it to Kate," replied Michelle.

"My mother has spent all her life as the dutiful wife, adoring her husband and revolving round him like a little satellite. All her energy went into being the perfect hostess, the perfect mannequin, the perfect wife. And wanting me to be the perfect daughter, too! Now that he isn't there to praise her efforts or notice her accomplishments, she's just falling apart. She keeps saying that it wasn't supposed to be like this. I'm very worried about her."

"That would happen to me if my David passed away. I know just how she feels," sympathised Jacky.

"Well, it's not healthy to be so focussed on one person. I keep telling you that, too. You need to widen your horizons," scolded Michelle gently.

"Perhaps you should bring your mother across, match her up with Jacky, wind them up and set them off in the general direction of Independence," said Kate, not entirely flippantly.

"Good idea. See if you can persuade Jacky to take time off for good behaviour," said Michelle.

"You make it sound as if I'm serving a prison sentence," bleated Jacky.

"Perhaps you are, ma petite. Anyway, I shall get Peter to work on David next time we meet up. Oh, Pete's my husband," she explained to Sally and Kate. "He's Jacky's cousin. But you probably know that already if I know Jacky! Peter and I are joint directors of my father's cosmetics business now, but it took us some time to feel at ease with working together at such a high level."

"You mean your husband didn't think you were quite as capable as he? Typical!" assumed Kate.

"On the contrary. He was always selling himself short, saying that I knew so much more about it than he did. Which was true, but he didn't take into account all the other experience that he brought to the job. He'd been an industrial chemist – well, he still is, I suppose. So he understands much more about the research side of the business. I'm good at marketing and style, and my accountancy training is invaluable; but I know nothing of the technical stuff. Together, we cover quite a wide spectrum."

"It sounds like a really good partnership," said Sally. "I expect it's a good marriage, too. I mean, I can't imagine that you could be so compatible in the business if your personal life was hell on wheels."

"You're right. The one feeds into the other. I feel very fortunate. I have my father to thank for it, really. He insisted on taking Pete into the firm, against my wishes at the time. I knew how diffident Pete was, you see, and I didn't want him to be subsumed by Daddy - or by me! But dear old Papa eased him in and gradually gave him more and more responsibility. In no time, he was worth his weight in gold. I sometimes wonder if Daddy had some inkling of his own illness. He seems to have ensured the continuance of the business very efficiently and smoothly. It was very prescient of him."

"You used to call him 'The All-Seeing, All-Knowing One' when we were in the sixth form. Do you remember?" laughed Sally.

"That was because he always seemed to know beforehand if you were planning to sneak out without his permission! The number of times he caught you tiptoeing down the stairs!" added Kate.

"I learned later that whenever I turned my bedroom light off, the one in the lounge dimmed for a moment. Every time it happened, he'd check the hall to make sure I was just going to sleep rather than going out. How we imbued our parents with knowledge they didn't really possess! Still, it did denote a certain wily cunning, I suppose, and I give him absolute credit for that. I miss him, you know. Very much."

"It doesn't seem fair that he's popped his clogs while my apology for a father soldiers on, making everyone's life a misery," said Kate bitterly. "My mum would be liberated by his demise, whereas your mum is imprisoned by grief. Fickle finger of fate."

"You're very hard on your father, Kate. Hasn't he developed any saving graces over the years?" asked Michelle.

"Don't start me off! This is not the time to talk about him. I want frivolity tonight, not soul-searching. Pour me another drink!" said Kate. "Whoops. We're on to the second bottle already. With any luck, we'll finish this one off, too, before anyone else can come and share it with us. Selfish connoisseur that I am!"

"It is good, isn't it?" agreed Sally. "Well done, Jacky."

"Well done David, actually. I raided his wine fridge on my way out. I didn't see why I shouldn't have some of the spoils of his soliciting," giggled Jackie.

"Attagirl! Could this be the burgeoning of independence? Or is it just the first hesitant steps on the road to dipsomania? Only time will tell," said Kate.

Imperious ringing of the doorbell announced the arrival of Pru and Mary, who had travelled together. They almost fell into the hall, bearing copious amounts of French bread and bottled water.

"Hope you don't mind water instead of wine," said Pru, "but I'm trying to give it up for a week or two. Detox and weight loss combined. But I'll probably succumb to something or other tonight, so I'm just fooling myself!"

"Why change the habits of a lifetime?" teased Kate, hugging Pru and then turning her attention to Mary. "Why, Mary, you haven't alterred one bit. It's as if you've just stepped out of the sixth form common room."

And, indeed, Mary did look just as young and gawky as she had back then. She was wearing jeans and a black T-shirt, with a black leather waistcoat over the top. Her long face was framed by fair hair in the same youthful style as she had worn since starting at comprehensive school. Only the glasses looked different, slightly more designer and smart, and they emphasised her large and vulnerable blue eyes. It was almost impossible to see her as the mother of an eight-year-old and Kate lost no time in telling her so. They hugged delightedly before Kate ushered both women into the lounge to go through much the same ritual with the others. On being offered champagne, Pru immediately succumbed, causing everyone to laughingly bemoan their own lack of tenacity when it came to resisting temptation. Suddenly, Pru became aware that there was a discrepancy in their clothing.

"Jeez, I didn't know we were going formal! Look at me!"

They all did. What they saw was a woman who had obviously been decorating in the clothes she stood up in. White paint streaked her denims and could even be discerned in her unruly hair.

"And I told Moo not to dress up, either. Sorry, Moo. Mind you, at least you look neat and tidy, whereas I'm a complete mess. Whoops. I was painting the bedroom walls this morning, and then I had this wonderful flash of inspiration for a poem and I just couldn't wait to work on it. I didn't stop until Mary came for me, and then I just picked up the bags and walked."

"And you think I haven't changed!" said Mary. "Hasn't Pru always been like that? I remember having to drag her into the exam hall while she was still trying to scribble down the last lines of a sketch she was writing for the end-of-term revue. If I hadn't been there, she would have missed the exam, I swear. And she would have made it sound as if she was the only one getting her priorities right!"

"I expect that's the mark of true genius," said Jacky with real admiration. "Nothing is allowed to come before the work in progress. I'm a bit like that when I get started on something. I was doing a marble effect in the bathroom a couple of weeks ago, and I nearly forgot to pick up the children from school. Can you imagine?"

"Yet another reason not to have kids!" said Pru triumphantly, neatly stemming the imminent laughter bubbling up in the others at Jacky's confident assumption that her faux paint effects were on a par with poetry. "Are we all here now?"

"No," replied Kate. "There's still Lyn. And you'll never believe this, but Cassie's coming."

"Cassie?" asked Mary. "That's wonderful. I haven't seen her since the very last day of term. We were all flitting around with autograph books and Cassie just swept out and stepped into a red sports car driven by a gorgeous-looking young man. Very fast!"

"The car? Or Cassie?" laughed Sally.

"Both!" they all chorused.

"She was such a complex character, wasn't she?" mused Sally. "Her father was so famous – always being asked to give talks about his biographies – and so bohemian. Lots of children would have shrunk in his shadow. Been embarrassed, you know. I would have been. But not Cassie. She acted like his consort rather than his daughter, entertaining all his friends as if she were decades older. God, I wanted to be like her."

"Surrounded by all those writers and artists, treated like an adult – oh yes, I know what you mean. I think we all secretly wanted to be Cassie," agreed Pru.

"I didn't," said Jacky decisively. "She was too young for all that stuff. Without a mum around, she had to pretend to be so grown up. You can't treat a kiddie like an adult unless you help them to be responsible with all the freedom. Cassie couldn't cope with it, really. She didn't just smoke the odd joint, like us, did she? I'm sure she was into all kinds of other druggy things as well. The state she was in sometimes! Her father did her no favours."

"Of course, I'd forgotten there was no mother around,"

agreed Michelle. "There were lots of women, mistresses I suppose, scores of them, and always different. But no-one to be the still point from which she could venture out knowing there was a safe haven to come back to. Oh dear, I sound a bit pompous, don't I?"

"No, you're right," said Kate. "But that's hindsight, isn't it? At the time, we thought she was so cool and sophisticated. Not many of us saw the vulnerable lost child underneath, not until we looked back later on. I wonder what happened to her."

"It won't be long before we know," said Sally. "We were so surprised when she got in touch. She really seemed to want to meet up. I'm still finding it hard to imagine that. It doesn't fit with my idea of Cassie as a wild bohemian girl roaming the world with a band of fellow artists."

"I don't think there was much chance of her being an artist, you know," said Pru. "I mean, she skipped more art lessons than she attended, and she didn't have any writing talent."

"Do I detect a touch of sour grapes?" asked Mary.

"Maybe," laughed Pru. "I remember feeling jealous that she had all those contacts, all that talent around her, and she couldn't put pen to paper. I wanted to be her, too, in the sense that I wanted to be in her ambience – well, her father's ambience, really. I often thought that if we'd lived in Elizabethan times, I would have been convinced that we were changelings, swapped at birth."

"Why Elizabethan?"

"Oh, you know, all those Shakespearean plots revolving round twins being separated and people assuming other identities," said Pru.

"Ah, but writers need to struggle. Garrets and all that. If you'd had Cassie's father, you probably wouldn't have been half as prolific," Mary said.

"But twice as published!" groused Pru.

"That's probably true," said Jacky. "My hubby always says that it's not what you know but who."

Kate opened more wine and ushered everyone to the table to pick up some food. They all loaded their plates, commenting on the abundance of goodies and the cleverness of Kate and Sally in assembling such a feast. As they settled with their food, there was a companionable degree of surface chatter about nothing in particular.

"It's as if we've never been apart," said Mary.

"It would be true to form now if Cassie arrived, catching us all with food in our mouths and mayonnaise on our chins!" laughed Kate.

"With salad caught greenly between our teeth!" agreed Pru.

Indeed, at that very moment, the doorbell rang. They all giggled and ostentatiously wiped their chins while Kate went to the door.

"Relax. It's only Lyn," she called from the hall. "Oh God, Lyn, that sounded so rude! We were expecting it to be Cassie catching us with our mouths over-full and looking down on us. But we don't mind if you see us with egg on our faces, literally."

Kate stood back to let Lyn through the door. She realised that she had been expecting to have to leave Lyn as much room as possible. Lyn had always been 'wider than the average chair', as they used fondly to misquote Yogi Bear. But the woman who came in was anything but wide. In fact, she could probably have got in through the letterbox if necessary.

"Kate! Precious! Sweetheart!" gushed Lyn. "You haven't changed a morsel."

"Well, you have. Lots of morsels, if I may say so. You look positively reed-like. Come through and show yourself off to the rest."

As Lyn insinuated herself through the lounge doorway, everyone gasped. There were cries of 'It can't be! But it is!' and 'That's just your shadow, isn't it?' amidst the hugs and kisses.

"You've either been cut in half by a wayward chainsaw or you've found the perfect diet. Do tell!" urged Pru.

"It's nice to know the change is visible," replied Lyn. "I sometimes wonder."

"Can absence be visible?" mused Pru.

"Where's the jolly, round bod that used to be our friend Lyn?" asked Jacky. "Where's all the fat gone?"

"As soon as I left home, I went on a serious weight loss regime. I knew it would be impossible at home with a mum who thought I was wasting away if she didn't give me chips every day. I lost four stone in three months!" she said proudly.

"That doesn't sound healthy, ma petite," said Michelle, with some degree of concern.

"Much healthier than being obese," retorted Lyn. "And that was just the beginning. I'm nearly at my target weight now. I'm seven and a half stone."

"How many kilo is that?" asked Michelle.

"Not enough," murmured Kate.

They all took a more searching look at Lyn. Although she was exquisitely made up, her cheeks were hollow and her hair was thin. There was the slightest suggestion of breasts on her concave chest, and her pelvis thrust forward without benefit of cushioning. Lyn's gamin haircut and abundantly mascaraed eyes emphasised her razor-sharp cheekbones. They caught one another's eyes and the word 'anorexia' was silently passed round.

"Let me get you a plate and a glass of wine," said Kate, voicing the wishes of them all, "while you tell us what's going on in your life."

"I've been modelling up to a few months ago," replied Lyn. "But I think I must have put on a bit too much weight, because the jobs have dried up recently."

They all thought that it was Lyn who had dried up, but no-one said so.

"Isn't there a bit more of a trend towards 'slim' rather than 'thin' nowadays? Maybe you should put a bit of weight on," suggested Kate. She handed Lyn a large plate and a full glass, hoping to encourage indulgence. "Here you go. Cheers! And help yourself. Sally and I have been slaving over a hot Marks and Spencer for this, so don't let us down."

"Don't worry, I won't. This looks delicious," Lyn replied, delicately parting lean chicken and crisp lettuce from everything else that had been piled on her plate. "But I foolishly ate before I came, so I'm not terribly hungry."

"So you've been modelling?" asked Sally. "How exciting! Are all those photographers as sexy as they sound?"

"Mostly they're egocentric bores. Models have a reputation for being self-obsessed, I know, but they're nothing compared with photographers. Believe me, I married one."

"That sounded a bit harsh. Do we take it that you're not married to one any more?" asked Sally.

"Oh, still married, but thankfully not occupying the same space. When I didn't produce his offspring on cue, he took himself off."

"Aha!" said Pru. "Another child-refusenik! Welcome to the clan."

"Well, it wasn't for want of trying, actually. I wanted a sprog, but Nature in her wisdom denied me. So... Anyway, it's all blood under the bridge now," Lyn said decisively, pushing the food round her plate without actually managing to raise her fork to her lips.

"Oh, I wouldn't be without my cherubs for anything in the world," sighed Jacky. "Would you, Mary?"

"Well, people are all different, aren't they?" said Mary uncomfortably. "Of course I love my son, but I can imagine a perfectly happy life without him. I mean, if I'd never had him. I wouldn't wish him away now, of course. But, you know, if my life had been different, I'd have been perfectly fulfilled without children. People are."

"Amen to that!" shouted Pru. "Tell you what: my feller should get together with yours, Lyn, and they could make a perfect couple to adopt a child. We'll carry on with our careers and let them bring up the infants."

"How _is_ your career?" asked Michelle. "Published any good books lately?"

"Well, I just happen to have in my bag … no, no, I'm joking. Thanks for asking, though. It's tottering a bit, but I am in print, and I'm working on a novel at the moment," said Pru.

"She's being modest," interjected Mary. "She has several published works to her name and she's nearly finished the book."

"Ooh, am I in it?" laughed Jacky.

"If you're not careful, you will be. I'm thinking of writing the next one about my childhood," replied Pru.

"I wonder if Cassie followed in her father's inkstains," said Mary. "She certainly would have had the right contacts, wouldn't she?"

"Can't you hear my teeth grinding?" said Pru. "If only I'd had her advantages… "

"I can't wait to see her," said Jacky.

"That's a shame, because that's all you can do," laughed Sally.

"Oh God. Miss Hewlitt used to say that to us! Do you

remember?" said Kate. "What a miserable cow of a teacher she was. Definitely the 'half empty' type."

"The what?" asked Jacky.

"You know, people either see the glass as half full or half empty, depending on their temperament. She was always so dour."

"We used to invent sad scenarios for her, didn't we, to explain her glum face. Boyfriends who ditched her at the altar, or illegitimate babies sent off for adoption whom she longed to trace," said Pru.

"Your explanation was the best, Pru. You used to say that she was a lesbian surrounded by gorgeous temptation – us girls! – and unable to do anything about it. Not that she ever did anything to make us think she really was gay," said Mary.

"But we used to say that all the unmarried staff were gay, didn't we?" recalled Jacky. "Somehow, we couldn't imagine women not getting married if they were hetero, could we?"

"I think we changed our views on that round the age of

fifteen. I know I did. After that, I could well imagine that life would be much better if you stayed unmarried!" said Pru.

"You have your wish, then," said Jacky. "You and Kate and Sally are the only ones here who didn't marry. I'm not surprised about Kate. She was always so bitter about her parents. And I'm not surprised about you because of your writing. But I'm really thrown by Sally still being single."

Sally looked so uncomfortable that everyone competed to fill the gap and save her embarrassment. Michelle won.

"What's the betting on Cassie's marital status?" she asked.

"Unmarried. Definitely," replied Jacky.

"Yes, I agree," said Pru. "She'll still be enjoying *la dolce vita.*"

"I'm not so sure," Mary mused. "I always thought she needed someone stable to ground her. Her father was too fey himself to do that job for her. I wouldn't be at all surprised if she were married."

"To an older man!" yelped Jacky. "Yes! Probably rich and famous, too. It'd be just like Cassie to outdo any of us in the marriage stakes."

"I didn't know it was a competition," said Kate wickedly, "or I'd have bucked my ideas up and given you a run for your money."

"The first thing I'm going to do when Cassie arrives is to look at her wedding finger for a ring," said Jacky.

And as if on cue, the doorbell rang.

Chapter 13

When Kate opened the door, she was astonished. She had been expecting peroxide, perfume, cigarillos. She had anticipated colour, movement, noise. She thought she would be overwhelmed. Instead, she saw before her the most ordinary of young women wearing little or no make-up on her earnest face, dressed in unpretentious black trousers and sweater.

"Cassie? Is it you?" she asked tentatively.

"Oh, Kate. How good to see you looking so well," replied a low, comfortable voice. "Yes, of course it's me."

"Come in. We've all been waiting for you."

"Oh dear, I haven't stopped you from eating or anything, have I? My bicycle had a flat tyre. Typical, isn't it? I swear it knows when I'm going out."

"A bike with a soul – now there's a thing," said Kate. "Come through and see the gang."

As Cassie went in, she was very aware of being the focus of everyone's attention. She was also very aware of their surprise when they saw her. She couldn't help laughing. This happened every time that she met someone she had known in the distant past.

"You should see your faces!" she said. "You look as if you've seen a ghost."

"It's just that we <u>haven't</u> seen a ghost, Cassie. You look nothing like your old self at all," said Kate.

"I know. Isn't it great? When I think of what I was back then… How did you ever stand me?"

She was exclaimed over and passed from person to person. They held her at arm's length and up close, searching for evidence of the old Cassie inside the new one.

"You've still got that twinkle in your eye!" said Pru. "The only way I would have known you, in fact, is if you'd been wearing a mask and I'd only been able to view your peepers."

"Actually, I think of myself as being masked back then. I

was trying so hard to be someone else, someone my father wanted as a companion. It was never who I really was. I was hiding all the time."

"We were just wondering what you were doing with yourself. You know, were you married, were you rich, were you an artist or writer of some sort? So put us out of our misery and tell us the story of your life, starting at the point where you drove off into the sunset with that handsome young man in the red sports car," said Sally.

"Green. The sports car," corrected Cassie. "And he wasn't handsome, just older. A man as opposed to a boy. Which made him seem special, I suppose."

"Anybody in long trousers was special to us!" laughed Mary.

"Not to you, surely. You were the one with the real boyfriend, Mary. If anyone was sophisticated, it was you and Gil," said Cassie.

"Not when you regaled us with tales of what went on during your weekends! My snogging on the sofa paled into insignificance compared with that."

"I probably made it all sound much more lurid and glamourous than it was. You know what a show-off I was."

"It wasn't the glamour that enthralled us, it was the dark undertones of sex and drugs and rock 'n' roll. I just wanted to be a fly on the wall," said Michelle, settling in to the sofa with a very full glass of white wine.

"I've left all that thankfully behind me. I'm a good girl, I am; I washed my face and 'ands before I come, I did," said Cassie, parodying Eliza Doolittle.

"So what do you do?" asked Jacky, with unashamed curiosity.

"I run a gallery in Kensington specialising in African works of art," she replied.

"Not exactly slumming it then," said Kate. "Oh, Gord, that sounded really rude, didn't it? I didn't mean it to come out quite like that. I mean, I took in the simple clothes and the fact that you came by bike and my mind went on to conclude that you were sort of poor. Oh dear, I'm making a real mess of this. It's meant to be an apology."

Cassie was giggling. "Dear Kate. You always jumped in with both feet, didn't you? Don't worry, I'm not in the least offended. But I think I'd better explain myself a bit, if that's all right."

Not only was it all right, it was an absolutely obligatory as far as everyone was concerned. They had all been waiting for Cassie with bated breath and felt that some explanation was needed for the definite disappointment they all felt at her sheer ordinariness.

"I've become accustomed to people remembering me for the flamboyant extrovert that I used to seem to be. I must have looked rather decadent to all of you, and I peacocked around loving every minute of my notoriety. Not all the gossip was true, of course, but enough of it was. I was quite a mess underneath, you know. I was always trying to pass myself off as a sophisticate, dabbling with drugs and alcohol, mixing with people who were way above my station."

"Au-dessous de ta gare," giggled Michelle. "Remember

that lovely sketch that Pru wrote where she took English phrases and translated them literally into French. What a hoot it was. I must admit I still do it, as you will no doubt hear as the evening goes on! And you were the star performer in that one, Cassie, because your accent was better than anyone else's. Even mine!"

"No, it wasn't. I just had more nerve than you. I rolled my Rs and pouted my lips and did my best to be like a French film star. It was all an act," laughed Cassie.

"Sounds like your whole life was an act," said Lyn perspicaciously.

"Too right," agreed Cassie. "It had to end. The act, I mean, not my life. Although if I'd gone on the way I'd started, it probably would have been my life as well. After leaving school, I persuaded Daddy to send me abroad for a year. I thought if I was away from him, I could straighten myself out a bit. Does that sound awful? I love my father, and I know he always did his best for me by his own lights, but he had whatever was the opposite of a Midas touch as far as I was concerned. I had to get away."

"Good for you," said Sally. "I always thought you had a strong backbone. Where did you go?"

"Paris. I thought I could get by with my schoolgirl French. It had always been my best subject at school. Not that I was much cop at any other language. Latin completely floored me because of the grammar. I could never get past pluperfect."

"There's no such thing as Past Pluperfect," said Sally, ever the teacher.

"No, no. I mean I could never get beyond the pluperfect tense. I mean, the past is the past. It happened. It's simple. How can you have a tense meaning a past before the past?" asked Cassie rhetorically.

"Well," began Sally.

"No, don't explain! I remember Miss Latham trying to tell me. The *plu* bit meant *more than*, but that made even less sense. More than the past?" Cassie went on.

"*Plus quam perfectum*," sighed Sally.

"*More than perfect* didn't help me one bit."

"It's the perfect tense, not perfection," said Sally.

"Well, I just couldn't get past it. How could something in the past be more than perfect? As far as I could see, all the perfection in my life was going to be in the future."

"But for lots of people, perfection is only in the past. They always look back with nostalgia at how wonderful things used to be compared with now," said Jacky. "In fact, we're all a bit like that, aren't we? Maybe that's one of the reasons why we're all here now. Schooldays, best years of our lives, and so on."

"Not for me," said Lyn. "Being fat and jolly was a misery. I longed to be slim and willowy, like the rest of you. And all I got was people saying how nice it must be not to care what I looked like."

"I still can't look back without pain and disbelief either," agreed Cassie.

"Thanks a bunch!" laughed Kate.

"*Merci un paquet!*" said Michelle. "Nice to know we contributed to the angst of your childhood!"

"Not you lot. You were the best, the very best. That's really why I was so thrilled to see you were having a little reunion. I wanted so much to thank you all for keeping me on the straight and narrow all those years ago. Without you, I'd have gone down the plug."

"Shucks! It was nothing!" said Kate.

"And I wanted you to know that I did come through it all."

"So what did you do in Paris?" asked Sally.

"Apart from drying out? Well, I discovered the love of my life."

"Hurray! A happy love-life at last!" yelled Jacky, adding rather sheepishly, "As well as mine, I mean."

"Not a man, though, not then," added Cassie. "Nor a woman, either, before you start jumping to conclusions. Africa. I fell in love with Africa."

"What? How?" asked Jacky, voicing all their thoughts.

"I fell in with a group of three students from the Congo. They were so different. I don't mean their colour – we were used to all shades of skin, weren't we? London's such a melting pot. No, it was their attitude to life. They had been educated in a missionary school financed by America, and they'd been so bright that the mission had raised enough money from the States to send them to study abroad. All they wanted to do was to learn and work and have fun and look around and absorb and enjoy …"

"… and you'd never seen anything like that before!" interposed Pru wickedly.

"I know that sounds insulting to you lot, but it isn't really. We took everything so much for granted, didn't we? Of course we were going on to further study, of course we were comfortably off, and of course we always had family to support us. Of course. It was all rather boring. But there were no 'of courses' in their lives. It seemed that everything was fraught with danger. The mission school should have closed down because of the tribal rivalries, the government out there didn't want the school to carry on, and it was a close thing every year as to whether it would survive. Literally. And here were these three amazing people, bright as buttons, who were determined to study hard so that they could go back and make a difference to their country. It humbled me, I suppose. But I also felt slightly jealous of them. Can you understand what I mean?"

"I think so," replied Sally. "They had a focus to their lives which you didn't have."

"That's it. Their futures were going to be really important. I wanted something like that. I wanted to make a difference, too."

"I think that's why I became a teacher," said Sally.

"Me, too," agreed Mary.

"It's why I was so dissatisfied with life in the advertising world," said Kate.

"It's why I think poetry's so important," said Pru. "The right words can free the mind and spirit."

"And it's definitely why I stayed at home with my

children," asserted Jacky rather smugly. "It may only be a small world, but it's where I can make a difference."

There was a silence as each of them thought about their lives under the spotlight of Cassie's conviction. The only person to have remained silent was Michelle, and she sighed deeply before speaking. "*Merde!* Guess who's the odd one out? The only changes I'm responsible for are the lipstick shades for next Autumn! What sort of a selfish pig does that make me?"

"You mustn't put yourself down, poppet," said Jacky. "What about all those policies you put in place about not testing things on animals? And using natural ingredients where you could? That's made a difference."

"Thank God! Now I can join the party again!" laughed Michelle. "Go on, Cassie. I want to know how all this connects with running an art gallery."

"Well, I fell in love with one of the guys. Jean-Paul," resumed Cassie.

"I knew it! Lurve rears its lovely head!" exclaimed

Jacky.

"He took me back to the Congo to meet his family. It was a shock. I had always revelled in slumming it, thinking I could adapt to anything. Nothing would faze me, I thought. But when you see real poverty – I mean bone-hard need – it makes you see how trivial your life has been. And how privileged. I was making grand gestures by living like a bohemian, but of course all the time my father was financing my Parisian garret and acting as my safety net. I was never actually hungry. But in Africa, things were altogether different. The meals they ate were filling rather than nutritious, and people really were on the point of starvation. When I thought about how much I used to spend on booze and cigarettes, to say nothing of drugs, I felt ashamed. It was the turning point of my life."

"But did you stay with Jean-Paul?" asked Jacky, wanting to steer the conversation away from such deep seriousness and get back to the subject nearest her heart.

"Dear Jacky," laughed Kate. "Do you still read Barbara Cartland?"

"I don't see what that's got to do with it," huffed Jacky. "I just wanted Cassie to be happy, like me. Is that so wrong?"

"Of course it isn't," soothed Cassie. "And yes, I'm still with him. In fact, we're married. He spends most of his time in Africa while I spend most of my time here, but we get together as often as we can, and when we do, it's like a honeymoon."

"I'm still having trouble with this art gallery scenario," said Kate. "It seems incongruous. Starving people at one end of the spectrum and art at the other. How does that work?"

"I know. In a way, it's not what it seems," said Cassie. "You see, we agreed that education was the only way to make permanent changes in people. The three students were all determined to go back to the Congo to set up schools - little local schools, nothing enormous. But even small ventures needed money, and that was the one thing they didn't have much of. My first thought was dear old Dad. He's not rich, but there's spare cash. Enough to do something. I flew back to England and started a massive begging session with him. That's when I learnt a bit more about my father than his seemingly open and bohemian life had led me to believe. The thought of his little blonde daughter marrying a 'bleck' was something up with which he would not put!"

"Whoops! Good old prejudice pops up again," said Pru.

"In the most unlikely of places. Really, I would never have assessed my father as prejudiced. His literary friends were all hues, shapes and sizes. But as a son-in-law? That wasn't acceptable."

"A different *bouilloire de poissons*," teased Michelle.

"So no money for black hubby, eh?" said Jacky.

"Not a bean. I tried to trick him. I said I was postponing the idea of marriage, and what I really wanted to do was set myself up in business. That pleased him much more. The only thing he insisted on was that the business should be in England and that all cheques from him would be made out to a business account."

"Foiled again!" said Sally.

"So Jean-Paul came up with the idea of setting up an art gallery exhibiting works by Africans. He would find them, ship them over, and pay the artist a good fee. I'd show them and charge silly prices. Whatever profit we made would be sent across to the Congo."

"Brilliant," said Kate. "And does it work? Silly question – obviously it does, or you wouldn't be telling us about it."

"Yes. It's great. We've established ourselves as being on the cutting edge of art. People like to buy from us because it proves what trendy folk they are, and they pay huge sums of money for the privilege. Oh, I'm not being fair. Quite a few of the customers buy because they know I send a lot of the money back over. They want to make a difference, too!"

"I think that's the best story of life bearing fruit this evening. Sorry, Jacky, I know you produced two children who are geniuses, but I think they have to give way to this," said Michelle.

Kate realised that Sally was looking wistful. She guessed it was the phrase about bearing fruit that had affected her. She was right in a way, but not exactly in the way she had thought. Sally wasn't grieving over babies, but over the lack of purpose in her life.

"Come on, everyone!" shouted Kate. "We've had enough seriousness – for this meeting at least. Let's all get tiddly and swap silly stories about a group of normal schoolgirls who became crazy adults!"

"You always did suffer from delusions of grandeur," laughed Pru. "But actually I don't see us as either normal or crazy."

"Surely we've got to be one or the other," said Lyn, curling her thin legs around her as she settled into an armchair. Within minutes she was fast asleep.

"We could be sub-normal, I suppose."

"What? With all our qualifications? I don't think so," said Mary.

"Qualifications do not a man make," hiccupped Jacky. Then she started giggling. "I think that's a sort of quotation, but I've no idea what from."

"Knowing you, it'll be Mills and Boon," snorted Michelle. "*Moulins et Faveur!*"

"Snob!" chided Jacky. "I won't tell everyone that I pass the old M and Bs on to you. I expect you wrap them up in a Proust cover."

"Just like we used to at school," Mary cut in. "We had *'Forever Amber'* in a Thomas Hardy cover. And Henry Miller was a great favourite, disguised as Jane Austen. We relied on you, Cassie, for all our forbidden stuff. Remember?"

"I do. Dad used to think it was a necessary part of my education to read such things, and I naturally passed them on. Oh, happy days, reading *'Tropic of Capricorn'* in the back row while Miss Fitt droned on about courtship in *'Pride and Prejudice'* with a nostalgic tear in her rheumy eye!"

"Poor old Misfit. Didn't she catch you once and ask what you were reading?" asked Pru.

"Yes. And I held up the cover – I think it was *'Emma'* –

which she took trustingly at face value and praised me for expanding my area of study!" laughed Cassie.

"Which was true, in a way. We learnt a lot from Henry Miller!" said Mary.

"Then you and Gil went and put it into practice while the rest of us merely imagined."

"I don't think our shy fumblings owed much to various Tropics, I can assure you," said Mary.

"And the rest of us did more than just imagine, didn't we? At least, we tried to. Oh, the things we did to get boyfriends. Shaming, now," said Kate.

"What was the name of that one you fancied from the boys' school next door?" asked Sally.

"Take your choice, there were so many."

"You wrote him a note asking him to meet you outside the cinema, which we dropped into his lap on the bus," supplied Sally.

"Oh, that was Tom Ring. We used to make all sorts of daft comments like 'Give us a ring' and 'engagement ring' and equally excruciating things," said Kate.

"You made me go with you to give you moral courage, and then you chickened out. Poor bloke was left waiting outside the cinema while we ran off home," said Sally.

"Why didn't you go through with it?" asked Jacky.

"I was all talk in those days. Scared of the real thing. And then there was the realisation of what my name would be if I married him."

"Mrs. Ring?" said a puzzled Jacky.

"Kate Ring," explained Kate.

"That well-known chef," laughed Sally.

"My hottest romance was with a pen-friend," said Michelle. "Remember how we all got one from our French lessons? They were all supposed to be girls, but mine got through the net because his name was Jean and the Secretary assumed that J-E-A-N was a she! We wrote to each other for ages, getting steamier all the time. In the end I was ready to leap into his arms and smother him with hot kisses. When I was next over in Paris with my parents, I took the metro to his district and watched outside his house for hours. This gangly, pimply youth eventually emerged. I ran back to the metro as fast as my fashionable high heels could take me. My mother never guessed I'd borrowed them! My next letter informed Jean that my father had supposedly found his last letter and forbidden me to write to him anymore."

"Another Dear Jean letter," quipped Cassie.

"And that was my closest thing to passion until I met this sexy accountant at Business School," said Michelle.

"A sexy accountant? Sounds like a contradiction in terms. Like that famous oxymoron Military Intelligence," said Pru.

"Don't you believe it. Most of them were so anxious to shake off the nerd image that they immersed themselves in the '*Kama Sutra*'. They were the best dates I ever had."

"Until you met Peter," corrected Jacky proprietorially.

"That goes without saying," agreed Michelle. "Well,

actually, no. Pete's not the world's greatest lover, to be quite honest. And if I can't be honest here with you, where can I? He's wonderful and I love him to pieces, but the bed department isn't his best bit."

"Bit? Mmmm, that conveys a lot, methinks," mused Kate. "Lie back on ze couch, my dear, and ve vill delve a little deeper. Unlike your husband!"

Raucous laughter erupted from Lyn, whom everyone had thought was still sleeping. She pushed herself up into sitting position from her previous slump and enquired if they were now ready to dish the dirt on their lovers, spouses or exes.

"I'll go first. Mine's a shit of the first order," she slurred. She then promptly fell down in a heap again and started snoring.

"I think Lyn may need a little more help than we can give her," said Pru soberly.

"She's terribly thin, isn't she?" said Jacky. "Anorexic?"

"Looks like it to me," agreed Sally. "We've had several cases in school. One of them had to be taken into hospital. She only weighed about five stone but she thought she was fat and her mother just couldn't get her to eat. Lyn sounded like that when she said she needed to diet although there's hardly anything of her. She's just not the real Lyn, is she?"

"But the Lyn we remember was the fat and jolly girl whom she says she never was. She was miserable when she was like that. So who is the real Lyn?" asked Pru.

"There's nothing wrong with dieting," asserted Jacky. "She just didn't know where to stop."

"Don't get me started on the dangers of modelling ourselves on men's fantasies of what we should look like," said Kate.

"Be fair. It's not just men's fantasies. Most fashion and beauty editors are women," said Michelle.

"Are there any fat ones? Or even plump ones?" asked Kate.

"Not that I know of. Thin as rakes, most of them. And waspish with it," replied Michelle.

"It must be hard to be sweet-tempered when you're half starved. So eat up, my cherubs, and open some more bottles. You can always sleep on the floor."

"Would that be *carpe diem* and then *carpet noctem*?" asked Pru innocently.

Chapter 14

Robin returned at midnight, turning the key as silently as he could so he wouldn't disturb them if they were still there. He started to tiptoe upstairs when he heard the whisper of voices. They had heard him, of course. He carried on up to bed, glad that the reunion must have been a successful gathering.

"Robin's home. That must mean it's late. Can anyone see the clock?" asked Kate.

"We can all see the clock, but its numbers seem to have blurred a bit," replied Sally. "Mind you, everything seems to have blurred a bit!"

"Midnight, the witching hour. All our secrets will now be revealed in golden runic writing on the mirror," said Pru. "Either that, or we'll all turn back into pumpkins."

"Mixing your fantasies a bit, darling," laughed Mary.

"And it was the coach that turned back into a pumpkin,

not Cinderella. Believe me, that story is moulded to my brain, the kiddies ask for it so often," said Jacky.

"Old Mouldy Brain. That's you," giggled Lyn.

"If it's really midnight, I must go. My hubby will be worried. I'm never out this late!" Jacky said as she struggled to get up.

"I wasn't mixing my fancies," slurred Pru. "I meant to imply that we were all modes of transport - transports of delight! Hence pumpkins underneath."

"I think we should all be going. Some of us have to work in the morning," bemoaned Michelle.

"But most of you need strong black coffee before you venture out. I'll make some." Kate leapt to her feet with more agility than she had anticipated herself capable of mustering.

"Not for me," said Jacky. "I was more abstemious than the rest of you. I take my responsibilities as a mum very seriously, you know – she said smugly! Anyway, I shall love you and leave you. But let me know when we're all going to meet again, won't you? Now we've found each other, we mustn't lose touch."

After numerous hugs, air kisses, protestations of undying friendship and stumbles over limbs that didn't seem to be quite in the right place, Jacky was gone. Kate came in with a tray of coffee and biscuits, which everyone decided was exactly what was needed.

"Good job Jacky's gone. Now we can dunk our biscuits without being told off about the crumbs!" said Kate. "Oh, I don't mean I wasn't really glad to see her, but she does go on a bit about 'hubby' and the 'kiddies', doesn't she?"

"But she sounded so happy and proud of them, didn't she?" said Sally. "It must be wonderful to be happily married."

"It is indeed," agreed Michelle. "But what makes you think that applies to Jacky?"

"Here comes the reality check," Lyn said with a sigh.

"That can't have been an act. She positively oozed self-satisfaction," said Kate.

"There are none so blind as those who will not see," Michelle replied enigmatically.

"You mean, she thinks that it's all hunky dory but you know something she doesn't? You can see something that should be obvious to her but she refuses to look at it?" asked Pru.

"Correct. Dear "hubby" has numerous weekends away on business, goes to meetings that drag on till late at night so that he comes home tired out, spends a fortune on what he calls corporate entertaining and generally treats her like a skivvy. Go figure."

"But that's terrible. Poor Jacky," murmured Sally, with half her mind on her own situation with its parallels.

"*Cherchez la femme*! And, true to form, there's a smart little cookie in his office with doe eyes," said Michelle.

"How are we spelling that? 'Doe' or 'dough'?" asked Pru.

"You've got it in one! There just happens to be a

secretary – oh, sorry, she terms herself his Personal Assistant – who concentrates on his every need before he even knows he needs it. She's also good-looking and elegant. I've watched her around him in the office, trying to hide the real situation from me because she's knows I'm close to Jacky. David isn't exactly *formidable* in the looks department, but he's certainly got plenty of money and that makes him overwhelmingly attractive, apparently. In my opinion, little miss Other Woman is a scheming bitch."

"Not all 'other women' are despicable," said Sally shakily. "Sometimes …"

Michelle cut her off. "If you could see Jacky as I do, and know her heart, you wouldn't make any excuses for the woman who wants to remove the one thing in her life that gives it worth in her mind. When it all breaks, and it must one day, Jacky will be completely wrecked."

"You can't build your life around a man," said Lyn.

"Well, you can. But perhaps you shouldn't," said Mary.

"She'll always have the children, though. They seem to

mean more to her even than David," said Cassie.

"You don't imagine a man like David wouldn't take the children with him, do you? He wouldn't leave his dynasty behind. He'll re-marry a much more 'suitable' woman who knows how to dress and entertain his important contacts, and he'll snigger with them about his first wife's frumpiness. He's so aware of what he thinks of as her shortcomings. Did you know he even wanted her to change her name?"

"What's wrong with 'Jacqueline'? I think that's really sophisticated," said Mary.

"Oh, 'Jacqueline' is fine. It's 'Jacky' that doesn't fit his bill. She resolutely refused to change it – she said it was who she was. He was willing to compromise if she agreed to spell it 'Jacqui' as he thought that had a certain je ne sais quoi. But she was having none of it. It was about the only time in her married life when she took a stand. He had to concede, but he hates it."

"What a dreadful snob", said Pru.

"It made me call her 'Jack' quite often, just to rile him

even more. Naughty of me, really."

"But surely he wouldn't take the children away from her?" queried Sally.

"He'll make damn sure the children prefer to be with him and his computers and swimming pool and villa in Tuscany."

"So it will seem like their choice, you mean?"

"I'd never do that," said Sally.

Michelle looked at her appraisingly, as did the others. No-one missed the implication of what had been said. Kate sighed. She had half wanted but half dreaded the now-inevitable confession from Sally. She thought it would help to have friends' opinions but she also knew there would be some lack of understanding and even criticism. She was relieved that Jacky wasn't there, feeling sure that there would be total disapproval from her. As Sally told her story, Kate added the occasional comment, trying to support Sally while also attempting to make her see the impossibility of her situation.

"So, his wife's expecting a baby?" asked Lyn. "Well, that's it, then. He won't leave now. Men seem to need their names perpetuated. Banquo and that long line of kings, you know."

"No, no. He doesn't want the baby. And he said his wife didn't. It was an accident. They were almost decided on an abortion. Maybe it was just an impression I got that she was glad about the child. In fact, I could well be wrong. I'm probably wrong. Don't you think so?"

There was a flurry of eyes raised heavenwards.

"Sal, you know better than that. I know it takes a lot of courage to face truths that you don't want to confront, but you must," pleaded Kate.

"*Ma petite*, you can't live in the past. What have we all been saying tonight? Live for something worthwhile and look to the future!"

"This sounds like a tremendous opportunity to me," said Cassie helpfully. "Just like my turning point in Paris. I knew that what was past had been harmful to me, and I needed to move on and change. Isn't that the same for you?"

"But I love him," wailed Sally.

"No," said Kate firmly. "You love what you thought he was. You love the man who was unhappy and wanted to leave his manipulative wife but who couldn't because he feared it would damage her. You love the man who was sensitive enough to worry about her health before grabbing the happiness he wanted with you. You love the man who was tender-hearted and kind. You love the man who had integrity. But that man doesn't exist. Poppet, he never existed. It was a fantasy he wove for you because you were too nice to have gone into a relationship with him otherwise," said Kate.

"I'm going to write a poem about this," mused Pru.

"You were always tender-hearted, Sally," said Mary fondly. "It was always you who picked up the injured birds. The lady at the PDSA was on first-name terms with you, wasn't she? You and your cardboard box were in there every couple of weeks."

"And you could never do the Biology experiments when

we had animals to work on. You gave the frogs names before you let any dissection go ahead!" said Cassie.

"Toughen up!" said Lyn decisively, slapping her knee with her open palm. "Ditch the bastard! I'm going to ditch mine. This has decided me. No more pleading for him to come back. No more whining apologies because I can't get pregnant. If he doesn't want me for me, I'm not going to try to change. It's his attitude that needs the alteration. If I can do it, so can you. We'll help each other to stay strong."

Michelle leaned over and took Sally's hand. "Sally, I'd hate it if any friends of his wife could talk about you the way I've been talking about David's woman."

"Yes, just imagine what they could say," urged Lyn.

"If it helps you to carry out the decision, call his wife 'Jacky' in your mind. Put Jacky's face on all your images of her. Think how Jacky will feel when her husband deserts her. That's what you'd be responsible for," suggested Mary.

That was the point at which Sally could bear no more. She lowered her head and wept, and somehow she just couldn't seem to stop.

"Oh, I'm sorry. Perhaps I shouldn't have said that," apologised Mary. "How can I know what you're feeling, or what's really going on in your relationship? I just poked my nose in – I thought it might help you, somehow. But I should have just kept quiet." She put her arm around the weeping Sally to try to ameliorate her previous words with a gesture of sympathy.

"No, you were right to speak. Giving Jo a different face, a face I know and wouldn't want to harm, is just what I must try. Then I can see what I'm doing more clearly. I've always worked so hard to make Jo anonymous. Hearing her voice over the phone the other day was a shock. She started to become more personal, a real woman, someone who can be hurt by what I do."

"At least the lucky woman is pregnant," said Lyn bitterly. "Even if he leaves her, she'll have a baby."

"Hey, I thought you didn't care about not getting

pregnant," said Pru. "I thought you and I were soul mates, forging our happy way through life unencumbered."

"Damn it all to hell!" said Lyn. "I've just blown my cover, haven't I? Still, I convinced you for a while, didn't I? Heart of stone, couldn't care less about kids, ditch the stupid bloke who wants them. Eh?"

"When really...?" asked Pru.

"Really I'd gladly give up everything to have a baby."

Pru sighed. "Bugger! Isn't there anyone around here who doesn't yearn for the patter of tiny whatsits? Kate? How about you?"

"I'm right there with you at the moment. Maybe one day I'll want sprogs. But first of all I have to exorcise the Ghost of Christmas Past – or rather, the ghost of father past," replied Kate. "Don't panic, I'm not going to burden you all with that little scenario right now!"

"What about you, Michelle?"

"I'm far too busy at the moment to give the slightest

whisper of a thought to having children. But one day, who knows? Maybe. It wouldn't break my heart if the business were my only offspring, though. Pete and I put so much into it that it's rather like bringing up a child. We watch a new line taking its first tottering steps and we feel so proud when it does well."

"And you've got your mother to look after now," said Mary.

"Well, not really. She's still pretty fit and there's no question of her not being able to cope physically. Emotionally, she's a wreck, but that will pass."

"Ah, but as she gets older she'll need you more and more. No husband to keep her company or look after her when she's sick. That will fall on your shoulders," said Lyn.

"Oh, thank you very much! Excuse me while I go and slash my wrists!" said Michelle.

"We're all getting a bit maudlin, aren't we? Perhaps this is the time to say farewell. When shall we seven meet again? What do you say?" asked Kate.

Everyone agreed that the evening had been great and they'd fallen so easily back into the old way of talking together without restraint but they realised that there was only so much soul-baring that could be done on their first reunion.

"Diaries at the ready, then," said Pru. "Except, of course, I haven't brought mine!"

The others had their phones, and Kate and Sally had their diaries, but it didn't seem right to make another date without consulting Jacky and Pru.

"We'll have to resort to good old e-mail. Or even that quaint old device called a telephone," concluded Pru. "So, out into the cold, cold snow!"

"Order the taxis, Jeeves!"

"Stand not on the order of your going," said Sally.

"Goodnight, sweet princess," declaimed Pru.

"Sshh. Remember Robin!" giggled Kate.

And the thought of him gave her an unexpected glow.

Chapter 15

Sally had felt too wobbly to drive to school next morning and then had been so worn out by the day, following on as it did from the reunion night, that she had persuaded James to drive her home on the promise of a cup of proper coffee in a proper coffee cup. As they opened the door they heard Kate singing as she loaded the dishwasher, mixing lyrics concerning 'ladies' and 'tramps' with the tune of 'Chicago'.

"Sinatra will be turning in his grave!" laughed Sally.

"Don't you believe it! I'm doing two of his numbers at once. There can't be a greater compliment than that," replied Kate, looking up to see an unfamiliar male with her friend. For a brief moment, she thought this might be a new man on the horizon for Sally, but she soon realised that that would have been totally impossible given Sal's state of mind and heart.

"James kindly acted as chauffeur so he needs rewarding.

Shall I make coffee for all of us? Oh, sorry, this is Kate. I keep forgetting that people I know from different areas of my life don't necessarily know one another. Kate, this is James."

Introductions over, James took his coat off and laid it over the back of a chair. He rolled his sleeves up and he started to stack dishes near the sink so that Kate could rinse them.

"Domesticated, too? Where have you been all my life?" asked Kate.

"Trapped behind the forbidding walls of the national curriculum," replied James.

"Now, now. No need for bad language!" said Sally as she set up the percolator. "This looks like the last of the decent coffee, Kate. We must have drunk a lot of it last night."

"I think we needed a lot of it last night. I was still feeling tiddly on my way to work this morning. I don't know how you coped with school today, but my work was definitely under par."

"The ghastly thing about teaching - well, one of the ghastly things - is that you can't tread water till you feel stronger. Every class, quite rightly, demands your full attention for the entire lesson time. No sneaking out for a loo break that stretches to ten minutes! No walking round with a clipboard pretending to be doing something crucial while really just getting your head together!"

"Yes, I can imagine. At least I could just do things in whatever order I wanted, and at half pace. No such luxury with kids baying for your blood."

"Oh, come on," said James. "They don't bay for blood. They just take it, very slowly, pint by pint, till you're a mere husk."

"Another happy teacher! The world's full of them!" said Kate.

"If only! Maybe we could fill all our vacancies then. My form has had no Science teacher all term, poor little cods. They tear the supply teachers to shreds every lesson, but you can't really blame them. Some of them really want to learn Science, believe it or not. Must be very frustrating," sighed James.

"At least they have lovely English lessons!" said Sally, loading the tray. "Come through to the sofa and let's relax."

The coffee seemed to hit the spot for all of them and they slowly unwound and threw off the day.

"Vol's been telling me about your school reunion last night. Sounds fun. Maybe I should get one organised for my old school crowd. Although it wouldn't be half so relaxed."

"Why not?" asked Kate.

"I went to a mixed school, so a reunion would include lots of women friends as well as men, so I wouldn't have the luxury of dishing the dirt with the boys without their wives and girlfriends getting to know what was said. I bet you lot had a whale of a time tearing us fellas apart in the knowledge that nothing would go beyond these four walls."

"Did we do that?" asked Sally uneasily.

"We did air a lot of grievances, and most of them were men-related!" replied Kate. "But we also gave praise where it was due."

"That's true. Robin got lots of plaudits. So did Michelle's Pete. But that was about it, wasn't it?"

"We were fairly gentle on Gil, I seem to remember," said Kate.

"We hardly mentioned him."

"Exactly. Ne'er a bad word was said!"

"Unusual name," commented James. "What saving graces did he have?"

"I told you about Mary and Gil getting married straight from school, then splitting up, then becoming good friends so that they see a lot of each other again. Remember?" asked Sally. "Well, he's always tried to be a good father to their son and he seems to have done a pretty good job, according to Pru, who sees a lot of them all."

"Aha! A good father!" exclaimed James. "I'd know cod all about that!"

"You, too?" asked Kate. "What was yours like then?"

"He was probably the most competitive man I've ever met. Everything was a competition, with him as the winner or there'd be trouble. He had to be the best, even when we kids were young."

"You mean that he competed against his own children?" asked Sally incredulously.

"It was one of the main reasons he had children, it seems to me. How else could you get a sense of superiority every single day? 'Race you to the next tree,' he'd say. And he'd let you think you were winning until the last minute, when he'd overtake and laugh."

"My dad would have done just the opposite," said Sally. "In fact, he probably went too far the other way so we never got an idea that there were people out there who could beat us at games and stuff."

"No chance of that with my dad. 'Life isn't easy or fair,' he'd say. 'One day you'll thank me.' But we didn't, of course. No child deserves to go into the world with an overpowering sense of their own inadequacy, which is what he did to us. It wasn't just to us, either. He and his brother, my uncle Thomas, were always feuding over something trivial. I remember when they both got new cars. Naturally, dad's had to be best. They ground away at each other all afternoon comparing horsepower and dashboard gadgets until the whole family was sick of it. The trouble was that everything about the cars seemed to be fairly equal, and dad couldn't have that. In the end, he took a steel rule out into the street and measured how long each car was. When he found that his was a couple of centimetres bigger, he was absolutely crowing with pleasure. I remember my mother remarking that he had always told her that size didn't matter, but her humour was lost on dad."

"He sounds incredibly petty," agreed Kate.

"It went beyond pettiness, though. We lived in a small village where he was a pillar of the church. So he had to be morally better than anyone else. I suppose that wouldn't have been so bad if it had just meant that he lived a good life and showed off about it. But no. He felt it was his duty to inspect everyone else's behaviour. It was only when he found people doing wrong that he could feel really superior. He used to ferret around trying to catch people out to see if they'd done something against the law. Then he'd inform on them."

"What do you mean?" asked Sally.

"Well, for instance, our next door neighbour let his car tax run out. So dad went into the local police station and put them on to it. This was in the Neanderthal days of paper tax discs."

"What a bastard!" exclaimed Kate.

"And the worst thing about it was that he actually boasted about it. He was proud of himself. He was upholding the law, so that gave him the moral high ground. He was the undisputed winner!"

"Bet he was popular!" scoffed Kate.

"It was poor old mum who really suffered for it. And we kids. Families who'd been shown up by dad's valiant striving for the truth would get back at him by ill-treating us in some way. So the butcher always slightly under-weighed our meat, and Mrs Next Door would chuck her snails into our garden. Johnny Hepton, whose dad was claiming dole as well as cleaning people's windows until dad reported him, always seemed to misjudge his aim when he was peeing in the school loo so that my shoe was soaked; and he couldn't help coughing up his phlegm down the back of my jacket."

"Gross!" said Kate.

"But I couldn't blame any of them. How else could you deal with someone like dad?"

"Didn't he ever transgress?" asked Sally.

"I'd love to tell you that he did and that we found him out in some major scandal. But no such luck. He even died smirking."

"How?" asked Sally.

"He was knocked down on a zebra crossing. His last thought must have been that he was in the right."

"At least he's not around to plague you any more.

Unlike my dear father!" complained Kate.

"It would really make me feel better to hear of someone else's paternal misfortunes," said James.

"How long have you got? I could go on all night," said Kate.

"Just a little helping would do," laughed James.

"Where shall I begin, Sally? You probably know just as much about Hater Scumilious as I do."

"Don't you mean pater familias?" enquired James, with a twinkle in his eye.

"I know what I mean!" chorused Kate and Sally.

"I take it this is a much-loved catch-phrase and I just fed you the cue," said James.

"Sorry, couldn't resist. But on to daddy dearest. He was a Jekyll and Hyde character. The outside world, and particularly his team at work, could be forgiven for thinking he was a jolly little optimist, always looking on the bright side, never letting things get on top of him. At home he was the absolute opposite. We never saw a smile, never heard a chirpy remark. He'd come through the front door and take off the smiley mask to reveal the tragic one underneath. We all used to love it whenever someone came to the door. We'd ask them in, whoever they were, just to get a bit of relief from the gloom."

"I bet the Jehovah's Witnesses had a field day!" said James.

"Funnily enough, they were the only ones we didn't invite in."

"Religious discrimination!" declared James.

"The trouble was that he'd be perfectly charming to them while they were in the house – and they were usually there for a long time, scenting the possibility of a conversion – but once they left, he really took it out on us."

"Verbally?" asked James.

"That's how it would begin. But if he was in a particularly foul mood, it soon turned more physical."

"Fisticuffs?" asked James, his eyes showing concern

behind the seemingly flippant question.

"According to dad, a good slapping never hurt anyone."

"I remember one occasion," interposed Sally, "when he said to my father – who was the mildest man you could hope to meet – that sparing the rod would spoil the child. He was smiling all the time he said it. My father thought he was joking and started to build on the humour, saying how he beat me nightly and twice on Sundays. Then my mum joined in, talking about the cat o' nine tails in the cellar. When Kate's dad said he'd never go that far, there was a slightly awkward moment when no-one quite knew who was joking and who wasn't. They all started laughing eventually, so the conclusion was that it was all said in fun. But Kate just looked at me, just for a tiny moment, and I caught that look. And I knew. I knew it wasn't a joke."

"Next day, I told you all about it, for the first time. And you cried," said Kate.

James shuddered. "Cruelty to children is something I find unforgivable."

"To say nothing of cruelty to wives!" flashed Kate.

"At least wives have some choice in the matter. Children are completely powerless," said James.

"That's the theory," rejoined Kate. "In practice, it's a little more complicated. I like to think my mother might have left him if she hadn't been more frightened of what would happen if he came after her. I mean, where do you go? How do you manage? It's not so easy."

"Your mum's solution was to steer away from trouble. You said she'd step in between you and your dad," said Sally.

"And take the blows herself, you mean?" asked James.

"I meant metaphorically more than physically. She'd try to distract him. Or she'd send Kate off on an errand," explained Sally.

"Many's the time I've been sent off for a loaf of bread only to find a full breadbin when I got back. But by that time dad would have cooled off so the trick had worked. Another thing she did was to bake cakes and biscuits and put them down in front of us whenever the atmosphere got a bit difficult. The theory was, I suppose, that we couldn't argue if our mouths were full!"

"I'd have expected you to be more nervous, or even cowed, after a childhood like that," commented James. "But you seem very confident. Even feisty."

"I know. I don't know where this temperament of mine came from. But I never let him get me down. I was always confronting him. I used to take the opposite view from him just for the hell of it sometimes. I knew I was risking a caning, but I just couldn't stop myself. How stupid can you get?"

"You weren't stupid," defended Sally.

"No," agreed James. "You were just young and hurting."

Kate sighed and bit her lip. Sally was afraid that the conversation had upset and depressed her friend, and James was quick to see the turmoil just below the surface.

"How do your parents get on now?" he said, trying to steer into less problematic waters.

"Much better," Kate answered. "I can't stand it. I keep wondering why they're happier now. How come my mother can forgive him so easily? Why doesn't she leave now that she doesn't have to stay for my sake? I want her to punish him for all those years of cruelty. I want her to stop him walking all over her. I want him to suffer."

"It probably wouldn't actually help you much," said Sally. "Not really. Although I feel very pious for saying so. Taking revenge corrodes the soul. Look at all those Shakespearean examples. He knew a thing or two about the human psyche, did our William."

"And on that too, too solid reminder of work, I must take my leave," said James. "Thanks so much for the coffee and sympathy."

"We're the ones who should be thanking you," said Sally, hugging James enthusiastically. "For bringing me home…"

"For listening to my turgid complaints about my father," added Kate. "I hope you'll come again when I'm in a lighter mood. You must come over for a meal. You'll like my partner, Robin."

"Thanks. Would the invitation embrace my partner? He's a good guy, too."

"Of course." She started laughing and felt the need to explain her mirth. "Sorry. I'm just thinking how my father would have loved to hate you! Homosexuality was an abomination in his book, the book being the Bible, of course."

"What a broad-minded upbringing you must have had!"

"Oh, my dad was so narrow-minded that he could see through a keyhole with both eyes! But say you and your partner will come. We'd love to have you."

"It sounds as if we'd have lots to talk about. Thanks so much. Vol and I will compare diaries tomorrow. See you in the morning, Vol."

When he had gone, Kate was silent and thoughtful for a while. She opened the fridge and started collecting together the remnants of the previous day's party, wondering how best to turn them into something edible for supper. She looked up decisively.

"I'm going to go and see mum this weekend. It's time we started to talk like adults, two grown women together. I really need her to explain to me why she stays with him. Maybe she still feels there's nowhere else to go. Maybe she needs me to help her make the move. Maybe..."

"Hang on, Kate. Don't start jumping to conclusions about what your mother wants before you even talk to her. Have the conversation first. That's going to be difficult enough, for both of you. Step by step."

"Step by bloody step!" she agreed.

Chapter 16

The next morning, a frantic Pru telephoned to ask if she had left a notebook behind on the night of the reunion. As Kate went to search the room, Sally continued to talk to Pru. It emerged that the book was almost irreplaceable because it had all Pru's running notes about poems, thumbnail sketches of potential characters in her novel, and first drafts of stanzas and chapters. When Sally was able to report that Kate had found it down the side of the sofa, there were triumphant yelps down the phone.

"The next problem is how to get it back to me," said Pru.

"Can't we post it? First class should be with you the next day or in two days at the worst. Can you cope without it for that much longer?" asked Sally.

"I think I'll be too scared of its going missing. If you could have seen the state I was in yesterday when I thought I'd lost it! Could I pick it up tonight?"

"The only problem is that Kate and Robin are going out tonight and so I was going to go round to my flat to check on the post and the phone messages. And do a little light cleaning, with emphasis on the light. I probably won't be back here till about nine," said Sally.

"Could I come to your flat? Tell you what, I'll bring an easy-cook meal. I'll even help with the light cleaning."

"That's the best offer I've had all month! You're on. 26 Malvern Street. There's a trendy wine bar on the corner which we might have to repair to if the dust gets too much for us!" laughed Sally.

"Six o'clock?"

"Well, I usually stay in school till six, marking and preparing for the next day. Could we make it half past?"

"Sure thing. Actually, there's a poem in the notebook that I'd like your opinion on if you can bear to be a guinea-pig critic."

"I sometimes think I've lost all my critical faculties since becoming a teacher – but I'm willing to launch them into action again. It will be rather nice to have some adult work to look at. Much as I love to encourage children's writing, I do feel the need for grownup experiences to analyse instead of teenage angst and once-upon-a-times. See you tonight, then."

"Missing you already," said Pru in a phoney American accent.

Sally managed the day rather well, she thought. She found she was feeling a little nervous about being in her flat again and she realised that her urge to clean it was to eliminate traces of Mark. She was glad that Pru would be there as it would stop her from brooding as well as making the work less irksome. She kept herself busy all day, throwing herself enthusiastically into her lessons and managing to be sociable at lunch and break time. Her need to finish her prep work by six kept her focussed after school and she was able to complete all her tasks successfully. She arrived at the flat at the same time as Pru.

"This is marvellous!" she said. "Now I don't even have to walk through the door on my own. It's still a bit of a challenge, I'm afraid, just getting in without bursting into tears."

"Of course it is. Memories soak into the walls. It's like the smell of after-shave long after the man has left the room. Redolent. What a lovely word that is!" said Pru.

"Come in! Welcome to the madhouse!"

Sally managed to push the door open over the mail that was piled on the mat. Pru helped her pick it all up and they dropped it onto the sofa unceremoniously.

"First things first – would you like a tea or coffee?" asked Sally, shrugging off her coat and going into the kitchen.

"You must be joking! The sun, as they say, is over the yardarm. I have no idea what that means, except that it's a signal for the corkscrew to be unleashed on an unsuspecting bottle," replied Pru.

"Glasses it shall be, then. And before I do anything else, I must give you the notebook. It would be just like me at the moment to go back with it still in my bag."

"I'm so glad it's safe. Not that my work is any great

shakes, but 'tis mine own. Remind me to show you that poem before we leave. It would be just like me at the moment …blah, blah, blah!"

Sally retrieved the corkscrew from the whatnot drawer and then realised that the bottle that Pru had thrust into her hands was a screwtop.

"Cheers! But you really shouldn't have brought the wine as well as the food, Pru. There's wine here already."

"Didn't know what sort of a state the larder would be in. So I decided to play safe. The only way I can tackle housework at all is if I'm slightly oiled, so it was self-preservation, really. Now, how shall we play this? Cleaning first, then meal? Or vicky verky?"

"Would you mind if I listened to the messages and looked through the mail first? It'll be mostly cold calling and junk mail, so it shouldn't take long."

"That's fine. Would you like me to go into another room in case there's something personal?"

"No, no. There'll be nothing you can't hear."

Most of the messages were just as Sally had predicted. There was a reminder that she needed to make a dental appointment, a book club wanting her custom, and a message from her mother which ended halfway through with her realisation that she was phoning the wrong number. Then there was the familiar voice that still managed to make her heart stop.

"Sally, it's Mark here. Just in case you've forgotten what I sound like. Look, I'm sorry about the other night at the pub. I did a bit of detective work and I realise now that the man you were with must have been your friend James. You've talked about him before and I know he's of the other persuasion. Still don't know why we had the pantomime, but blood under the bridge. Let's just forget it. What I wanted to say was that you'll find a letter from me on the mat. Please, don't just throw it away. You must read it, darling. It contains some great news that I really can't tell you in a phone message. You know how I hate these things. They seem to make me talk in monosyllables. And this news needs to be in purple

prose. Read it, darling. Then call me. On my mobile."

Sally sat down unsteadily, staring sightlessly at the pile of mail. She looked up at Pru with a lost expression on her face.

"You look like me whenever the phone bill arrives," said Pru. "Sort of needing to open the envelope, but also afraid of what it contains."

"What good news could there possibly be in our situation?"

"There's only one way to find out. Unless you've already decided that you'll accept no more communications from him of any kind."

"I had decided that. But now..."

"I have to admit that in your position, I wouldn't be able to stop myself from opening the letter. Just to put it to rest. It'll be buzzing through your mind constantly otherwise, tantalising you."

"You're right. I need to know. Even if I go on rejecting what he has to say."

Sally sifted through the envelopes, throwing aside all the obvious circulars until she was left with the proper mail. From there, it was easy to sort out Mark's letter, with his distinctive and, she still thought, beautiful handwriting on the envelope. As she tore it open, her hands were trembling violently. Before unfolding the single sheet of paper, she looked up at Pru.

"This may seem a strange request, but would you mind reading it first, just in case it's a nasty joke, a way of taking some revenge by upsetting me?"

"Would he do that?" asked Pru uncomfortably.

"I didn't think so until recently, but I'm not so sure any more. Would you mind?"

"All right. Hand it over."

Pru read it silently first, then sighed. "Shit!"

"What does it say?" pleaded Sally.

"He says he's left his wife. So he's looking forward to moving in with you."

Sally grabbed the letter from the unresisting hands of her friend. She read Mark's words, which were rather more romantic than Pru had indicated by her bald rendition, and then she hugged the note to her heart, crying. Pru refilled the wineglasses and sipped thoughtfully until Sally recovered some of her composure.

"So the world's back in turmoil. Just when we thought it was safe to get back in the water…" mused Pru. "Look, this is obviously unexpected, to say the least. Shall I just go so you can contemplate for a bit? It's Kate you'll really want to talk to. Though I think you said she's out tonight. So maybe we should eat together as planned? We can't have you making life choices on an empty tum. We needn't talk about Mark and the letter if you'd rather let it sink in for a while. And we can definitely say 'Sod the cleaning!'"

"Sod the cleaning! Yes, let's have some supper. I'm suddenly starving."

"I'll take care of it while you open the rest of your mail."

True to her word, Pru had brought an almost-instant meal: pasta with a ready-prepared sauce and pre-washed salad. She had been going to make garlic bread, but decided that under the circumstances it would be just as nice to have the French stick unadulterated. The table was swiftly set and the steaming plates set down. Sally ate with relish, hardly speaking except to thank Pru for her care. When they were wiping up the remains of the delicious sauce with the bread, Sally broke into more personal stuff.

"Do you mind my talking about it, Pru?"

"Course not. Use me as a sounding board."

"You said 'Shit!' when you read the letter. Why was that your reaction?" asked Sally.

"Well, to be quite honest, I hoped that you were making progress in your attempts to put Mark out of your life. This makes it messy again."

"You mean you thought I'd done the right thing in breaking with him. But things have changed if he's left Jo, haven't they?"

"Are you sure about that?" asked Pru uncertainly. "He's the same man, isn't he? The one who deceived his wife, and not just this once with you? The one who told you his wife was going to have a termination when she was actually having a scan?"

"But if he's left her, then surely he must have been doing some thinking and decided that he wanted to be with me more than anything else?"

"So he's willing to leave a woman who's a few weeks' pregnant. That makes him an O.K. guy, does it?" she asked tentatively.

Sally sighed uncomfortably. "We don't know what all the background is yet. There may be all sorts of ramifications to this pregnancy. Suppose the baby's not his. Suppose I was wrong about Jo sounding pleased about it. Suppose she's already had a termination. Suppose they've talked it all through and it's an amicable arrangement. There are so many things that might be happening. I shan't know till I phone him. Don't you think I ought to do that straight away?"

"No!" yelped Pru. "Don't do a thing until you've talked to Kate! I've come into this situation late and I just don't know all there is to it. Kate has far more knowledge, about you and your predicament. Wait till you see her. Pretend you didn't come back here tonight, so you haven't yet got the message or the note. I know that's hard to do, but just try to put off doing anything irrevocable for another day."

"Maybe I could phone Kate's mobile?"

"Sally, think about that. They could be in a cinema or a theatre, in which case she'll be the most unpopular girl in the stalls. Or they may be enjoying a romantic meal, relishing the fact that for tonight there's just the two of them. Even if Kate's in a position to talk, how can she possibly concentrate on something as important as this without having you there in front of her? Phones are great, and I wouldn't be without them most of the time, but there are moments when communication just has to be up close and personal."

"You're right, of course. I'm being stupid and selfish. Kate and Robin need time away from my constant whingeing. One more day won't make any difference. I've just got to be a bit more disciplined about this. Oh, but it's hard! I just want to know NOW!"

"Course you do. I understand. So let's give ourselves something else to do. Do you think you could concentrate on my draft poem? It might help to take your mind off things."

"I'll try, Pru. I don't promise to be much help but I'll give it a go. Lay on, Macduff!"

"That makes it sound rather as if I'm about to deliver a few body blows. I hope it won't be quite such a formidable experience. But who knows?"

Pru quickly turned the pages of her notebook until she found the poem.

"Would you mind reading it aloud to me?"

"Here goes. It's called 'Wearing Mother's Clothes.'

As a child

The thrill, the excitement,

Of wearing mother's clothes.

The dress

Studded with pearls like tiny stars.

For dancing.

The hat

Fluffed with feathers like fallen

petals.

For weddings.

But most of all

The shoes.

Slipping tiny feet

Into shiny satin

With heels like ice cream cones.

Growing taller, and therefore

Growing up.

Pretending.

How strange and wonderful

To be my mother.

Now

I still have the pearl-studded dress.

Its stars have faded a little.

The hat is moulting, petals

dropping,

But still it has its shape

Retaining the spirit of the past.

The shoes have gone.

I have worn these memories

As if on a stage,

Actor finding confidence

In pretence,

Hiding behind a role.

Still a child dressing up,

Trying to appear

Star-studded and feather-decked.

But I'll never fill

My mother's shoes.

That's it. What do you think?" Pru asked diffidently.

Sally was silent, gazing into the corner of the room as if she could see the mother standing there.

"Let me look at it. I need to see the words in front of me

to take in the images properly. I haven't retained it all just hearing it."

Pru handed her the notebook and sat quietly waiting for Sally's considered thoughts.

"My first reaction is that I love it."

"I've worked on it a bit, but I'm sure there's a lot more to do to it. Just say whatever comes into your head as you read it through."

"All right. First of all, I can relate to the child dressing up. Probably everyone can. My mum used to have a dressing up box for me, full of weird and wonderful stuff. But the best kind of dressing up was when she let me put on her clothes, especially the floaty chiffons and the smooth satins. And you're right, it was like becoming mother and being grown up. Oh, I've just noticed that you've used 'tiny' twice – tiny stars and tiny feet. Maybe change one of them? Keep tiny feet because that 'tiny' rhymes with 'shiny' on the next line. How about 'minute stars'?" suggested Sally.

"Good point. But in print 'minute' could be read as a

unit of time. You know, second, minute, hour."

"What about 'miniature' then?"

"Better. I like it. Go on."

"I like all the images you use to describe the clothes. They're all things that children relate to – stars, feathers, petals, ice cream cones. And then I like the way those images deteriorate with age, so the stars fade and the feathers moult and the petals drop. I'm not sure about the hat, where you say it still has its shape and retains the spirit of the past. Not sure about those words."

"Yes, I'm not quite happy with that. I'll work on it," said Pru.

"I really love the way you take the dressing up idea into adult life. 'All the world's a stage' sort of thing. We do play parts and hide behind our poses, don't we? And then back to the picture of star-studded and feather-decked. Lovely."

"What about the end?" asked Pru eagerly.

"Yes. You've already said the shoes are missing, so

literally you can't fill them. But there's also the meaning of not being able to live up to your mother. That's great. I'm sure lots of women will relate to all these sentiments, Pru."

"So, it's worth pursuing, is it?"

"Absolutely. I really love it. I feel so privileged to have seen this first draft. I don't suppose my comments are much help..."

"Oh, but they are!" insisted Pru.

"Well, I'm thrilled. I'll be your critic anytime. Are there any others you'd like me to see?" asked Sally.

"Not tonight. You've done enough for one session, thank you."

"What made you write it? Did you physically find something that belonged to your mother?"

"No, I came at it from the other end. I was thinking about my mum, what a wonderful person she was and how I'd never be able to be such a loving and self-sacrificing mother myself. I'd never fill her shoes.

Actually, if I'm really honest, my partner thinks this comparison with my mother is one of the reasons why I'm so against having children."

"And is he right?"

"It's hard to say. I don't think so, but I'm willing to concede that Freud would probably have a field day roaming through my psyche!"

"You seem pretty together to me. Mind you, I'm in such a mess myself that Salvador Dali would appear normal at the moment."

"Let's just wash up the dishes and get you back to Kate's, shall we?"

"I certainly can't face doing any housework now, but I would like to wash the dishes. I couldn't bear to come back to dirty plates on my next visit."

They cleared the table and Sally immersed her hands in soapy suds while Pru dried and piled the dishes on the table for Sally to put in their appropriate places.

"I'm still happy to pop round with you next time and do the dusting, you know. I always have the image in my mind of Doris Day and whoever-it-was flicking their little dusters in 'Calamity Jane' and making everything all spick and span with no visible effort!"

"Oh yes! 'A Woman's Touch'"

"Terribly sexist stuff, isn't it? But I've always loved that film. I'm not sure why."

"Me, too! It was one of the films that my mum and dad watched with me – it was thought 'suitable'! Actually, dear Doris slapping her buckskinned thighs was more likely to encourage me to be a lesbian than anything else!"

"Ah, but you forget Howard Keel. That barrel chest and deep sexy voice. He certainly made me wet my knickers!"

"Pru! What a thing for a sensitive poet to utter!" laughed Sally.

"I have to have nights off or I'd be far too earnest for this world."

"Feel free to be as ribald as you like."

"I shall certainly make use of you, both to let off steam and to rehearse my inimitable stanzas. That's what friends are for."

"It is. And you've been a good friend to me tonight. Thanks so much, Pru."

Chapter 17

Kate and Robin had once again performed their usual trick of not being able to agree on a film to see and so going to a restaurant instead. Once seated, they both agreed that this was exactly what they really wanted to do anyway.

"I adore Sal, you know that," said Robin. "But it's wonderful to have you all to myself for a while."

"I know I've been a bit distant lately. Partly it's because I'm worried about Sally, but there's something else as well," said Kate.

Robin felt the muscles round his stomach tighten considerably. He was constantly expecting Kate to realise that he was unworthy of her and he thought the time might have come when she finally saw him for the fool he was. He braced himself.

"I've decided that I've got to talk to my mother – I mean

really talk. Not just the surface chat we usually have when we avoid anything remotely important," Kate went on.

Robin silently thanked his Guardian Angel for the prolongation of his relationship. He passed the menu to Kate, suddenly realising just how hungry he was.

"I'm tired of ignoring the past and pretending that I had an ordinary father who actually loved me. It's time mum and I faced reality."

"I've thought for a long time that you needed to confront your daemons, darling. I often feel you start a quarrel with me merely because I'm the only available man, while the person you really resent and want to challenge is your father."

"I'm not sure I'll ever be able to do that. But at least I can make mum face up to the truth about my childhood. And who knows where it will go after that."

Luigi, the waiter, approached them, addressing them as long-lost friends. "So, you return to Luigi, eh? Where you been? I been feeding the whitebait, I been suckling the veal, I been whipping the zabaglione. For what? For customers who don't appreciate the fine tastes in this ristorante! Now you back, we can put the genius back into the food!"

"And the food back into the geniuses," quipped Robin.

Kate laughed. "Sorry, Luigi. We've been snowed under with work and worry. But it's really good to be sitting here now."

"When you got worry, that's when you need food. You should be in here more, not less. Now, what about tonight? We got some Specials up on the board as well as the usual favourites. What's your pleasure?"

"I'm going to have whitebait, followed by veal in that lovely creamy mushroom sauce. I can't have either of those with Sally – she can't stand the fishy eyes looking at her, and she makes me feel thoroughly guilty about little calves reared in the dark," said Kate.

"Is not happen no more," asserted Luigi. "The little calves, they live outside. The meat not so pretty white, but the flavour better."

"I'll have the *tonno e fagioli*, followed by *saltimbocca*. We'll have a large bottle of fizzy water and a bottle of Frascati," said Robin.

"I bring wine straight away so you uncoil," said Luigi, retreating quickly to the bar.

"I think he means unwind. Though, actually, maybe uncoil describes what I need to do more graphically!" said Kate.

"It's so good to be here. I hadn't realised how much I've missed it and how important it is for us to come."

"You used to say that the only time we really talked was when we were opposite each other in a restaurant."

"It's true. You're always leaping up to do something at home. I also used to say we talked when we shared a bath. Again, you had to look me in the eye and you couldn't rush off."

"Darling Robin. We haven't had any of those lately either, have we?"

"Well, it's never seemed quite right with Sally around."

"That Baptist background of yours! You'd have thought water immersion would please you!"

The water and the wine arrived and they toasted each other with their usual "Health and Happiness!" The first course was put in front of them with a flourish and Kate began to stab at the innocent whitebait with abandon.

"I'm pretending it's dad on the plate," she explained.

"It is indubitably time you delved a bit with your dear mama," Robin said through a mouthful of tuna.

"I'm hoping I might be able to encourage her to leave him. She may be scared of making that sort of move without help. I'll give her all the support she needs if only she'll do it."

"Screw the old courage to the sticking point, eh?" said Robin.

"Place," murmured Kate.

"What?"

"It's screw your courage to the sticking-place," she explained. "Sorry, but Sal has corrected me so many times on that one!"

"She'll be thrilled that you actually listened to her. But back to your dear mama. Are you sure she's that unhappy? She's always struck me as being quite contented with her lot."

"That may just be a front. If she feels there's nowhere to go, then it's better to stay where she is. But if she knows I'll support her…"

"How would that work? I mean, where would she live if she left your dad?" asked Robin.

"I suppose to begin with she'd move in with me, us. Would that would be all right with you?"

"I suppose so."

"You don't sound very enthusiastic," said Kate, beginning to prickle.

"Don't misunderstand. It would be fine for a while, but I

just know you and she would get on each other's nerves after a time. You'll need to have a plan for what happens after that. Well, before it really. I mean, it would be better not to get to the friction stage at all."

"I see what you mean. Yes, well, dad would have to provide some sort of settlement so she could get her own place."

The waiter approached hesitantly, making sure they were ready to have their main dishes. This process gave Robin time to appraise Kate's mood and assess how in touch with reality she was. He knew that she often took off with an idea, assuming that she was right and that everyone with any sense would feel the same as she did. She was often wrong in that assumption. Robin wondered if her view of her mother was coloured more by her own feelings towards her father than by a real knowledge of her mother. He knew he would have to tread warily around her emotional eggshells. He smiled at her and the waiter as their plates were cleared and their main courses were placed steaming in front of them.

"I give you a mix of the vegetables," explained Luigi. "The baby courgettes in the tempura, the baby carrots glazed in the butter, the baby potatoes with the salt and the rosemary. Eat! Enjoy!"

"It's all babies tonight," sighed Robin.

"Don't start on that one!" warned Kate. "This is definitely not the time!"

"Only joking. The thought of sharing the house with your mother and a springoff is too much to bear."

"Don't you mean offspring?" asked Kate, feeding him the line.

"I know what I mean!" he completed. "But we may be jumping ahead too quickly. Your mother may have no secret thoughts of escape at all. Don't get too wedded to the idea of rescuing her, Kate. She may be perfectly happy."

"We'll see. I just want to give her the chance to get away if she wants to, that's all. But enough of me! What's new in the field of advertising?" asked Kate.

"It may well be fresh fields and pastures new," said Robin enigmatically.

"That's actually 'fresh woods and pastures new'. But ignore the pedantry! What's going on?"

"It looks as though we may be merging with Thomasson & Haywood. There have been rumours flying around for some time now, but today the MD actually acknowledged that there were talks going on."

"How would that affect you? Is your job secure?"

"Oh yes. No worries there. Freddy even hinted that there'd be promotion for me."

"Great, Robin. You certainly deserve it. So what's the problem?"

"The thing is that Thomasson & Haywood is where Jo works. You know, Mark's wife."

"Of course it is! I'd forgotten that. That might be a bit awkward for you."

"I overheard some of the guys chatting at lunch time, and there's a bit of a bombshell coming. Brace yourself."

Robin took a deep breath. "Rumour hath it that she has left him!"

"What? Are you sure? Why? When?"

Kate's mouth was in grave danger of disgorging its half-chewed contents. Robin smiled at her flabbergasted face, glad to have grabbed her attention so completely.

"It appears that somehow she found out that he'd been playing the field on several occasions. So she ordered him to vacate the premises. Immediately."

"Who told her about his affairs?" asked Kate.

"No idea. Either a friend who couldn't bear to see her made a fool of, or an enemy who wanted to hurt one or other of them. It wasn't you, was it?" asked Robin.

"Of course not. I only behave like God in our relationship, not in anyone else's. Was anything said about her being pregnant?"

"No. I don't think that's common knowledge yet."

"What on earth's going to happen now? I'm sure Sal doesn't know about it. Oh Lord, I do hope this doesn't change her mind about seeing him again. I mean, he'll be footloose and fancy free now, won't he?"

"In his opinion, he always was. But it's bound to have an impact on Sally, isn't it? Like you, I hope she doesn't slip back into a relationship with him. I can't see him as anything but thoroughly bad news. Sally deserves so much better."

"With his track record, he wouldn't stick with Sal for long anyway. So she'd have to go through all the angst over again when he moved on to the next conquest. Let's just hope she doesn't find out," concluded Kate.

However, on returning home they found a flushed and agitated Sally pacing the room clutching a letter in her hand.

"Oh, I'm so glad to see you two. I've had a note from Mark. He says he's left Jo and he wants me to ring him. Pru didn't think I should do anything until I'd spoken to you. So I've been like a wild animal caged in a zoo waiting for you."

"I thought the pacing looked familiar," said Robin.

"Give us a chance to get in and take our coats off, Sal!" Kate ordered, a little peremptorily. She glanced at Robin and saw that he was afraid of the same thing as she was. They both took off their jackets, making the operation last as long as possible without seeming strange so that they could gather their thoughts.

"Can we recap for a moment? You say Mark has left Jo? Not the other way round?" asked Robin.

Sally stopped in her tracks and regarded Robin levelly. "Why do you ask that?"

Robin shuffled his feet uncomfortably but caught Kate's nod of approval to go on.

"I heard a rumour at work today that Jo had chucked him out," he replied.

"There's a big difference, isn't there?" said Kate. "Don't you think we should find out the answer before you talk to him?"

"What's wrong with asking him directly?" challenged

Sally.

"For some reason, 'trust' is the word which comes to mind. Sorry, Sal, but I'm not sure you could safely take his word for it," said Kate acerbically.

"So how else would you propose we find out?" said Sally. "I'm telling you right now, Kate, I can't wait until tomorrow over this. I'm going out of my mind here."

"How about phoning his home number and seeing who answers?" suggested Robin.

"Would that tell us anything? If Jo answers, it could either mean that Mark has walked out or that she's chucked him out. It doesn't get us any further," said Kate logically.

"If we asked to speak to Mark, we might get some information from her reply," offered Robin.

"That's true. And she doesn't have to know who we are or anything," said Sally, seizing on the suggestion with alacrity. "Would you do that for me, Robin? She might feel more at ease with a bloke asking for Mark rather than a woman."

"Hoist by my own petard. Maybe it's not such a good idea."

"Please, Robin," pleaded Sally.

"All right. Hand me the phone."

While Sally got the number, Kate finally took her coat and hung it up in the hall. She felt weary at the thought of what would probably turn out to be another late night looking after Sally, but she felt that she had to be strong enough to take it on. When she returned to the room, Robin was speaking on the phone.

"Oh, I see. Well, don't worry. I'll try him at school tomorrow," he said before hanging up.

"Well?" said Sally eagerly.

"No luck. All she said was that he wasn't there."

"Back to square one," said Kate. "Wouldn't it be better to wait till tomorrow? Robin could ask around at work in the morning."

"At work? What do you mean?" asked Sally.

"Ah. Yes. Well, what you don't know yet is that my firm and Jo's are merging and I heard a rumour that Jo was no longer with Mark because she'd heard about his extra-marital pastimes," explained Robin diffidently.

"Why didn't you say so straight away? Oh God, I hate all this behind-the-back whispering. Why can't people mind their own business? And what have you been saying to your buddies?" accused Sally.

"Not a word. Honestly. I just listened in on a conversation, that's all."

"Don't start attacking Robin, Sally," said Kate loyally. "He's done nothing but support you since you moved in and he doesn't deserve your jumping at him as if he's betrayed your confidence in some way."

"Sorry, Robin. I know you wouldn't... I'm just over-wrought."

"It's all right. Don't worry about it. The question is: what do we do now? Couldn't you wait till I can find out something tomorrow? Surely that would be best."

"I don't think so. I'm sorry. I know I sound pathetic,"

moaned Sally.

"Let's get it over with, then," said Kate resolutely. "We have to ask him. But, Sally, I really don't think you should do it yourself. Look at the state of you. How about if I phone as a go-between and get him to tell me?"

"I don't think he'll talk to you. He knows you don't like him."

"Tough. It's the only option we'll give him. He either talks to me or no-one."

"It's worth a try. Go on then."

Sally wrote down Mark's mobile number and then explained that she couldn't stay in the room while Kate talked to him. Robin enlisted her help to make a pot of tea in the kitchen and Kate got on with the unpleasant necessity, as she thought of it, of speaking to Mark. He answered the phone immediately, as if he'd been waiting for the call.

"Mark? It's Kate here, Sally's friend. Look, I know I'm

probably the last person you thought you'd be hearing from at this time of night, but I'm phoning on Sally's behalf."

"Can't she speak to me herself? Is she all right?"

"She's really too upset to talk to you. She asked me to find out what was going on."

"It's simple. I've left Jo. I've done what Sally wanted. We can be together now. Tell her…"

"Wait a minute, Mark. You say you've left Jo. But we've heard that she threw you out."

"What difference does it make? The point is that I'm free now. So Sally and I…"

"It makes a huge difference," interrupted Kate. "One way, you've made a conscious decision and taken action yourself to ensure you can be with Sally. The other way, you're unwillingly homeless and searching around for a convenient shelter."

"For goodness sake! Of course I'm choosing Sally. Jo and I are finished."

"And the baby?"

"That's entirely Jo's business. She's free to do what she wants about it."

"You'd just walk away from it, would you?"

"Look, Kate. I think you're being a bit intrusive here. I can't see that this is any of your business. All you need to report to Sally is that I'm free and wanting her. Can you do that?"

"Sally and I have been friends for a very long time, Mark. I want to protect her from hurt if I possibly can. And frankly, I have a bad feeling about all this."

"You've never liked me," he said petulantly.

"That's not the point. I just don't want you to mislead Sally with half-truths. Either you left your wife or she asked you to leave. Which was it?"

"None of your damn business! Put Sally on the phone. I want to speak to her, not her so-called friend."

"I think we've come to the end of this conversation, Mark."

"Don't you mislead her! I want her to know I love her and I want to be with her. You tell her that!"

"I shall faithfully pass on the whole of our conversation to her, don't worry about that. It'll be up to her after that. Goodbye."

Kate found that she felt furious about Mark. Her gut instinct was not to trust him, yet it was no more than a feeling and in a way he was right when he'd said it wasn't her business. She knew she must simply report back to Sally without overlaying the conversation with any of her own misgivings, and she felt like a journalist in a war zone. When Robin and Sally returned with the tea, she calmly relayed everything and waited for Sally's reaction.

"So he didn't actually tell you who had left whom? Just that it didn't matter."

"That's right."

"You've got to decide whether it makes a difference to you," said Robin.

"What do you mean?"

"Well, let's suppose first of all that Jo ditched him. He's out in the cold, nowhere to go, sees you as a nice warm place of refuge," said Robin.

"Thanks! Very complimentary!"

"You'd never know if he was really committed to you, would you? You'd be afraid that if Jo hadn't found out about his affairs and therefore hadn't thrown him out, maybe he wouldn't have left her," Robin went on relentlessly.

"I'd feel like a last resort rather than a first choice, you mean?" said Sally quietly.

"Exactly. And frankly, judging by his past behaviour, you'd constantly be watching for him to do it again – find a new woman because he got bored with the status quo."

"What do you think, Kate?" asked Sally.

"Exactly the same. I think it's vitally important that you find out the truth."

"And if I find out that he left of his own accord?"

"Then you've got to decide how you feel about a man who could leave a pregnant wife and show no concern for his baby, implying that it was just Jo's business from now on. But let's find out first, and then see where you want to go from there."

"Burn that bridge when we come to it, you mean? Let's face it, Kate. You aren't going to feel happy about my being with Mark no matter what. Are you?"

"No, Sally, I'm not. But that really doesn't matter. It's you who needs to make this decision and my feelings don't come into it."

"Correct. It is my decision. But you're my best friend and I know you only want what's good for me. As far as I know, you haven't got a hidden agenda. Though I sometimes think you want to punish all men because your father was a pig."

"No, no," interrupted Robin. "She only wants to punish me!"

"Enough, already," said Kate, trying to lighten the mood a little. "I know men have feelings – but like, who cares?" she laughed.

"As you say, enough. I'm just going to have to wait until tomorrow, aren't I? Do you think you can find out more for me, Robin?"

"I'll do my best. I'm being sent over to her building in the morning so I'll delve a bit. Leave it in my culpable hands."

"Don't you mean capable?"

"I know what I mean! So there's no more to discuss now. I suggest we all worry about it horizontally rather than vertically. To bed!" said Robin.

Sally dragged her way almost painfully up the stairs, leaving Robin and Kate to contemplate her retreating form in silence. The tea had been untouched and sat on the tray accusingly. Neither Kate nor Robin really wanted it. When they heard Sally go into the bathroom, Robin said, "You know, I think Mark is one of those bad things that sometimes happen to good people."

Chapter 18

It took Robin two days of undercover sleuthing to find out more about what he called the Mark Matrimonial Muddle. He contrived to be sent over to Jo's building for a meeting with one of his counterpart Account Executives, and found to his surprise that it was Jo herself. Robin was impressed by her appearance and presence. Everything about her was neat, from her smooth haircut to her kitten heels. Robin glanced at her tummy area surreptitiously but could discern no bump, realising that of course there would not yet be any sign of pregnancy anyway. Her handshake was firm and she made eye contact with him. Robin was always wary of people who didn't look at him when they greeted him and was pleasantly impressed with Jo. They established a friendly rapport immediately as they discovered that they had a similar attitude to the ethics of advertising. Both of them refused to do cigarette ads and both kept a careful eye on the use of sexual persuasion. After two hours of examining their respective present campaigns, they felt optimistic about working alongside each other in the soon-to-be-amalgamated agency.

Jo suggested that they relax over coffee and sandwiches before she introduced Robin to other members of what she called her 'squad'. He had noticed that she had referred earlier to her immediate boss as 'Coach', and to her assistant as her 'Sub'. He commented on her sport vocabulary.

"That's my father's influence, I guess," she laughed. "He played lots of games himself when he was young, then took on the role of teacher with his children. I was the only girl so I was treated as an honorary boy – if you can call it that! – so I learnt alongside my brothers. Daddy took it all very seriously and his attitude even dribbled down into everyday life. We all had our separate chores to do around the house but Daddy emphasised that we were all part of a team pulling together. Every time we finished a job, we yelled out 'Goal!' and Daddy would cheer. It was quite sweet, really."

"It sounds like a very cunning way to get you to do the work," agreed Robin. "He must have been quite a psychologist."

"He was. Housework has never been such fun as it was back then. It was great training for life as well. I always think of myself as a member of a group rather than as an individual. It comes in handy in my job."

Robin took a deep breath and decided to take the opportunity to delve, as Kate would have him do. "So, you were part of a big family, were you? How many brothers do you have?"

"Only three actual brothers, but my mother's sister had been killed in a car crash when her children were quite young, so there were her three boys living with us most of the time as well."

"You must have felt completely outnumbered."

"Actually, no. I thought I was a boy most of the time! I loved playing all the games and I was really good at them, too. I was the best spin bowler, and I was a really speedy fly half. I even threw myself around fearlessly in goal. I loved it."

"A happy family with lots of kids to play with. Sounds idyllic. I expect you want lots yourself, then," ventured Robin with his heart in his mouth, wondering if she felt comfortable enough with him to talk about such a personal issue.

Jo busied herself with pouring the coffee for a few minutes. Her back was towards Robin but he could sense stiffness in her movements. He thought he'd moved in too soon and was cursing himself for his lack of patience.

"Oh heck!" she sighed. "I might as well start the ball rolling with you as anyone else, I suppose. The thing is, Robin, I am actually pregnant. For the first time."

"Well, congratulations. That's great." He paused. "Isn't it?"

"Yes and no."

"I don't quite follow. Is something wrong?" asked Robin carefully.

"You could say that. You see, I'm separated from my husband."

"Ah. I can see that that might present a problem."

"The sad thing is that we'd been trying for a baby for ages, with no luck. Then suddenly we score a goal, jubilation all round."

"Where's the snag?" asked Robin.

"I just felt I had to call time out."

There was a silence while Robin pondered on how to prolong the conversation and Jo pondered on whether she should end it.

"Do you want to talk about it?" asked Robin gently, realising that he wasn't just curious for Sally's sake but was genuinely sympathetic to Jo as a person in her own right.

"Actually, I wouldn't mind just testing it out on someone. Would you referee for me?"

"I don't promise to do that, but I'll certainly listen."

"I don't know why I feel like telling you this. Maybe it's because you don't know any of the people involved so you can see it from the outside," Jo began.

"Well, we don't know that for sure, do we?" Robin hastened to say, feeling uncomfortable about his possible duplicity. "I mean, I might know your husband and not realise he was your husband – if you see what I mean."

"True. I'll just call him X so you won't be in a compromising position. X and I – oh dear, it sounds like an equation! – have been married for five years. And we were childhood sweethearts long before that. Actually, I've never really had any other relationship. He was one of my brother's friends who used to join in our games in the local park. I loved him for his swerve balls!" She giggled. "Then we started going out as teenagers, and it lasted all through our separation to different universities. For me, there was never anyone else. And I thought it had been the same for him. I discovered I was wrong about that."

"Ouch! What happened?"

"Someone told me he'd been playing away. Not just once. There was even a permanent fixture somewhere else. I didn't believe it at first. But I did a bit of checking and I discovered that quite a lot of my friends knew all about it and hadn't said anything so as not to upset me. A couple of them even assumed I was aware of it and that we'd agreed to have an open marriage. They said we always looked so happy when we were together that they just thought we were – what was it they said? Oh yes, 'terribly grown up about it'. Can you believe it? Infidelity is grown up!" she scoffed.

"I've never understood that either," agreed Robin. "It must have come as quite a shock."

"That's the understatement of the year. Especially as it came just after hearing I was finally preggers."

"What did your husband have to say?"

"About the pregnancy? He was delighted. I'm sure that wasn't feigned. He really was pleased. Then I learnt about his away games and I confronted him with it. He denied it at first, said it was sour grapes on the part of the so-called friends who'd told me because they were jealous of our perfect relationship. But when I named a few names and said I was going to go to them and ask them point blank if they'd ever had an affair with him, then he backed down. He said they had all been the equivalent of adolescent flings. They were over; he was with me and would stay that way forever. Begged forgiveness. All that."

"You've already said you're now separated, so I assume you didn't believe him," said Robin.

"I don't know about not believing him. He was very convincing. He said that we should have had other relationships when we were young, before we got married, and that that was what happened to most people. He said we'd always considered ourselves lucky that we'd met and fallen in love so young, but maybe it wasn't really fortunate. Maybe we should have done a bit more talent spotting before we settled down. He's got a point, hasn't he?"

"It's certainly what usually happens. Most people don't

stay with their first dates. But I would have said you were lucky to have been so sure of each other straight away. <u>You</u> obviously didn't feel the need to sample anyone else, did you?" asked Robin.

"No. I've always been sure that … X was the one for me. However, he says he felt a bit cheated, even though he realises now that that was really immature. He saw all his mates having a great time seeing all kinds of different girls, especially at College, and he felt he wanted it too. Can you relate to that?"

"I suppose I can, if I'm honest. One of the biggest learning curves at University had nothing to do with what I was studying. It was experiencing sex for the first time. Finding out what I wanted in a relationship."

"You see, I can forgive that. At College, we were miles apart and it must have been very tempting for him. It didn't happen to me, but I was still living at home when I went to Uni. I was always so busy, helping to look after the house and my brothers as well as studying. There weren't any gaps in my life that needed filling. It was different for him."

"But it didn't stop after University?"

"No. That's the bit I'm having trouble with. I would have thought that once we were together again – and we started living together almost straight away and got married quite soon – it would have blown the whistle on any other involvements."

"What does X say about that?"

"That he was weak, that he was wrong to do it. He says he's desperately sorry about it. None of it was important compared with his feeling for me. He's now mature and ready to settle and he'll never look for a transfer again."

"Do you believe him?"

"That's the whole crux of the matter, isn't it? He sounded completely sincere. And he really was thrilled about the baby. He was desperate when I threw him out, crying and everything. I want to believe him. I really do. For the moment, he's on the bench. But I know there's no sub for me."

"So he's in the Sin Bin."

"More like the Blood Bin," said Jo.

"Will you let him back on the field?" asked Robin.

"If he can clean himself up. Yes, I think so. To be absolutely honest, the thought of life without him is intolerable, especially with a child."

"You wouldn't consider an abortion, I suppose?"

"Absolutely not."

"That would seem to be it, then. You've made up your mind already."

"I have, haven't I? I didn't realise that I had until I talked it through with you. Thanks so much for letting me. I hope I haven't embarrassed you so much that you'll never want to work with me."

"Course not. I'm only too happy to have been a sounding board. Er… how much of all this is common knowledge? I mean, I'm not going to gossip, but I'd like to know what you want me to say if the subject comes up."

"Oh, the grapevine has been very efficient. People know

that my husband and I are experiencing some difficulties at the moment. They know we're not living together. No-one knows I'm pregnant, so please don't mention that. When we get back together again, I'll make a sort of public announcement. But I'll keep the baby secret for as long as possible. I don't want people warming up to take my place in the team until the last moment. Once I have one baby, you see, I'm going in for several, so it'll be goodbye work for quite some time."

"Well, congratulations. Everything seems as if it will work out fine for you both. When will you tell X the good news?" asked Robin.

"Oh, I want him to stew for a bit first. There's nothing like losing something to make you want it desperately! Let him realise what he's got with me and think he might have done something to make himself lose it forever. So I'm relying on you to stay zipped up until rumours reach you about our reconciliation. Is that all right?"

"Of course. You know, I feel really flattered that you've trusted me with this. I won't let you down. There's just one thing. Would you mind if I told my partner? We never hide anything from each other and I'd feel really awkward about keeping something back from her."

"I can understand that. As long as she keeps it all to herself, that's all right by me. I don't suppose she's likely to meet my husband. Although there's this theory – what's it called? Six degrees of separation or something? Anyway, it sort of proves that you're likely to be connected to any complete stranger. Who knows, your partner might be my husband's second cousin twice removed, or they may have lived next door to each other as children," said Jo.

"Unlikely," said Robin, masking how close she was to the truth.

"Thanks. I really appreciate all this. I was very unsure about this merger of our two companies, you know. Mergers so often mean massive redundancies and people competing with colleagues for fewer jobs. I've been assured that that won't happen. In fact, I'm told that the new company will actually expand. And I'm really happy about this meeting with you. We seem to have the same attitude to all the important things. It'll be good to have an ally on the ethics front!" said Jo.

"Even if you won't be around for long."

"A few months is a long time in advertising!" laughed Jo. "Are you ready to meet my Squad now? They're working on a fast-tanning product for next summer. I'm sure they'd love a little relief from jolly brown beauties."

"Lead on!" said Robin.

On arriving home that night, Robin was praying that Kate would be there without Sally. He knew that Sally was waiting impatiently for any news that he could glean about Mark, but he wanted the chance to give Kate the full information before offering the expurgated version to Sal. He was determined to honour his promise to Jo and only reveal to Kate her decision to take Mark back. Fortunately, Kate was already home when he opened the door. Her voice sailed down to him from the study.

"Hi, love. I'm just sending out an email to the gang about our next reunion. I'll be down in a minute."

Robin busied himself with the ritual of tea-making until she careered into the kitchen.

"I'm so excited," she said. "We're going to have another reunion next week! Everyone really wants to make it a regular thing now we've started it. Isn't that great?"

"It certainly is. It'll help with Sally, too."

"Oh dear, that sounds ominous. What gives?"

"Well, I had a very interesting meeting today with my fellow account exec, Jo, and she's one of the nicest and most genuine people I've ever come across in this slippery advertising world. We had a long talk about work and then I managed to get her to open up about her personal life."

"Well done. My favourite sleuth! Tell me all."

They sat comfortably with the ubiquitous tea, Kate snuggling up to Robin companionably.

"She'd found out that her husband – she called him X just in case I knew him – had been having affairs all the time they'd been together and also that he was involved with someone now. So she'd chucked him out…"

"I knew it!" shouted Kate. "The slimy bastard didn't leave her so he could be with Sally at all! Bastard sod, as they say in the Classics."

"Wait. There's more. She's going to take him back."

"The fool! Why on earth…"

"She really loves him. They were childhood sweethearts and all that. He's convinced her that he's truly sorry and that he'll never stray again."

"And she believes him?" asked an incredulous Kate.

"She does. The prospect of life without him doesn't bear thinking about, she says, especially with a baby on the way."

"Oh well, much as I feel sorry for her, it will make life easier for Sally. She won't have to make any decisions at all. It'll be taken right out of her hands. Mr X will be safely ensconced with wifey and scared to death of stepping out of line again."

"There's a snag, though. Jo's not going to tell him

straight away that he's forgiven. She thinks he needs a bit of anxiety first to make him realise where his heart lies. She's right, too."

"Why's that a snag? We can inform Sally that Jo will be forgiving him and taking him back, so…"

"We can't," Robin broke in. "I promised I wouldn't tell anyone about that bit. At least, I got permission to share it with you as my all-knowing partner, but I swore I wouldn't spill the beans further. I also promised that you wouldn't, either. So we can't actually tell Sal what the future holds for Mark."

Kate harrumphed and clattered her mug onto the table.

"Damn. But we can tell her that Jo chucked him out rather than his making a noble choice in Sally's favour, can't we?"

"Yes, Jo knows that's grapevine knowledge."

"That should be enough, shouldn't it? I mean, the fact that he's lied to her yet again should put her off once and for all, shouldn't it?" asked Kate, but there was an edge of anxiety in her voice.

"For most people, that would be a clincher. But I'm not so sure about Sally. This man seems to have the power to make women forgive the most heinous crimes."

They both stared into space contemplating all the possibilities.

"We'll have to emphasise the lying…" Kate started.

However, she got no further, because Sally hurried through the front door and burst into the kitchen.

"Did you find anything out today?" she asked Robin straight away.

"I did, as a matter of fact," said Robin, taking a deep breath.

Kate poured tea while Robin reported as much of his conversation with Jo as he was allowed. Sally didn't say anything at all while he was talking, and then she just sipped her tea for a minute or so before letting a moan escape from her lips.

"I'm sorry," said Robin. "I know it must be tough to find out that he lied to you."

"Again!" said Kate before she could stop herself. "I mean, I'm sorry, too, Sal. I really am. But I can't honestly say I'm surprised. We were sort of expecting it, weren't we?"

"Speak for yourself," replied Sally rather frostily. "I was giving him the benefit of the doubt, on the basis that all men are innocent until proven guilty."

"Most men are nothing of the sort," snorted Kate. "Take my father – please!"

"Perhaps this isn't the right time to digress onto your father, darling," said Robin tactfully. "Sally needs to concentrate on how Mark has treated her badly in this."

"Right. Sorry. You must be feeling really shitty, lambkin. Of course you wanted to believe he left his wife so he could be with you. You must feel second best, to say the least, when it's obvious that he only wants you because he's homeless."

Kate knew she was being brutal but she wanted Sally to see things clearly.

Sally started crying and did nothing to wipe the tears from her miserable face. Kate grabbed tissues and started to mop her up gently. Robin felt extremely uncomfortable in the presence of such raw misery. He shuffled his feet and cleared his throat before mumbling something inaudible and leaving the room.

"So it was all a lie," cried Sally. "He's made a fool of me again."

"No, he hasn't. You haven't been in touch with him since his letter and the phone call. So for all he knows, you've just stuck to the decision you made when you parted company with him. You can pretend to the outside world that you're well over it and never entertained the slightest thought of going back to him. No-one need know that you're upset, least of all him. You don't have to get in touch with him. There's nothing to say."

"It's over. Finally and completely," sobbed Sally. "Finally and completely."

Chapter 19

Kate seemed to spend most of Friday 'organdising' things, as Rabbit would say to Winnie-the-Pooh. First of all, she had determined to see her mother so that they could have a soul-searching talk. She spoke to her over the phone, trying to sound confident and friendly, arranging to go over on Saturday. Then she had to co-ordinate the reunion. Making sure that everyone was indeed free on Tuesday proved to be a time-consuming task but eventually it was settled. Unfortunately, Sally had a Parents' Evening that day, but would join them as soon as it was over at 8.30 or thereabouts.

When Kate arrived at her parents' home on Saturday, she knew her first task was to get her father out of the way for long enough for her to be able to talk to her mother. As she walked up the familiar path, her head was full of strategies, none of which filled her with much optimism. Her final recourse was going to be a head-on request for time alone with mum; but she had no idea how he would react to that, and feared that it might just drive him into suspicious refusal to leave the house. Her mother opened the door before Kate even reached it. Her arms gathered Kate in just as they had done when she had come home from school every day. It was as if she had tried, always, to make Kate's first steps into the house happy ones. Kate took in the neat and prim woman who was her beloved mother: the pale blue twin set adorned with the obligatory pearls; the pleated grey skirt covered by the pristine floral pinny; the fluffy slippers whose pale lilac colour reflected her well-cut hair. She was the perfect example of the well-groomed but slightly out of date woman whose complete attention was focussed on herself, her home and her husband.

"Darling! How splendid! I've sent Daddy off to do some house repairs for Auntie Jean, so we've got all afternoon to ourselves!"

Relief surged through Kate. With that first hurdle negotiated comfortably, she felt that the omens were good for the open and frank talk which she longed to have so that she could show her mother the support she obviously needed to change her life. Kate felt optimistic about the outcome, thinking that this could be the day that freed her mother from the ogre who kept her chained. She didn't want to rush in too quickly and frighten her, but it was hard for her to allow all the usual rituals to happen. First, her coat had to be hung up on a padded hanger - "those wire things make such a mark on clothes, don't they?" – followed by the comfy chair in the kitchen and the obligatory slice of newly-baked cake.

"You're looking a bit thin, darling. Are you eating properly?"

Kate laughed. "Oh, mum. You won't really be happy until I'm the size of a house, will you? It's all right to be slim, you know. It's more healthy, actually."

"There's a difference between slim and thin. I used to tell you that when you went through that awful teenage phase of dieting all the time. You and Sally were as bad as each other. Rabbits, I used to call you, eating nothing but lettuce and raw carrots. If God had wanted us to nibble on that stuff, he'd have given us..."

"Buck teeth and bobtails, I know!" finished Kate. "So you used to say. I could never get you to see the sense of salad. If a meal didn't end with pudding, it wasn't a meal to you. And if I didn't tuck myself round a piece of cake as soon as I got in from school, I was well on the way to anorexia!"

"You used to love my confections, you and your Dad, when you were smaller. It was just those teenage years that changed you. Nothing was ever the same again. Your Dad used to say…"

"Mum," interrupted Kate. "That's what I want to talk to you about: Dad."

"I know, dear. That's why I sent him out."

Kate took a moment to register what her mother had said.

"How did you know? I didn't say anything."

"I'm your mother. I could tell by your voice. I've been waiting for you to want to talk to me for a long time now. And I could tell that you were ready this time."

Kate was nonplussed. The thought that her mother had

been waiting for her to be 'ready' threw her. This seemed to be completely topsy-turvy. Surely she, Kate, was the one who had been waiting for a chance to talk to her mother, not the other way round.

"It's time we thrashed it out, Kate dear."

"An unfortunate verb, under the circumstances," said Kate.

"Perhaps not. Let's get right on with it, before I go to pieces. We must talk - while we can."

Kate watched as her mother consciously stilled her fidgeting hands and placed them neatly in her lap. She could see the effort involved and her heart went out to the older woman.

"Oh, mum. It must have been awful for you all these years. I don't know how you've stood it. That man!"

"Let's talk about you first, pet. Tell me how you've been feeling all these years. Let's see if we can clear up some of the misery you've carried around with you." She took a deep breath. "How do you feel about Daddy?"

"Well, that's pretty easy and completely predictable. I hate him, of course. How else would I feel? He oppressed and bullied us right through my childhood."

Her mother's hands fluttered and she stroked her frosted fingernails. "Is that how you remember it?"

"It's how it was! When I think of my father, I think of the cane!"

Her mother took a sip of her tea and Kate noticed that the delicate hands that put down the cup were trembling.

"Can you remember the first time he caned you?"

Kate pondered. All the incidents seemed to blur into a general picture of shouting, hitting and crying. She seemed to remember later incidents with clarity, but not the earlier ones when she was small.

"Was it when I trampled his daffodils?" she asked uncertainly.

"No. He didn't actually smack you for that, you know – just threatened to. No, it was earlier than that. You were about five years old…"

"You mean he caned me when I was only five?" asked Kate incredulously.

"Wait a minute, dear. Just let's see what you remember first. If I say the word 'honey' to you, does that conjure up any pictures?"

"Honey? No, nothing at all."

"This is quite important, darling. So I'm going to go into quite a lot of background detail. Don't jump down my throat like you usually do. Just listen for a minute."

"Mum, I don't jump down your throat. You make me sound so bad-tempered!"

"And you think you're not?" asked her mother innocently. "Anyway. All this happened when you were about five. Your father had a good job and he was proud of being able to earn enough for his wife not to have to go to work to make ends meet."

"You mean he was glad he could tie you to the house so you had no independence!" Kate exploded, full of righteous indignation on her mother's part.

"That's not how it was, darling. You're imposing your views on it. It was me who chose to make a career out of being a housewife. I liked being at home. I wanted to be there when you were growing up. Making the home nice and teaching you how to do things made me happy. Reginald tried to make sure that I could do that. He didn't tie me down, darling. He freed me."

"That's your hindsight kicking in," said Kate.

"I don't want to get side-tracked on this. Let's concentrate on the honey incident. Where was I? Oh, yes. Your father had a good job. But it was a constant strain on him. He was very conscientious, very particular about doing things neatly and getting them right."

"Anally retentive," muttered Kate.

"There was always the fear that he wouldn't be able to keep it up, that someone else would come along who'd do it better so they'd get rid of your father. He was always worried."

"I think I've got the picture, Mum. Get on with the

story," Kate said impatiently.

"Not until you calm down a bit, dear. Please eat some cake – it's one of your favourites. And drink some tea."

Kate released a pent-up sigh and did as she was told, nibbling her cake, which she found was really delicious, and sipping at her tea in its porcelain cup. No mugs for Mum, she thought. When she had partaken sufficiently to please her mother's hostess eyes, she looked meaningfully up to encourage the continuance of the story.

"Well, his firm gave him a briefcase. It was lovely leather, really good quality, with the firm's monogram on it. Daddy was so proud of it. It symbolised his status, somehow. They only gave these briefcases to valued employees, you see."

"Bully for dad!" sneered Kate.

"Kate, you aren't helping. Please. One day you took a jar of runny honey and poured it into his briefcase."

"What?" Kate was astounded. "Why?"

"I only wish I knew. I was hoping you'd be able to enlighten me now. You certainly had no explanation at the age of five."

Kate racked her brain to try to recall the incident, but she couldn't picture it at all.

"What happened?"

"Well, your father was quite beside himself. There was this sticky mess all over his papers and coating the inside of his case. He just lifted you up and spanked you, right then and there. You screamed blue murder. It was such a shock for you, I suppose. You'd never been smacked before, and then suddenly you were spanked with real anger, real frustration. I had to take you away from your father and comfort you until you stopped crying. Then I had to deal with his panic. The papers were ruined, of course, but he could re-type those easily enough. It would take him several hours, but it could be dealt with. But the briefcase! We wiped it, we washed it, and we scrubbed it. But there was no way we could remove that stickiness. We knew that every paper that was put inside that case would be ruined, and the outside was indelibly marked. It was completely unusable. So all evening he worked on the documents, and all night he worried himself sick about how he was going to tell his boss that the precious briefcase would have to be thrown away. I'm sure it was the start of his ulcer."

"Surely he could just have been honest about it. I mean, it wasn't his fault. His little child had done something naughty without even realising she'd done something wrong. Everyone would understand. Most people would laugh, surely."

"Your father didn't think so. He felt it would show that his home life was chaotic and out of his control. He felt it would reflect badly on his ability. Try to understand, darling. He didn't feel secure in his job, yet he desperately needed to keep it so that he could pay the mortgage and everything. Smacking you was perfectly understandable. I think most people would have reacted the same way."

Kate was taken aback and was trying hard to come to

terms with the incident.

"I suppose everyone would have been cross. Maybe. So what happened at work next day?"

"The boss wasn't pleased, but after treating your father like a naughty schoolboy, he wrote out a chitty for him to have a second briefcase on the understanding that he'd take greater care of this one. Your father felt humiliated, as if he'd been sent to the Head's study for a good telling off. And it was made worse by the secretary letting some of the others know about it. She thought it was hilarious. She made a point of calling him 'Honey' from then on and it spread to others in the firm as well. He felt they used to snigger behind his back. He was determined not to let it appear to get to him at work, but when he came home he used to worry about it. He used to walk in the door with a sociable grin on his face, and then when the door was closed he would relax and let the burden of the day slip away. He could only be normal when he'd shut the world out."

"You mean he became a miserable sod as soon as the door was closed! All I remember is his moaning and his long face. But I don't remember the honey episode at all. Although, now I come to think of it, I do recall his briefcase always going straight up on top of the wardrobe in the hall as soon as he came in."

"That's right. He was terrified that you would get your hands on it again. He just couldn't have overcome another honey attack."

"So I'm supposed to forgive him for hitting me, am I?"

"I hoped you might be able to sympathise…"

"All right," Kate conceded grudgingly. "I can actually understand his panic over that. And yes, I might well have reacted the same way. But it didn't end there, did it? It wasn't as if he never laid hands on me again, was it?"

"After the honey, he did change towards you, it's true. He could never understand why you'd done it. I think he felt you harboured some sort of grudge against him and that you wanted to hurt him. He thought that you were jealous of his closeness to me, that you wanted me all to yourself and so you disliked him. From then on, he was constantly looking out for trouble. He used to ask you what mischief you'd been up to every night when he came home. It was how he greeted you. And he'd never trust you near his things."

"You mean he was always threatening to wallop me if I touched anything! It got so as I'd touch things just to spite him."

"You did lots of things to vex him, you know. It was as if you wanted to drive him to hit you."

"So now I'm a masochist, you mean?" scoffed Kate.

"No, I don't mean that. But you knew it was wrong of him to hit you, so you pushed him and pushed him until he did it just so you could say he'd done something bad. Kids are like that, aren't they? Surely in your job you've come across situations like that?"

Kate got up and took her plate and cup to the sink. She found that it was her hand that was shaking now.

"I suppose I did drive him to lash out, and then I'd feel

all self-righteous about it. Come to think of it, there's a client at the Clinic who does that sort of thing. I can't tell you his name, of course. But his parents split up and he blames his mother for the break-up. Every week he comes up with things his mum's done wrong. And time and again he's the one who's pushed her into it."

"That sounds familiar. Are you allowed to tell me what he does?"

"Last week she bought him some trainers," answered Kate.

"Oh, poor thing!"

"Yes, but they were the <u>wrong</u> trainers. You know how important it is to have the right ones so your mates can't make fun of you."

"If it's that important, I don't see how the boy's in the wrong for that. She should have made sure she was getting the right trainers."

"The full story is that she took him to a big shopping centre – Lakeside, Bluewater, somewhere like that. They went to shop after shop after shop, and he wouldn't have any of them. In the end, after five hours of it, she just bought the next pair that fitted. And the point was that some of the trainers he'd tried on were the trendy ones, but he wanted her to be in the wrong and him to be the martyr. 'Look what my awful mother bought me! That's the sort of cow she is!' Then he goes on to say, 'If dad was still around, this would never have happened!' And he so wants it to be true that life would have been better if his parents had still been together that he forces his mum into situations where she just can't win."

"Can you connect that to what you did to Daddy?" asked Kate's mother gently.

"You think I might have been doing the same? Driving my Dad into a corner where he had to come out fighting and then crowing over the fact that I'd made him lose his temper?"

"That's exactly it. And you used to blame him for things that weren't his fault, you know, just like your boy at the Clinic."

"What do you mean?" asked Kate, not liking at all the

way this conversation was going.

"Well, if ever we made plans that had to be changed, it was always Daddy's fault. If we planned a picnic and then it rained, you railed at him for the weather. Even if we tried to do something equally nice that didn't need us to be outdoors, it was never good enough."

"You make me sound like an absolutely ghastly child!"

"You had your moments, darling. But I feel responsible for some of it."

"Oh, Mum. For goodness sake don't start taking the blame for him. Being a Good Wife doesn't mean taking on the sins of the father, you know."

"But there were times when I encouraged your resentment of your father. It was wrong of me – a sort of collusion, really. If ever Reginald and I had an argument, which wasn't often, before you leap in with thoughts of wife-beating, I used to enlist you for my army. It was so easy to do. You wanted to see him as the enemy and I sometimes encouraged that. Do you remember that sort of thing?"

"I remember my happiest times being when you and I were in full agreement about something and pulled together to change his mind. Like the trip to France."

"Yes, now that is a good case in point. Let's think about that. It was the first time that I wanted to go abroad for a holiday, when you were about ten."

"You mean you hadn't been abroad before that?" interrupted Kate. "Unbelievable!"

"That had been my decision, Kate. I wanted to have holidays that were best for you, and that meant not too much time spent in travelling and lots of seaside when we got there."

"Bloody Frinton!"

"You loved it at the time. Don't start getting pretentious about it now. Anyway, when you were ten I thought you were ready for foreign travel. So I suggested France. Daddy disagreed. He said his French wouldn't be good enough and it might lead us into awkward or dangerous situations. We talked about it quite amicably for quite some time, but then he came up with the argument that always got my goat, that of his being the only breadwinner so he had the deciding vote. I hated it when he did that. Probably because I always felt slightly guilty about not getting a job when you were grown up enough not to need to come home for lunch every day. I resented his throwing my dependence on him in my face as if it were a weapon. So I worked on you, painting pictures of how wonderful France was and how you'd have a huge advantage at school if you already knew some French before secondary school. I encouraged you to think that Daddy was spoiling your chances. We took him on in a two-pronged attack and we got our way. But it was wrong of me to have done it like that. I took advantage of your natural antipathy towards your father. I even encouraged it. I feel so guilty about that now."

"My 'natural antipathy', as you call it, was based on the fact that he was a bully!"

"But don't you see? He didn't know how to control the things in his life that threatened to overwhelm him - things at work mostly - so he exerted his authority over the nearest available underlings. At least he could control his family. Or so he thought."

"Kick the cat! My memory of it is somewhat different. You make it sound as if you deliberately enlisted me so you could win against him, but my feeling is that you were constantly stepping in to save me from him."

Kate's mother went to the sink and started to re-wash the crockery, not trusting her daughter's standards of cleanliness after years of watching her slap-dash attitude to dirt.

"There was quite a lot of shielding you, too. You're quite right about that. I felt like the Thames Barrier sometimes, ready to hold back the flood if it threatened to happen. I could understand your resentment at the way he treated you and I could see also how utterly impossible you were. I used to tear myself apart sometimes, trying desperately to explain each of you to the other. But you used to drive him to distraction and he could never control his temper. It was like a battlefield every night."

"That's how I remember it. Shouting and smacking and

tears before bedtime."

"It's wrong to hit a child, Kate. There's no shadow of doubt about that. But you really were a trial. And he didn't hit you very often, you know."

"What? Of course he did. I remember that very clearly!" asserted Kate.

"There were plenty of threats, I grant you that, but not many actual incidents."

"Oh, Mum, come off it. There were lots of 'incidents'. The cane was deliberately kept behind the larder door when I was little so that he had easy access to it."

"But it was there as more of a warning than anything else. He used to say he'd cane you if you were naughty, but I think he only caned you about ten times in your entire life."

"Ten times too many!"

"Yes, probably. But children do need some discipline, you know. They need lines drawn and kept to."

"Absolutely. But good parents do that without recourse

to GBH."

"My point, darling, is that you've exaggerated. And you aren't taking full responsibility for your own part in it."

"I was a child! I was just a child! I may have been wilful and naughty, but he was the adult and he should have had more understanding. His indifference to me – no, his dislike of me – was what drove me to challenge him. Why couldn't he just love me, like you did?"

"I think he tried. But he never ever understood the honey incident. He couldn't get beyond it. It seemed so unreasonable, so hurtful. He never trusted you again, and he never believed you could love him if you did that to him."

"And I never believed he could love me if he did that to me – threatened me, caned me."

"It was a complete impasse. We should have gone for help, of course. Your Clinic might have been able to sort us out. But we were too proud to admit that we were having trouble with our only child. Daddy would have felt particularly humiliated."

"Oh, poor Daddy! We can't have him humiliated, can we? Heaven forfend!"

Kate felt her mother's arms wrapping her and she realised that she was crying. In fact, they were both crying. They each stroked the other's back lovingly and comfortingly until they felt able to continue. Kate led her mother into the little-used front room and sat her down on the plush sofa. She flopped down beside her and repaired her mother's eye make-up with a tissue, brushing the tears carelessly away from her own cheeks as well.

"So on we went. Your teenage years were decidedly sticky. But at least you were never caned then."

"Only because I broke the cane. Don't you remember?" said Kate.

"You didn't break it, darling. Daddy did."

"Don't be ridiculous! Do you really think I could forget that momentous day!"

"We'd had a meal with Sally and her parents, and we'd talked rather flippantly about sparing the rod and spoiling the child. Sally's father was joking, of course, and obviously thought it was perfectly ridiculous to even contemplate 'the rod'. I think it made Daddy aware that threatening a teenage girl with a caning was utterly unacceptable. So the next day he took it out into the garden with you and he broke it in two and put it on the bonfire. He told you that now you were an adult he expected you to behave more responsibly and so the stick wouldn't be needed any more. You even had a row about that, with you shouting that he should never have used it in the first place. It went on and on. I just couldn't stand it, especially out in the garden."

"What would the neighbours say?" asked Kate sarcastically. "Anyway, my memory is that I broke it in half and put it on the fire."

"That may well be so. But he actually took it out intending to destroy it. His intention was to stop using it as a threat. But you couldn't give him any credit for anything, and you still can't. The constant rows were so wearing. It got so that I longed for the day when you'd leave home permanently, just so I could enjoy some peace and quiet. It's a terrible thing to say, but I was at my wit's end."

"Is that why you didn't want me to go to university? Because I'd be home every holiday?"

"I feel so guilty about that. You were so bright. And all your teachers wanted you to go. Every Parents' Evening, they'd talk about how you'd get good results and needed to go on to further study. But you weren't keen to go..."

"All I wanted was to get away from home, too."

"So when you mentioned a secretarial course, I thought that would be just the thing. You'd be through it in six months and then you could get a job and become self-sufficient."

"You couldn't get rid of me fast enough. I remember that all right."

"Because of all the trouble, Kate, not because we didn't love you. I just couldn't take much more. I think your coming home from University after every term would have been the final straw. I'd have been dreading it every time, and I really think I'd come to the very end of my strength."

"An oeuf is an oeuf, as they say. I always thought it was Dad who wanted me out of the way and that he bullied you into wanting it, too. So it was your decision all the time. Well, what an eye-opener," said Kate bitterly, hiding her hurt behind a show of sarcasm.

"Even when you come home to visit now, I feel that old dread coming back. I keep wondering how you and Dad will treat each other. Even though I know he's a completely different man nowadays, it's still enough to make me sick the night before."

"What do you mean, a different man?"

"Oh, come on, Kate. You must have noticed how gentle he is with you. Almost deferential. He walks on eggshells whenever you're here. He's desperate to try to make up for being such a bad father to you. He'd do anything to turn back time and do it all again."

"But that's the trouble, mum. He would do it all again.

There'd be the same tensions, the same thunder and lightning, the same temptations to hit out. He'd be no different."

"He'd be different if he knew then what he knows now. And Dr Gray has helped a lot."

"You mean he's on blessed tranquilisers?" asked Kate sarcastically.

"I suppose that's what they are. They certainly calm him down. If only he'd had them years ago."

"You know, I came here today with thoughts of rescuing you. Knight in shining armour stuff. I thought you might need help if you were to leave Dad after all these years."

Her mother's face registered her shocked disbelief.

"Why on earth would I want to leave him? He's my husband."

"Yes, but he hit you. He hit me. He used to take out his bad temper on us. It really doesn't matter that I provoked him. There isn't a teenager in the world that doesn't provoke parents. It's part of growing up, feeling your independence. It's not an excuse for a man to hit out."

"The quarrels were never-ending, I grant you that. And you generally got him to walk out and slam the door. And threaten to tan your hide, or some such expression. But, as I've told you, actually hitting you was very rare."

"That's not how I remember it," said Kate stubbornly.

"Perhaps your memory isn't quite as clear as it should be, Kate. There were threats aplenty, but very few actual blows. And he never hit me, you know."

"That's just not true, Mum. I haven't fantasised about that! I remember really clearly..."

"There was one occasion, darling, only one. Reginald was going to smack you, I stepped in between you both to stop it happening, and his hand caught me instead. We were all devastated. Reginald was beside himself with the shame of hitting me, you were incandescent because I'd been hurt, and I felt that I'd simply made things worse when I'd been trying to help. You never forgot it and you never let him forget it either."

"Are you trying to tell me that that was the only time he hit you?" asked an unbelieving Kate.

"Yes. That was the only time. And it was a mistake."

"It would have been all right if he'd managed to hit me, I suppose?"

"Of course not. You're deliberately misunderstanding. I'm just trying to tell you that Daddy was not in the habit of mistreating me. I'm sorry if that spoils your image of a wife-beating father. You seem determined to cling to that, whatever I say to the contrary."

"This is too much, Mum. I know he hit you. Why are you lying for him?"

"I'm not! It's just that you seem to want to believe he was irreparably bad."

"Well, he wasn't good, was he? You can't call him a good father, can you?"

"Not good, no. But he tried to be a good husband and he would have tried to be a better father if you had given him half a chance."

"I don't believe this. You really are blaming me for it all!" exploded Kate.

"I just want you to take a share of the responsibility, dear. You weren't a perfect daughter. You seem to think your behaviour was normal, that all children did the things you did. But I don't think that's so. Sally never spoke to her father the way you did to yours."

"Sally hasn't got any time for my father, either. She knows what he was like to me. She was nice to her own dad because he was kind to her. He never hit her, you know."

"I think you'll find that she had her fair share of smacks when she was little. All children were smacked back then when you were a child. It was the way of things. It's only fairly recently that there's been all this kerfuffle about smacking. Personally, I think the odd smack is normal and natural. It can be a loving act, to protect your child from danger and to teach them something important about safety. I smacked you several times, you know, when you ran out into the road, for instance. I did it because I wanted you to learn about road safety.

Honestly, Kate, there isn't a parent alive who has never smacked their child to teach them a safety lesson."

"Mum, we aren't talking about little taps on the arm or leg. Maybe those are normal, as you say. Though I don't think I'd want to do it to a child of mine. However, what we're talking about is much more than that. Caning, Mum. Not smacking."

"Why can't you understand what I'm saying? It didn't happen very often, Kate, not half as often as you seem to think."

"Your memory seems just as skewed as you say mine is."

"Perhaps both of us need to ponder on the past with a more even gaze, darling. Shall we both agree to try to do that? I want so much to be able to talk about nice things in the past. Most families can do that, you know."

"It's hard to be nostalgic when you're told you can't remember anything!" snapped Kate. "All right, Mum, let me ponder what you've said and see if I can re-arrange the past into something more to your liking."

"Oh, darling. Why so sarcastic?"

"Mum, our views of the past are completely at variance. How am I supposed to react to the things you've said? You remember it one way, and I remember it another. You're asserting that you're right and that my childhood recollections are mistaken. You're implying that I've deliberately maligned my father all these years. Whereas my feeling is that you're softening everything so that you can continue to live with the man. I mean, how could you consciously decide to stay with a bully who hit his only child? So your subconscious takes over and does a clean-up job on the past. That's what I think is happening."

"Just promise me that you'll really try to examine the incidents you think you recall. Get Sally to help you."

"All right, I promise. We're having another reunion of old school chums soon and I'll see what all of them remember, too."

"I don't like the idea of your discussing your father with all and sundry. What happens inside a family should be private."

"These were all close friends, Mum. I need their help to get to the bottom of this. That is, if you seriously want me to delve. If you say my memory is faulty, then they may be able to shed some light on things I think I remember."

"Well, if it would help, dear. But I don't like the idea of your blackening your father's name in public."

"Your loyalty does you credit, Mum, even though I think it's misplaced. Shall we stop now? How about another slice of that gorgeous cake?"

"That's more like my little girl! And what about another nice cup of tea to go with it?"

Chapter 20

The reunion was at Jacky's house, and Kate arrived
promptly at 7.30. Hampstead Garden Suburb created
certain pictures in her mind, and the exterior of the house
was no disappointment. The Arts & Crafts features
impressed her, but she walked up the path in some
trepidation. She realised that she was unsure enough
about Jacky's taste to feel some fear about what she
might have done to the interior. Thoughts of excessive
'improving' with marble or wood effects, rag-rolling and
stencilling filled her mind. She was somewhat reassured
when Jacky threw open the door and she saw the
splendid hallway with its original banisters complete with
an inverted heart pattern. There was a charming cast-iron
fireplace with green tiled surround and Jacky had
thoughtfully lit a log fire so that the ambience was warm
and softly lit.

"Welcome to my humble abode," gushed Jacky, hugging
Kate enthusiastically. "Let me hang up your bottle and
open your coat," she laughed. "Michelle's here already.

I expect you'd like to see round the house, wouldn't you? I'll wait till the others arrive, and then do a Grand Tour."

"Come through and have a drink," called Michelle.

"I'm on my way!" replied Kate, stepping into a rather grand front room. She just had time to take in the tasteful and decidedly period furniture and pictures before Michelle pressed a large glass into her willing hand. "Wow! This is quite something."

"Jacky's dying to show you all the full splendour of her good fortune!" said Michelle with a fond smile.

Pru and Mary arrived at that moment and were soon joining Kate with equally impressed looks on their faces as they surveyed the scene. Jacky bustled in, pink and proud. They all toasted each other with good champagne served in expensive crystal flutes and found that they were giggling straight away.

"Sally's coming later after her Parents' Evening," explained Jacky, "and I'm sad to say that Lyn's in hospital and there'll be no Cassie. So we're all here."

"What's wrong with Skinny Lynny?" asked Pru.

"Sounded like a collapse due to anorexia to me. Apparently, she passed out in the street and an ambulance was called. They must have taken note of her appearance – they probably weighed her! – and decided she had to stay in. I've told her we'll all visit and bring her lots of fattening chocs," said Jacky, rather heartlessly. "Now, who's for a tour?"

It would have been impossible to refuse, of course, and in fact none of them wanted to miss seeing the house in all its glory. Nor were they disappointed. Fears for Jacky's taste were groundless, even though not a surface had been left without a paint effect. Fortunately, there was a subtlety in the colour schemes that complimented the furniture agreeably. Pru was heard to whisper to Mary that it was a pity that the good taste in decoration didn't spill over into Jacky's wardrobe. When they reached the "Nursery Rooms", as Jacky grandly called them, they all expected to have their way barred because of sleeping children. However, Jacky threw open the doors to reveal rooms stencilled to within an inch of their lives. This was the only place where Jacky's decorative techniques had run amok and overwhelmed the room, and as it was 'for the kiddies' the friends forgave her over-enthusiasm.

"Where are the children?" asked Mary, who had been looking forward to meeting them.

"Oh, the kiddies aren't here tonight," replied Jacky. "My hubby thought it would be nice for me to have the house to myself this evening. Bless him. So he's taken the babes to our cottage in Norfolk for the night."

"I'm impressed!" said Kate. "Here's a man who earns alorradosh and can also look after the kids himself!"

"Oh, his PR is with him to give him a hand," said Jacky airily.

"Don't you mean his PA?" asked Pru.

"She knows what she means," replied Michelle, and her eyes met Kate's meaningfully. They both busied themselves looking at toys.

"Let's go downstairs and start on the food. I hope you're

all hungry."

They were! Everyone swooped on the array of food as if eating had suddenly come back into fashion. For a while, the only sounds were those of munching and swallowing, along with the sort of small talk that that necessitates. The sound of Kate's mobile phone ringing was an annoyance and she apologised for not having switched it off. It was a number that she didn't recognise and she almost ignored it, but she could not quite make herself do so. She was surprised to find out that the caller was James. She left the room so that she could take the call more privately.

"Sorry to interrupt your evening revels," said James. "I'm at this ghastly Parent Sieve and this is the first opportunity I've had to get away momentarily to phone you. I'm afraid there's been a development here with Sally and You Know Who."

"Mark? Oh no. What now?"

"He turned up just as we were setting up for the meeting."

"Bastard! Why can't he just leave her alone?" moaned Kate. "What happened?"

"I refused to leave her so he had to speak in front of me, which didn't please him at all, as you can imagine."

"Good for you!"

"The upshot is that when Vol said she knew that Jo had chucked him out so why didn't he just jolly well stop lying to her, he started laughing. He said that he had <u>allowed</u> Jo to say that so that she wouldn't lose face in front of her friends. He said she hadn't wanted it to look like she couldn't keep her man. He was willing to go along with the lie to protect her. Can you imagine? There he was, casting himself as Mr Magnanimous!"

"But surely she didn't believe him?" asked Kate.

"She practically fell into his arms! They've arranged to meet after the Parents' Thing. I'm panicking – sorry – because it seems to me as if they're planning to go back to Sally's place and renew their sexual intercorsets. It'll be disastrous for her. I'm stuck here, feeling like a spectre at the feast. What can we do?"

"Bugger!" said Kate.

"My inclinations exactly!" said James mischievously.

"I'll try to get hold of Robin. If he came over to the school, could you and he together tackle Mark and keep them apart?"

"We can try. Oh, sorry, I've got to go! Next parental soul-search is due. I've never met Robin, but I'm sure I'll know who he is by the set of his determined chin! Tell him to wear a green carnation, too!"

Kate returned to the room feeling decidedly wobbly. It was obvious to them all that something was wrong.

"Not bad news, I hope?" asked Michelle.

"It's the continuing saga of Sally. You remember that she was heartbroken that her lover had decided to stay with his wife after she announced her pregnancy? Well, there have been further developments. I can't remember how much you all know, but the latest is that the wife chucked him out after finding out about his serial affairs – including Sally – but he's managed to convince Sal that it was he who did the leaving voluntarily so that he could be with Sal. One of her colleagues has just phoned me to say that Mark turned up before the Parents' Evening and more or less swept Sally back into his arms. We've got to stop her going off with him tonight. I just know she'll regret it. She's not allowing enough time for sensible decision-making."

"But what can any of us do? She's a big girl, Kate. She needs to make her own mind up about her life," said Pru.

"But there's more to it, stuff that I can't tell you. Sworn to secrecy and all that! But believe me, it will all end up in even more of a mess if she sets up house with him. He will leave her and go back to his wife, I'm absolutely certain about that. So Sally will have a double helping of grief and abandonment to cope with. I've just got to phone Robin. I'll be back in a minute," said Kate, running from the room again with her mobile at the ready.

Kate held down the Instant Robin button, and just prayed that he'd have his phone turned on. To her great relief, he answered straight away.

"Robin? Thank goodness. Listen, I've just had a call from James at Sally's school. Mark turned up and he's convinced her that he's allowed Jo to say she dumped him so she could save face. What an arch manipulator that man is! Anyway, he's going to collect her at the end of the meeting. We've got to stop that happening. I told James you'd get there and would help him keep them apart. You could do that, couldn't you?"

"Hang on a minute, darling. Let's think about this. Fisticuffs won't convince Sally that he's a heel. It'll just make her angry with us for interfering, won't it?"

"You're right. She'll hate it, but I can't think what else to do."

"No. Oh well, into battle! At least I'll have James to help me. Sally might just listen with two of us urging caution."

"James says you should wear a green carnation."

"I like him already! I'll phone you when there's something to report."

Kate returned to the room and replaced the mobile in her bag. She knew the phone wouldn't ring again for quite a while and she didn't want the whole evening to be focussed around its presence.

"I don't really understand what's going on," said Jacky plaintively, and it was only then that Kate realised that Jacky had not been present when the revelations about Sally's relationship with Mark had been dissected by the group. She gave her a simplified and sanitised version, and saw the approval on Michelle's face. They all had to be careful about Jacky's husband's possible infidelity, she realised.

"So he's really messing her about," said Jacky. "There are some really horrid people around, aren't there? She'll be so much better off without him."

"But she won't see that for a while. In time, she will. But for now we'll have to provide her with lots of support," said Michelle, imagining that the same might apply to Jacky herself in the not-too-distant future.

"In the meantime," said Kate, "We can take our minds off that by concentrating on something else – well, someone else, really. Me. I need you all to help me with a bit of remembering the old temps perdu. I need a bit of delving into my past."

"Does the Past make you Tense?" joked Pru.

"And Pluperfect to you, too!" replied Kate. "No, really, it's a serious matter. You see, I went to see my mother this weekend. I'd decided to talk to her in depth about the way my father treated us both. Robin convinced me that the problem of my relationship with my father was souring me. I was forever having a go at Robin simply because he was a man! My resentment of my father always seemed to get between us."

"You never had a good word to say about him," agreed Pru.

"Actually, it got a bit boring. You were always going on about how horrid he was," agreed Jacky.

"So I'm right!" said Kate triumphantly. "You all remember that he was awful."

"Hang on," said Michelle judiciously. "It's not exactly that, is it? I mean, what we remember is your ranting and raving about him. As far as I can recall, whenever we met him he seemed charming. He always had a smile on his face."

"Yes, those Christmas cracker jokes he was always telling! Always trying to make us laugh when we called for you," said Jacky.

"But that doesn't mean he wasn't cruel to Kate when we weren't around," said Pru. "Lots of people present a mask to the outside world that isn't their real selves."

"That's it exactly," agreed Kate.

"But how can we help you delve into the past if we only ever saw your father's public face?" asked Mary.

"Can you remember any incidents at all?" insisted Kate.

"What? Like bruises, or something?" enquired Jacky.

"Well, yes, I suppose so. Or even atmospheres that were hard to explain. I mean, did you ever see any vicious looks or involuntary raising of a hand or a fist?"

"I saw your rudeness to him. And I often thought you'd gone too far in what you said to him. But when you told us that he hit you, I assumed that your rudeness was because you were getting your own back on him while we were there to sort of protect you. I always thought it was a bit daft of you, though, because surely he'd punish you later for what you said to him in front of us," said Michelle.

"We used to talk about that, didn't we?" agreed Jacky. "We said we'd never dare speak to our dads like that or we'd get a good hiding, and then we said that that was exactly what you did get. I must say, I always thought you deserved it!"

"Well, thank you very much!" said Kate.

"I think what Jacky means is that we all thought the "hiding" you got was the same as the "hiding" we would get for saying what you said. No more than a slap round the backside and a sending to bed for the evening," interposed Mary.

"You mean your fathers used to hit you?" asked Kate

incredulously.

"Not really <u>hit</u>. You couldn't call it hitting," said Mary. "I've tapped my son a few times when he's been really naughty. I defy anyone to keep calm all the time when dealing with kids."

"My father never hit me at all," said Pru.

"There you are!" said Kate triumphantly.

"No," continued Pru. "It was always my mother."

"What?"

"She was the disciplinarian. My dad was away so often with his job that mum had to take on the role. It was no use her saying 'Wait till your father gets home' because that could be a fortnight away. So she had to get used to dealing with it then and there. I remember her slapping me round the face when I was about fifteen. I'd been particularly obnoxious and she just reacted. But it shocked us both, and I must say she never did it again."

"My parents never smacked me," said Jacky.

"Sometimes I almost wished they had."

"What do you mean?"

"Well, they always used to 'talk things through' with us if we did anything wrong. And that often took hours and hours. A good sharp smack, a few tears and forget it would have been lovely!"

"I can confirm the hours of talking-to," smiled Michelle. "You remember that I used to stay with Jacky quite often when my parents had to go back to Paris for the business. I was always included in the tutorials! But it felt good to me. They were such kind people, always treating me as one of the family. I came to love them almost as much as my own mum and dad. In fact, I had a much better relationship with Jacky's father than I did with mine. I always resented dad going back to France. It always felt as if he was abandoning me. I used to row with him constantly when he was around, and I got hit a few times when he couldn't stand it any longer."

"But we aren't talking about the same sort of 'hitting', are we?" said Pru. "I take it that you're saying that your father did more than smack you lightly, Kate. You're talking about beating, aren't you?"

"My mother insists that I wasn't beaten, but my memory convinces me that I was. Mind you, I firmly believe that children should never be smacked at all – not even tapped. Jacky's parents' talking it through seems right to me. I've always felt very strongly about it, even as a child," said Kate.

"So perhaps even the lightest chastisement would have upset you. Could it be that you exaggerated what happened because you were affronted by even the threat of violence?" asked Michelle.

Kate sighed and sipped her wine contemplatively, glad to see that some unknown hand had replenished her glass. "I don't know any more. I was hoping one of you would step forward and say, 'Yes, I remember those lash marks on your back.'"

They all shook their heads, almost sorry that they couldn't confirm their friend's memories.

"Maybe I have blown it out of all proportion," said Kate.

"Poor Robin! I may have made him pay for masculine behaviour that perhaps never happened."

"Poor Dad, as well. You've made him pay, too," admonished Jacky.

"I'm still not completely convinced, you know. My father has a lot to answer for, even if physical violence isn't as big a part of it as I thought," insisted Kate. "I shall need to …," she faltered as the phone rang. "Sorry, folks, I need to answer this. Hello, Robin? Oh, it's you, James. What's happening?"

Kate listened while Jacky passed round another bottle so everyone could top up their glasses. They were as quiet as possible, wanting to hear the conversation.

"So she's with Robin? And they're coming here?" Kate asked. "Thanks, James. I'm sure all will be revealed when they arrive. We'll 'grid our lions' and be ready for it. Thanks again."

She replaced her mobile and looked up at the circle of anticipatory faces. "It must have worked. Robin is bringing her here. I don't know more than that. But I think we can safely assume that Sally will be distressed."

"Pile up your plates and chow down. An army marches on its stomach, and I have the feeling we're about to engage in battle!" ordered Jacky.

Chapter 21

When Sally arrived, she was indeed deeply upset. But instead of the weeping that most of them expected, she walked in as if in a dream. She was obviously in a state of shock and her empty eyes rested on each of them without recognition. She allowed her coat to be stripped from her as if she were no more than a limp rag doll, and she accepted the drink thrust into her hand without comprehension. While the others fussed round her, Kate drew Robin into the hall.

"Was it awful? How did you manage it?" she asked.

"Mark didn't turn up," replied Robin stonily. "The bastard raised her hopes and then just left her dangling."

"What? I must say, that's the last thing I expected. I was visualising you and James being highly physical!"

"All the way over there, I was working myself up to kidnapping her with James pinning Mark to the ground as

I carried her off. I thought she'd hate me for it until she came to realise in a few weeks' time that it was for her own good. But when I got there, the meeting was over and James was talking to her, obviously trying to persuade her not to be too hasty in going back to Mark. I could see he wasn't having much success from the set of Sal's mouth – you know how she looks when she's really determined on something. I breezed over to them pretending I knew nothing, saying I'd turned up to give her a lift over to Jacky's so she wouldn't miss out on too much. She accepted that without question, thank goodness. But then she said there was no need because Mark was picking her up. I had to listen to the whole story as if it was new to me. Then I joined James in trying to convince her not to jump too quickly. We were all still there when the Caretaker came round jangling his keys and wanting us to go. Sally looked at her watch and realised that Mark was fifteen minutes late. She rang his mobile and guess what? It was switched off."

"Bastard sod!"

"Exactly. James said much the same. I really like him,

by the way. He genuinely cares about what happens to Sal. Anyway, we stood outside the locked school gate for a further five minutes, and I swear you could see the life draining out of her as the seconds ticked by. She just let me lead her to the car. I had to put the seat belt on her and everything. She's like a zombie."

"It's the shock," said Kate. "Robin, you've been marvellous. Thank you so much. But you'd better go on home now. We'll manage Sally. Sorry, but it wouldn't be right for you to stay."

"Of course not. I won't go to bed till you come back, though, just in case you need a strong arm again. Are you sure you'll be all right?"

"You're a brick!"

"Don't you mean prick?" Robin teased.

"I know what I mean," said Kate, hugging him.

When she went back into the room, there seemed to have been little progress in the thawing out of Sally, who still looked frozen and lost. Kate decided to take the initiative and spoke to Sally in a matter-of-fact tone: "So Mark didn't turn up."

Sally's eyes slowly focussed on Kate's. Then she looked around as if she had only just understood where she was and how she had got there. She raised the glass to her lips and sipped slowly. Thinking better of it, she gulped thirstily and drained the glass, holding it out to be refilled, which it duly was.

"I don't understand what happened. I thought the nightmare was over, Kate. Now what?" she said.

"I couldn't begin to count the number of times I've been stood up," began Pru.

"I remember the first time I went out with my hubby," said Jacky, "he was half an hour late! The only reason I was still waiting for him was because I couldn't find a taxi."

"Maybe I didn't wait long enough!" squealed Sally. "Maybe he's had an accident!"

"And maybe not," Kate said decisively, restraining Sally

as she tried to struggle up from the all-encompassing sofa. "Let him go, Sal."

"Can I borrow your phone? I just want to make one call," pleaded Sally, finally extricating herself from the sofa and making her way to the telephone. There was no way Jacky could stop her, although they all groaned inwardly, watching Sally fumble with the buttons and then turn away as she shielded the phone from them. They all assumed that she was phoning Mark's mobile again and that it was still turned off because they saw her shoulders slump before she replaced the receiver. She stayed where she was, facing the wall. Her voice was tiny when she spoke, but they had no difficulty in hearing her because they were all completely concentrated on her.

"He was there," she said.

"Who was where?" asked Jacky.

"Mark. At home," Sally replied.

"But how did he get in?" asked Kate. "Robin changed your lock."

Sally turned. She looked steadily at Kate before replying: "No, I mean at his home, not mine. I just phoned Jo's number and he answered."

There was stunned silence for a moment. No-one could quite take in what was going on.

"But I thought they'd separated," puzzled Jacky. "I'm getting really confused."

"Wait a minute," said Mary. "What on earth is happening here? He says he's left his wife, he says he's meeting you after the meeting, then he doesn't turn up and the next thing we know is that he's back with his wife. Have I got that right?"

Sally nodded.

"What's he playing at?" asked Michelle.

"It seems to me that he's deliberately trying to hurt you, Sal. Why else would he leave you stranded like that?" said Kate.

"He's also given his ego a big boost," added Pru. "He

first makes sure you still want him, then he returns to wifey, who also invites him in. Wow! Two women falling over themselves for him! What an incredibly attractive man that must make him feel!"

"Well, I don't want to sound too suburban here," said Jacky, sounding suburban, "but shouldn't we be glad he's gone back to his wife? I mean, she is his <u>wife</u>. And she's pregnant."

"Poor cow!" said Michelle.

"I suppose I'm naturally supporting spouses here," continued Jacky, "because I know how I'd feel if ever my hubby left home. Not that that's at all likely, of course," she added smugly.

No-one said a word, which Jacky took as agreement rather than the embarrassed awkwardness that it actually was. Michelle raised her well-groomed eyebrow at Kate.

"I don't have any horses running in the Marriage Stakes," said Pru eventually. "So I'm making no Till Death Do Us Part judgements. Frankly, I feel sorry for Jo, but if she still wants him then I think it's only right that she should have him. Sorry, Sally."

"I'm not taking a moral stance either," said Kate. "I just don't feel he's to be trusted, so I'd rather Sally was free of him."

"But none of you really knows him," pleaded Sally. "You're looking with jaundiced eyes, from the outside. You're turning him into the stereotypical married man having an affair. It's not like that."

"No. It's more like a married man having lots of affairs and lying to everyone along the way," said Kate.

"You jump to conclusions, all of you. And now I'm doing it, too. You're destroying my faith in him and I'm allowing you to do it! There's a simple explanation here, I'm sure of it now I come to think of it. Perhaps Jo phoned and asked him to go round. He's such a softy, he wouldn't want to hurt her if she was in pain or in trouble – or just in one of her depressed moods. Or he might have gone to collect something he needed and thought he had enough time to do that before picking me up, but Jo kept him talking. She may be pleading for him to go back to her, and he couldn't just walk out on her. He'll phone me as soon as he can and explain. I've just got to be ready to leave as soon as he collects me," Sally said decisively.

"For heaven's sake, Sally, get real!" exploded Kate. "Are you saying that Mark couldn't have phoned you before now to let you know what had happened?"

"How could he phone me in front of Jo? He's far too sensitive to do something as crass as that!"

"Put yourself in his position," reasoned Kate. "You'd be desperate to communicate with him. You'd be imagining him waiting for you in the cold, wondering what was going on, doubting your commitment. What would you do?"

"I know what I'd do," said Jacky. "I'd make an excuse to go to the little girls' room and phone on my mobile."

"Exactly!" said Kate.

"Yes, I agree," Pru joined in. "Somehow, I'd phone you."

"But you're women. Men don't think like that," said Sally defensively.

"But you just said how sensitive he was," said Mary. "Gil would have found a way to ease my mind. And he's not the tenderest flower in the bunch."

"And can you imagine Robin leaving me there without a word?" added Kate.

Sally crumpled under their onslaught and her eyes misted over as she spoke. "I keep hoping. I just try to keep hope alive. I do a fair job of it until I think of Robin. He's become my touchstone. 'What would Robin do?' 'What does Robin think?' And every time I do that, I see Mark in a different light."

"I'm just beginning to realise what a treasure Robin is," said Kate. "I must have been blind before. Or maybe I was blinded by my experience with my father."

"But not all men are as wonderful as Robin. Mark isn't in his league. So why am I expecting Mark to do what Robin would do?" said Sally, visibly sitting up straighter as she entertained hope again.

"We aren't talking about the reactions of a superhero," said Pru gently. "We're just talking about the normal reactions of a normal man. Robin's on a pedestal, but the rest of us have experienced the dizzy heights of ordinariness. Would any of our lesser specimens leave us stranded like this?"

She looked around at everyone for reaction. They all shook their heads decisively.

"I'd put my hubby alongside Robin on that pedestal, so perhaps it isn't fair to ask me. But the rest of you must know what it's like to have ordinary men," smiled Jacky.

Everyone laughed, except Michelle, who bit her lip and sighed. Remarks about tact interspersed with snorts of disbelief. Eventually, Jacky became aware of the insult to the others buried in her faith in her husband, and she had the grace to giggle as she apologised.

"I think we're all agreed, *ma petite*," said Michelle. "There must have been some way to contact you. But let's give him the benefit of the doubt and wait till the end of the reunion. If he hasn't phoned by then, we must surely consign him to the rubbish pile."

"So let's beguile the shining hour, or whatever it is, and have some more shampoo," said Jacky. "We've been very niggardly with it so far. There are three more bottles in the wine fridge."

With that, she went scooting off to the kitchen and she returned with a bottle in each hand. She handed one to Pru to open, and the other to Michelle. "All this talk of virtuous men has made me want to phone my hubby. I hope you don't mind. Just to say goodnight."

The companionable pop of corks and the laughter accompanying the strategic placing of glasses underneath the frothing bottles made even Sally lighten.

"What is it about champagne?" asked Michelle. "It never fails to inspire happiness."

"Shush, everyone! I don't want David to think there's an orgy going on!" shouted Jacky.

Giggles were stifled and everyone listened in to Jacky's phone call, which was probably what she had wanted them to do so she could show off her uxorious man.

"Could I speak to David, please?" Jacky enunciated carefully, turning to smile at them all. Everyone heard the female voice at the other end call out "Dodo, it's for you!" Jacky's smile faltered slightly before she got into her stride. Michelle caught Kate's eye, not for the first time that night.

"Darling! It's little old me! Is everything all right? … Of course I know you can cope perfectly well, sweetheart. I just wanted to hear your voice. … I'm not shouting, am I? Sorry. I'm just enjoying such a nice evening with my old friends. … No, there wasn't anything in particular, darling. I just wanted to say nighty-night. … Do you miss me? … Well, I know it's only been six hours, darling. But you know how I count the minutes when you're gone. … Oh, sorry, sweetheart, I didn't realise I was interrupting business. I'll see you all tomorrow, then. Kissy, kissy!"

Kate was reminded of the way that her soon-to-be-boss Dr Moran treated poor Betty Troop. She could almost feel the arrogance and dismissive disdain of Jacky's not-so-doting husband oozing from the phone. Could Jacky not hear it? Was she making the best of a bad job or did she really believe that she had a paragon? People's ability to fool themselves where relationships were concerned never failed to astound her. But she was intelligent enough to know that she, too, was part of the self-deluding masses. Only in her case, she realised that she had been denigrating Robin as yet another untrustworthy man instead of rejoicing in his goodness. She and Jacky were at opposite ends of the delusional spectrum.

When Jacky left the room to get a mop-up cloth for the spilt champagne, everyone exchanged glances. Mary whispered, "Just listening to her end of the conversation you could tell he was being horrible to her!"

"I don't think it's going to last much longer," sighed Michelle.

"I don't know. I have a boss who treats his secretary like that all the time and she absolutely adores him. He'll never get rid of her because she massages his ego. It might be the same with Jacky and David," whispered Kate.

Jacky rushed back in and started dabbing damp patches on the carpet. "Luckily, champagne never seems to stain. Or maybe we're just too drunk to see the blotches!"

As the evening progressed, with no phone call from Mark, Sally sank lower into the sofa. She rallied once or twice when something dear to her heart was being talked about, but mostly she was a passenger who watched the night flash by her train window. When the time came for phones and diaries to be produced, she reached listlessly for her shoulder bag. A date was chosen in a week's time and she dutifully wrote it down. There was no enthusiasm from her, unlike the surprised delight that the others felt in commandeering a date so close to this one. They had not envisioned meeting so regularly and they knew the frequency of their reunions would probably fall off in time, but at the moment there seemed to be so much to share that they wanted to meet frequently. Pru offered her flat as the next venue, along with laughing comments about sublime to ridiculous. That decided, they made departure sounds. Hugs, kisses and protestations of lifelong affection buoyed them all to the door. Sally was led to the taxi like a tired child after a party and was bundled in without protest. She didn't speak at all during the journey, and after a while Kate stopped trying to make her respond. When they arrived home, Robin was still up, as promised. He could see at a glance that Sally had reached the bottom of her resources. He wisely desisted from making any fatuous remarks about their evening. Sally checked the machine for messages and trailed listlessly up to bed.

"Tomorrow," said Kate as she watched the sadly ascending figure of her friend, "you've got to find out what's going on!"

Chapter 22

In fact, it was two days before Robin could get hold of Jo. She had taken a couple of sick days, according to her 'Sub'. When she returned, Robin arranged to go over to her building on the pretext of checking some important merger documents with her. There were indeed some queries that he wanted to talk to her about, but frankly they could have been aired over the phone.

"Robin! How nice of you to take the trouble to come over. Tea's on its way. I hope you don't mind if I don't offer you coffee, but the mere smell of it nowadays seems to stimulate barfing!" laughed Jo.

"Who'd be pregnant, eh?" replied Robin.

"Well, I would! I don't mind the slight nausea really. It's well worth it. I'm at First Base already and I can see my way clear round!"

"You sound extremely cheerful. Do I take it that all is

progressing well on the reconciliation front?"

"Absolutely. I'm a respectable married woman again!"

"Aha! The black sheep has been returned to the fold, then?" asked Robin jauntily, matching Jo's mood.

"I know it's much sooner than it should have been, but I just couldn't stand it any longer. I rang him up and I asked him to come round straight away. Then we just fell into each other's arms. It's been like another honeymoon ever since. I can't tell you how happy I am!"

"I think I get the picture! You're absolutely glowing with delight. I'm really glad for you."

"Thanks. Actually, I caught him just in time."

"What do you mean?" asked Robin, fearing that Jo knew about Sally's lonely wait.

"He was just about to write a letter of resignation. If he'd handed that in, he would have been jobless at the end of term just when it was really important that he had a stable income to see me through to the end of the pregnancy. It's his career that's going to be the major one for a while. So his being on the transfer bench would have been disastrous."

"Yes, I see. Of course, they'd probably have let him withdraw his resignation," said Robin.

"I'm not so sure about that. His Head of Department is a bit of a dragon, apparently. Mark says she'd quite like to see him go."

Robin thought that Mark had probably hit on her and all the other female members of the Department. No wonder she'd be pleased to see his departure.

"So it's all settled? You're back together in the matrimonial home and all that?" asked Robin, just to 'cross the eyes and dot the teas' as Kate would say.

"Oh, yes. He moved straight back in that night. He'd been camping out very uncomfortably with a mate of his so he was overjoyed at the prospect of a good night's sleep. Not that we slept much! Whoops! Too much information! I'm sure you don't want to hear all about my love life."

"It's just good to see you happy. Is it too early to ask

about your long-term plans?" asked Robin, wanting to lay as much info as he possibly could at Kate's feet.

"This is absolutely *entre nous*, Robin. I'm going to take my very generous maternity leave, but I'm not coming back at the end of it. Or only for a very short while just to ensure that I don't have to pay anything back! Then it will be Baby Two and move out of noisy old London. We both want to bring up our children in the country, so we'll look for a Head of Department job for Mark further north. I shall become what I've always wanted to be, a full-time mum with lots of gorgeous kids!"

"Complete with jam-making kit! I can see it all!" laughed Robin.

"Bit of a stereotype, isn't it? But to me it sounds blissful."

"Then I hope it will be."

When he arrived home that night, he found Kate in the throes of cooking for the dinner party they had arranged with James and his partner, which Robin had completely forgotten about. He imparted his news as he rolled up his sleeves to attack the vegetables.

"I knew it!" exclaimed Kate. "Being with Sally was better than dossing down on a mate's lumpy mattress, but she was swiftly cast aside when Jo re-opened the door. God, he's a rat of the first order, isn't he? Dice the carrots, love. Shall I roast the parsnips?"

"Only if you coat them with Marmite first - and the roast potatoes, too. Suddenly, I'm starving! The smell of roast beef always reminds me of Sunday din at home when I was a kid. We only had roasts on a Sunday and I looked forward to it all week. Mum made a mean Yorkshire pudding. She used to say that her grandmother told her that when she was a child, she had had that as a starter to the meal, sometimes covered with jam! Can you imagine!" laughed Robin.

"That was to fill them up, I suppose. Then they wouldn't be so hungry when the meat came along. They'd get away with a smaller joint. Good housekeeping if you've got limited money."

"Her mum certainly compensated for it when she was grown up and managing the purse strings and that was carried on to the next generation. We may only have had one joint a week, but it was massive. Looked like half a cow to me!" said Robin, carefully dicing carrots.

"Did you go on having it all week? I remember getting so fed up with cold meat on Monday, mince on Tuesday and soup on Wednesday. Every bloody week!" said Kate.

"My mum sometimes branched out into spag bol or goulash – which we called ghoulish, of course!"

"Very adventurous!"

"But she wasn't very adventurous over the veg. Dear old mum! If the sprouts weren't boiled for ten hours, they weren't cooked!"

"Oh yes, I remember that. Christmas sprouts went on in November. And the smell of cabbage pervading the house every week," agreed Kate.

They heard the front door slam. Sally rushed into the kitchen laden with Marks and Spencer bags.

"Sorry I'm late. I just had to finish marking before I went shopping. Then I was in the wrong queue again – why does that always happen to me? I swear the woman in front of me was a robot on slow speed trying to pay in buttons. Anyway, I've taken the easy way out tonight and bought the pudding. The thought of getting home and trying to whip up a zabaglione didn't appeal. I got a cheesecake, which I know James likes, and a nice selection of smelly cheese. Is that all right?"

"Perfect. We've got ten minutes before they arrive, and everything's done in here. I need to change – I expect you do, too – then it's out with the pretzels and on with the music. Table's all laid, wine's being chilled," said Kate.

"And I'm opening it straight away," said Robin, heading for the fridge.

By the time the women came downstairs, Robin had filled glasses for all three of them. They only had time for a toast to the success of the evening before the bell sounded. Robin felt slightly apprehensive: he'd met James, under rather unusual circumstances as 'minders' to Sal, but he knew virtually nothing about Lloyd. All Sally had said was that he was "absolutely lovely", which didn't convey too much to Robin, and that he directed plays. Oh well, he thought, all to find out! The large figure of James fell into the room first, followed closely by a tall and very handsome man. Robin immediately thought of Don Quixote as he surveyed the greying hair and goatee beard which decorated – there was no other word for it – the face of Lloyd. An elegant black linen suit, Nehru style, completed the picture. Robin found himself shaking a be-ringed hand and gazing into startling blue eyes. It was all slightly camp but not excessively so. James wore jeans and a checked shirt, which might have looked too casual had the shirt not been ironed to perfection and the jeans virtually new and expensive-looking. They made a very attractive couple, thought Robin. He felt Lloyd's appraising eyes on his work suit, which he had not had time to change, and wondered briefly if he should excuse himself to nip upstairs and don something more fashionable. He then realised that Lloyd's blue eyes were actually appraising the ample muscles beneath the suit! It was a compliment, he thought, without being flirtatious. Bottles and chocs were accepted, glasses poured and greetings exchanged before they all sat down comfortably.

"Sweet Geezers! I've had one of those days," sighed James. "I was just telling Lloyd in the car. Only he stopped me so that he wouldn't have to endure listening to it twice."

Lloyd laughed. "I don't remember mentioning the word 'endure' – although it might well have been on the tip of my tongue!"

"Do tell us," said Kate. "I always find that it helps to burden everyone else with my troubles!"

"Well, it all started to unravel at morning registration. Jenny Anydots arrived just as the pips went for the first period."

"That can't be a real name," interposed Robin.

"No, it's Enditz, but James has pet names for most of his form," replied Sally.

"She hurtled in with this story about her father being sick, which elicited heartfelt sympathy from me and an enquiry about his diagnosis. It turned out that when she said 'sick', she really meant it. Literally. All over her homework, apparently. The worst aspect of it was that the homework was for me – an essay on Romeo and Juliet."

"Ah, lovesick!" quipped Lloyd.

"She proceeded to reach into her bag and I had a nightmare vision of pages festooned with diced carrot. Fortunately, it was merely a note from Mrs Anydots to explain the lack of homework."

"I don't know how you stand it," said Lloyd. "At least with adults you only have to suffer their own outpourings, not their parents' too."

"Do I take it that you teach at a college?" asked Kate.

"Indeed. I'm in Adult Ed, for my sins. I teach Drama," replied Lloyd.

"Ah, I thought Sally had said something about directing. I suppose you do productions with your students. That must be … interesting," said Robin.

"I notice your hesitation," smiled Lloyd. "Yes, 'interesting' is one word for it. Another might be 'painful' or even 'agonising' at times. There's a Chinese curse, isn't there, which says 'May you live in interesting times!'"

"Take no notice of him. He loves every minute of it. But attention back to me, please. Period 1 was passable, but Period 2 was Poetry with Year 7. Why do so many littlies come to us from Primary wanting poetry to rhyme all the time? Any old word will do as long as it rhymes! We were thinking about weather, so of course you get all sorts of matches for 'colder' – you know, bolder, shoulder, older. But today we had: 'The winter was colder, the sun was golder.' Cross-questioning (very cross) elicited that young Wayne thought the sun became more golden in the crisp cold of the winter months. And no amount of persuasion would have him write 'more golden' because it didn't rhyme. The whole class agreed with him so I was fighting a losing whatnot. It ain't poetry if it don't rhyme!"

"I think they may have a great career in advertising ahead of them," said Robin. "We're always looking for rhymes. All God's chillun got shoes, and all good jingles got rhymes."

"I shall in future pass the best on to you for your delectation and delight," said James.

"It doesn't sound a bad day so far," prompted Sally, handing round the pretzels.

"That's because it hasn't quite reached its nadir. That acclamation must be reserved for my Sixth Formers destroying 'Hamlet.' Toby Macdonald had the effrontery…"

"Oh no!" laughed Lloyd. "Toby or not Toby…" he declaimed.

"As I was saying, Toby had the effrontery to suggest that Hamlet was a poofter – his word – and that was why he couldn't make his mind up to act because, of course, all poofters are cowards."

"Limp-wristed, too. Makes it hard to hold the sword," added Lloyd.

"You wouldn't believe the sexist rubbish that ensued. It turned into a full-scale attack on gays. Or, rather, on 'homophones', as Toby called them."

"Sounds right!" quipped Lloyd.

"Do they know you're gay?" asked Robin.

"Not openly. It's difficult to come out as a teacher nowadays – some would have it that that constituted promoting homosexuality. So it was a tough lesson to get through. I don't actually think it matters whether Hamlet's homosexual or not. It's often argued that his mother's hasty jump into Claudius's bed stimulated a latent misogyny and made him realise he's gay – hence his rejecting Ophelia so brutally. Well-argued, it can be a fascinating discussion. Unfortunately, we couldn't get round to viewing it intellectually. We just got outpourings of homophobic trash from boys who aren't too sure of their own sexuality and are terrified that they might be gay themselves!"

"Now they've got it off their chests and made sure everyone knows they're acceptably macho, they'll be able to look at it more coolly. You'll see," said Sally reassuringly.

"Watch this space," said James, unconvinced.

"We've got time for all of us to have one moan about our day before we go through to the table," said Kate in organising mode. "All right? Can I go first? Then I can disappear to the kitchen and do cooky things. My bad bit was my needing to make a decision about my job: whether to stay on as Senior Secretary under a new Head of Unit whom I loathe, or let my colleague take it on. She adores him, so although she doesn't really want the responsibility she also doesn't want to lose him. I should explain that I work in a psychiatric clinic where the clients are all adolescents and the psychiatrists and psychotherapists share the secretarial time of two of us, me and my assistant. The senior secretary, me, looks after the Head of Unit. I've been really happy with that, but my man is retiring and the guy stepping into his shoes is a big-headed prat."

"Don't hold back – come right out with it!" laughed Sally.

"Adolescents, eh? Watch out for the name Toby Macdonald!" said James. "What was your decision?"

"I decided to stand down. It means I'll take a drop in salary so it's a big step. A big step backwards."

"But you'll be a lot happier," said Robin supportively. "That's far more important than mere money."

"O.K. I'm convinced! Now your turn while I work my magic in the culinary sphere."

"Need help?" asked Sally.

"In a minute. I'll give you a call."

Kate departed and Robin took up the complaints mantle.

"Mine's job related, too," he said. "We were told today that the merger with another Ad Agency will mean redundancies, even though we were promised that that wouldn't happen. We're all looking at one another with speculative eyes. It's not a good work atmosphere. We all feel we should have been told the truth."

"An advertising agency telling lies?" said Sally, mock-horrified. "Whatever next? Perhaps we ought to include that in our Media course."

"You mean you don't already?" asked Robin innocently.

"Yes, of course we do, Robin dear. We just study it as 'persuasive language' instead."

"What was the low point of your day, Lloyd?" asked Robin, not wanting to get into a castigation of his profession when he knew that he would have no-one to support him.

"I suppose it would have to be one of my actors dropping out of my production of 'A Midsummer Night's Dream'," sighed Lloyd.

"The Bottom dropping out of your world?" asked James

mischievously.

"Actually, it was Oberon. He totalled his bike last night and wasn't wearing a crash helmet. Fortunately, it's not too bad, but he won't be treading the boards."

"A case of 'No helmet by moonlight, proud Titania'," intoned James. "What about you, Sally?"

"Oh, just about everything, really," she began.

Kate called through from the kitchen that she was about to bring in the fatted calf and needed help to transport the vegetables.

"Let's go through to dinner before I get the chance to bore you all," said Sally, leading the way into the dining room as Robin hurried to help Kate.

James and Lloyd sat where they were told and commented on the luxury of having linen napkins instead of paper ones. Kate carried in the joint triumphantly and plonked it in Robin's place.

"Now help yourselves to veg while Robin carves," she

said.

"I'm a hopeless carver," said Lloyd. "James always says it's like watching Dr Livingstone machete his way through the jungle."

"Carving was a sacred art in our family," said Robin, "passed down from father to son. When I reached dubious maturity at the age of sixteen, my father gave me the carving knife and fork and told me to 'Be a man, my son.' It was a rite of passage."

"I've never like Kipling," said Lloyd.

"I've never kippled," giggled Kate. "Though I'm told it's ruddy 'ard!"

"Whoever said that old ones were the best ones?" asked Robin. "Now, to maintain this jovial mood – ho, ho – we must all come up with a good thing that's happened to us today. I'll go first. I've been assured that my job's safe in the coming re-shuffle!"

"And he believes them! Bless!" said Kate. "My best bit was very simple. Betty Troop, my secretarial colleague, called me 'Kate' today."

"That needs some explaining. Is she mentally retarded and remembering your name was a triumph? Does she usually call you 'Fred'? Do enlighten us," said James.

"She has a pathological reluctance to say anyone's name. I'm always her 'little colleague' or something. So saying 'Kate' is a mark of acceptance and respect."

"The katemark!" laughed Robin, doling out expertly cut beef slices.

"My outstanding moment was finding a better Oberon than the one who crashed out. There was a real chemistry between him and Titania. It's going to be all right," said Lloyd.

"That's Lloyd-speak for marvellous," explained James. "Choosing my best would probably be another moment from that same A Level lesson. Jug-eared Toby opined at one point that he was conservative with a small 'c', to which lovely Amanda said, 'Well, something with a small 'c' anyway.' I shall give her a Distinction, whatever the quality of her prose."

"And you, Sally? The best part of your day?" asked

Lloyd.

"That would have to be right here and now," said Sally.

"Flatterer!" said Lloyd. "It must also be a relief to know exactly where you stand with Mark, now that he's definitely returned to his wife."

His words dropped into the conversation like a pebble thrown into a still pond: the ripples gradually touched the whole expanse of water. After several beats of silence, Lloyd realised that he had said too much too soon. "Sorry. Not my place to… I just thought… Damn and blast!"

"What exactly do you mean?" asked Sally, putting down her fork and looking with narrowed eyes at the benighted Lloyd.

James came to his rescue, explaining he had heard that afternoon from a friend in Mark's school that a reconciliation had taken place.

"And just when did this happen?" pursued Sally.

"The night of the Parents' Evening," replied James uncomfortably. "Sorry, Vol."

"I'm getting quite used to being the last to know about momentous decisions in my own life," said Sally bleakly.

"My fault. I should have given Lloyd more information – or none," said James.

"Don't start blaming yourselves. Believe me, someone would have told me soon enough – and I'd much rather hear it in the company of friends. In a crazy sort of way, it is a relief to know, Lloyd. My life's been like a demented lift for some months now. I press Ground Floor and want to get off, then find myself going up again to the top – symbolising my Heaven, my zenith, a possible life with Mark. I'm dizzy with excitement. I'm almost there, when suddenly I'm plummeting down again. I've been stuck between floors for a couple of days. And no doubt I'll be heading for the Basement tomorrow when it all sinks in properly."

"Well, it's our job to keep you on the Ground Floor for a while," said Kate. "Feet on the ground, and all that."

"Before we launch you into the upper reaches of the store. Women's Lingerie!" said James.

"And he talks about others being sexist!" said Sally. "Oh, come on, everybody. If I'm honest, I knew this was going to happen. As soon as he didn't turn up for me, I knew. I just wish he'd had the courage and decency to tell me himself."

"I propose a toast: to the liberated Sally. May she live to look back with relief on her escape from servitude and despair," said James.

"To Women's Lingerie!" said Sally, smiling bravely.

Chapter 23

Kate arrived at work early next day. She realised that she had to make known her decision about the job. She was resolved to let Betty Troop take the senior secretarial post and stay with Dr Moran. It sounded terribly unselfish but actually Kate knew that she couldn't work with the man and stay sane. What she didn't want, however, was for Betty to think that Kate was making a magnanimous gesture. Betty feeling constantly beholden would be irksome, to say the least. Having finally got her to say 'Kate', she didn't want to slide back into being the 'little colleague' again – or worse, she thought with a start, as it could become 'generous little colleague' accompanied by Uriah Heap hand-rubbing. She had to make sure that Betty knew it was a positive choice to take the more junior role. How to do that would take some quiet contemplation, hence the early-to-work stratagem.

It did not work out quite the way she had planned. When she arrived, Dr Tailor was already there. He must have been clearing up his files and case notes, she thought. How typically kind and professional it was of him to want to leave everything in good order. Kate offered to help him and he accepted gratefully.

"I'm consigning the really ancient case notes to strong cardboard boxes which I shall endeavour to store in my attic. I can't quite allow myself to jettison them," he said ruefully.

"The boxes are going to be awfully heavy. Won't you need some help transporting them?" Kate asked.

"Is that a veiled offer of assistance, my dear?"

"Well, my partner…"

"Robin," he broke in.

"Yes, Robin would consider it a simple work-out, so you wouldn't be imposing at all."

"In that case, I shall gratefully accept. Dr Moran has offered but I think his motivation is to free more space for himself rather than having any sympathy for my plight," he smiled.

"Well, he's got to make room for all those books he's going to write, hasn't he? I wonder if the world is quite ready for his learned outpourings."

"Now, now, my dear. I'm sure Dr Moran has many valuable insights to impart to the unsuspecting public."

"Poor Betty!" laughed Kate.

"Surely it will be your burden as senior secretary?"

"Ah, well... um... The thing is, I've decided to swap jobs with Betty. She's really good as Dr Moran's secretary. She knows all his little idiosyncracies and she just loves working for him. It seems eminently logical to allow that to continue. I'd be much happier, too. I would always be making unflattering comparisons with you and getting discontented. I shall really miss you. It's been a privilege to work for you. Oh, lawks-a-mercy, I'm getting quite tearful here. Sorry!"

"Thank you, Kate. What a lovely thing to say."

They worked quietly for a while, each contemplating the admirable qualities of the other.

"You know, I've been wondering for some time if I could ask you to do some private work for me," ventured Dr Tailor. "I had decided not to ask simply because I had thought that Dr Moran's workload might be overwhelming, but if you really are sure that you want the junior post then perhaps you might feel able to accept some work for my private practice. I shall be expanding it once I retire from the clinic and my wife doesn't want to take on any more. She services my private work at the moment, you see. What do you think?"

Kate knew that Dr Tailor had a private practice but she had assumed that retirement meant that he would be cutting back rather than expanding it.

"In fact... Oh, I don't want this to sound as if I'm a professional head-hunter, but actually my wife would love to hand over all the practice's workload to someone else. If you felt that you might like to transfer your skills to my Hampstead home full time, I should be delighted."

Kate sat down with a thump. She felt the beginnings of joy bubbling up inside her. She had dreaded Dr Tailor's leaving, not only because she disliked the bumptious Dr Moran but also because she really appreciated Dr Tailor, both as a 'boss' and as a person. Handing in her notice at the clinic would also provide an easy way for Betty to step legitimately into the senior role.

"I'd be delighted, too," she said, beaming. "Thank you very much."

"That is splendid news. My wife will be much relieved. It was she who thought I should approach you and she has been chipping away at my misplaced ethical reluctance for weeks. You see, I thought it was not altogether moral for me to offer you an alternative post. I'm not at all sure how Dr Moran will view it."

"Actually, I think he'll be pleased. He's so used to Betty massaging his ego. I shouldn't really say that, but I'm sure you are aware of Betty's ..." She stopped, looking for the right word to sum up Betty's feelings.

"Devotion?" offered Dr Tailor. "Yes, I know what you mean. You may well be right. Your acerbic quality – which I value as a means of keeping me safely tethered to the sensible high ground – would perhaps be more of an irritant to him. Let us trust that all will work out for the best for everybody."

"In the best of all possible worlds!" added Kate. "Very 'Candide'."

"Now, are you sure? Perhaps you would appreciate more time to consider."

"I'm sure. I think the possibility of leaving the clinic must have been sloshing around in my head without my recognising it, because as soon as you suggested it, I knew it was what I wanted."

Meanwhile, Sally had been equally early getting into school. Kate's morning ablutions and attacks on the kitchen cupboards in search of breakfast had woken her and, having woken, she didn't want to spend time in pensive reflection on her own misery. She had always been an optimist, and the now-inevitable break with Mark would sorely test her natural resilience. She had determined to get up and out and into work so that her mind would not wander into the uncharted waters of despair. The English Department office was untidy but it had a certain charm and there were definitely no uncharted waters. Sally sat at her desk and looked at the list of reports that she needed to tackle. How strange, she thought. Normally the idea of reports made her wince visibly; but right now they provided a therapeutic focus. She preferred still to write them in longhand before using the computer program. She found that her thoughts flowed more smoothly through hand and pen, probably because the act of writing was itself a smooth motion rather than the jerky tapping of the computer keys. However, she had hardly started before James burst onto the scene, overcoat undone and scarf flying.

"Vol, don't tell me you've moved in to this what-a-dump place! You haven't been here all night, have you? It is surely impossible to contemplate anyone arising before me! The veritable crack of dawn! Whose desk did you kip under?"

"Actually, I slept on top of yours. Can't you see how rumpled the sheets are," Sally laughed.

"Those sheets are merely well-thumbed. The surface of my desk is the physical embodiment of my mind…" James began.

"Untidy and flamboyant?"

"Many-layered and gaily caparisoned. And certainly not anally retentive, as some un-named person's overly tidy space shows abundant evidence of."

"Ha! You ended with a preposition!" trilled Sally.

"I think that more than proves my point," replied James. "Now, first things first: Lloyd and I had the most wonderful time last night and we thank you copiously."

"It was great, wasn't it?"

"Secondly, have you gunned the kettle into action?"

"Not yet. But I wouldn't say no to a coffee if you're making one."

"Bloomineck!" exclaimed James. "There's no milk. It will have to be black."

"Fine, as long as there's honey to go in it," said Sally.

"Let's see: 'And is there honey still for coffee?'" he intoned. "It doesn't have the same ring to it, does it?"

"Why are you here so early, James? Don't tell me your day is unprepared!"

"Metaphorical finger-wagging? If you must know, Vol of my heart, I am indeed somewhat under-prepared. Lloyd and I had quite a session last night."

"T.M.I." interposed Sally. "Keep your sexual fumblings to yourself!"

"That's exactly what Lloyd said. No, no, rest assured. There will be no startling revelation to cause a maiden blush. I merely meant that we talked ad infin-night-time."

"Happily? Productively?" enquired Sally.

"Indeed to goodness. We started off talking about you and ended up analysing our own relationship. It was very satisfactory."

"It's nice to know that I'm still a useful object over which to leapfrog."

"Sorry, Vol. That didn't quite come out right. We were very sympathetic to your pain, believe me, but you know how it is: other people's sadness throws your own joy into sharper relief. We realised how fortunate we were. Sorry – I'm making this worse!"

"Only opening your mouth to change feet, you mean?"

"Something like that."

Sally sighed. "It's all right. I'm pleased if I've shown you how lucky you are. Honest, guv!"

"We investigated my green-eyed monster and he did his best to reassure me. But I know it's going to be really hard imagining him with all those gorgeous young actors that he can manipulate to his will."

"His willy?"

"La, milady, thou dost lower the tone somefink awful!"

"Lloyd obviously adores you. It shone from his every pore," insisted Sally.

"I just want those paws all over me."

"Steady, Fido. You won't be able to concentrate on 9B."

"Do you really think he loves me?" asked James, with more seriousness than Sally had expected.

"I truly do," she replied with equal candour. "What do you think?"

"I hardly dare think it, let alone voice it," he said quietly. "But I do think it."

"And now you have voiced it."

"The Monty Python foot doesn't seem to be squashing me for my audacity."

"The ground certainly doesn't seem to be opening up to swallow you."

"Careful, now. I've studied too many Greek tragedies to want to tempt the gods too much. One buskinned step at a time!"

"Weren't they for comedy?"

"Let's hope so!"

Chapter 24

Getting through the week was a struggle for all of them. At school, James was still apologetic because Lloyd had spoken too soon about the Mark revelation but Sally gradually reassured him that she really had anticipated the situation and did not hold any grudge. In fact, she said, she had really enjoyed his company and was confident that their friendship was going to last and grow. Sally seemed genuinely to have come to terms with 'the end of the affair' but then she would regress into a panic over where her life was going and this would send her spinning. First she decided that she was going to stay in her home and in her job; then the thought of the ghost of Mark living alongside her and the fear that all her colleagues might soon know absolutely everything made her want to leave it all behind and go somewhere far-flung and exotic. However, she was sensible enough not to carry out any hasty plans.

Kate meanwhile had a difficult time at the Clinic. No-one could believe that she was voluntarily leaving her job. Betty Troop was convinced that Kate was sacrificing herself to allow Betty to stay close to Dr Moran; Dr Moran was incredulous that she should be turning down the inestimable opportunity to work with him as the new Senior Clinician and concluded that Kate must be reluctant to work as hard as he would require; Dr Tailor kept politely quiet. Robin picked his way carefully through rumours of sackings and redundancies over the prospective merger, and each day seemed to provide reasons to hope or despair about jobs and accounts.

On the evening of the next Reunited Rendezvous, Sally and Kate chose plain clothes in deference to Pru's obvious nervousness about people who 'dressed up'.

"I hope Jacky doesn't do the Christmas tree option again. Baubles would definitely be out of place at Pru's," said Kate.

"Smart casual is the order of the evening – or even casual casual. What will you wear?" asked Sally.

"Got any paint-splattered jeans? No, I didn't mean that. Pru only wore what she'd been painting in because she ran out of time, I know. I don't mean to hurt."

"But you do, Alfie, you do," quoted Sally.

"New leaf. I promise I won't be acerbic at all this evening," assured Kate, then added, "I'll save it all up until tomorrow."

"Gee, thanks. Will jeans be all right?"

"As long as Jean doesn't mind if you wear them and as long as you haven't ironed a crease down the front."

"I'll leave that to Jacky. Whoops, hush my mouth! Now who's being acerbic?"

"Have you been to Pru's place, Sal? When you returned her notebook, did you go there?"

"No, we met at my flat, so I've no idea what her place is like. I imagine it's rather bohemian and arty."

"Joss sticks and candles, you mean? I suppose it rather depends on her guy. I mean, his personality will be stamped all over the place as well. We'll just have to wait and see."

Robin had volunteered to run them over to Pru's and to pick them up as well so that they could drink without driving or needing a taxi. When they arrived, it was Mary who opened the door. Smoke was billowing behind her.

"Sorry about this. Pru decided to prove to us all how domesticated she was but then she got stuck into another chapter and forgot all about the cake she was so lovingly and uncharacteristically baking! We're going to pretend that the smell is joss sticks, though we haven't actually used them since our bohemian days."

Kate and Sally exchanged a smile as they were ushered into the living room. The walls were spectacular and drew exclamations from them both: a collage of magazine snippets, chosen for their colours and artistically juxtaposed, covered all the walls and were a feast for the eyes. Blues shaded into turquoise, yellows into lime, lilacs into purple. The actual pictures were irrelevant as the shades of colour were the whole point of the arrangements.

"Wow! This must have taken ages to put together," exclaimed Kate. "It's wonderful. Highly idiosyncratic."

"Brave!" said Sally. "Not everyone could get away with this, but I think it's splendid. It really works."

"Mind you, it reminds me a bit of Joe Orton and Kenneth Halliwell. Halliwell decorated their place with illustrations cut out of library books, didn't he?" said Kate. "Let's hope we don't have the same conclusion here!"

"Indeed," agreed Mary mock seriously. "Splatters of crimson would ruin the colour scheme."

"Gruesome!"

Mary laughed. "If you look carefully, you'll see that there are poems in amongst the colours," explained Mary. "Pru's, of course."

Pru rushed in and hugged them. "I'm nearly with you! I've just got to don the motley. Make yourselves at home."

With that, she vanished with a whiff if not a puff of smoke. She re-emerged minutes later in a multi-hued jumper that was reassuringly quirky.

"I've got to be seen to be artistic," she laughed. "Don't tell anyone, but my mum knitted it. Her eyesight's not what it was so she now produces these strange colour combinations without realising that at last she's accommodating my eccentric taste. She has no idea that she's created something fit for the artist that she wishes I wasn't!"

When they settled themselves in the over-stuffed sofa and chairs, Sally turned to Mary and asked, "How are Gil and Conrad?"

"Both well, thank you. Gil and I are getting on like the proverbial house on fire at the moment. It makes me wonder why we ever bothered to get divorced!"

"I can answer that," said Pru. "When you were tied to each other, you were always getting in each other's way and resenting the freedom you thought the other one had."

"That's so true. It seems crazy now, but every time that Gil went out I found that there were myriads of things I needed to do that required me to go out and then I got really angry when he wouldn't change his plans and stay in with Conrad. I'm sure with hindsight that I did it deliberately, trying to assert the importance of my life and my career. Maybe I thought I was being a feminist. I don't know. Of course, he was doing the same thing, asserting himself by resenting my times out."

"Was Conrad aware of all these manoeuvres?"

"Kids are like little sponges, aren't they? They soak up whatever is around. We weren't aware of his prescience until we realised that he was acting as a referee. 'Mum, it's Dad's turn to go out tonight' or 'Dad, Mum had to take me to the dentist last time' and so on. He was so damned sensible that it made us feel ashamed. It was as if we were the kids and he was the adult."

"That's when you decided to stop living together," said Pru. "Mind you, I'm still not sure why you felt the need to divorce rather than just live separately."

"It seemed fairer. Neither of us could have started a new relationship if we had had to explain constantly that we were still technically married. I mean, how many men have used the old 'My wife doesn't understand me' line?"

There was a momentary silence, followed by Mary's attempt to apologise for her gaff while Sally tried to reassure her that she wasn't upset.

"I just didn't want Gil to have to fill that stereotype. It wasn't a true picture of who he was."

"And Conrad was all right with it?" asked Kate, steering the focus of the conversation to the child rather than the parents.

"He was unbelievably clear-eyed. He said he had such a nice time with me when he was with me, and with Gil when he was there, that he was glad he didn't have to struggle with times like those when we had been together!"

"He actually said 'struggle'?" asked Kate.

"He's a very articulate child," replied Pru. "Probably because he has me for a godmother!"

The doorbell announced the next arrival, which alerted Pru to the fact that she hadn't offered her first guests a drink as yet. Mary was given the task of putting that right while Pru went to the door. The arrival turned out to be plural as Michelle and Jacky arrived together. Michelle, casually elegant in denim, led a dishevelled Jacky in by the hand, whose appearance was doubly shocking in contrast. Her hair was wild and her dress was creased. What make-up she wore had been applied hurriedly and probably the day before. She looked bewildered. Michelle led her solicitously to a chair and indicated that wine was a medical necessity. Mary hurriedly filled a glass and pressed it into Jacky's trembling hand.

"Has there been an accident?" asked Pru, because that was the conclusion that they had all separately come to on seeing Jacky's obvious shock.

"Would you like me to tell everyone?" whispered Michelle, kneeling at Jacky's feet.

Jacky nodded miserably as she took her first gulps of wine.

"Jack's husband David has run off with his bloody P.A."

"The one who was helping him look after the children when we were all together last time?" asked Sally, aghast.

"The very one. She obviously proved to be invaluable, the little darling," snarled Michelle.

Jacky began to cry, quietly at first but soon with great hiccupping sobs. She was immediately surrounded by her sympathetic friends. Sally stroked the hand not holding the wine glass, careful even then about the possibility of a spill; Michelle, still at her feet, eased off her grubby shoes; Kate brushed away the wayward hair from her face; Mary supplied her with a handy box of tissues; Pru left to answer the door and admit Lyn, informing her succinctly about the situation while hanging her coat over the bannisters.

"The world is full of bastards," philosophised Lyn.

"Why didn't I see it coming?" sobbed Jacky disconsolately. "How did I miss the signs?"

"You have a sweet and trusting nature, darling," replied Michelle.

"You mean I'm a blind fool!"

"No, I don't mean that at all. You trusted him completely and that makes his betrayal even worse. He took advantage of your innocence."

Pru and Mary brought plates of neatly cut sandwiches

and bowls overflowing with crisps from the kitchen, figuring that this might well be a long night needing constant re-fuelling.

"I couldn't eat a thing," moaned Jacky, proceeding to chew her way through several sandwiches at once.

"Funny how emotional occasions make you ravenous," said Kate, smiling indulgently at Jacky.

"Did I neglect him?" asked Jacky.

"Of course not. You couldn't have been more attentive to his needs," assured Michelle.

"You mean I was a doormat!" wailed Jacky, grabbing a handful of crisps.

Kate remembered that that was exactly what she had thought about Jacky, but she would not have dreamt of saying so at this juncture.

"Perhaps I put the kiddies first when I should have concentrated on my hubby," bemoaned Jacky, reaching for another sandwich.

"Children should always come first," pontificated Lyn,

entering the conversation for the first time. "You mustn't blame yourself for that."

"But hubbies need their egos massaged. Don't you think so?" asked Jacky uncertainly.

"I'd massage his bloody ego," snarled Kate, "and then I'd kick his balls!"

Jacky giggled and then started to choke on her wine, spilling some down her awful dress.

"Now look what I've done. All down my best dress."

"Remind me to take you shopping, ma petite," said Michelle, "as soon as possible."

"When did all this happen?" asked Mary, refilling Jacky's now-empty glass.

"Yesterday. All my troubles seemed so far away. Macca understood the hurts of the heart," slurred Jacky. "I believe in yesterday, too. I wish I could go back and do it all again, only better this time. I'd get it right instead of making a mess of it."

"For God's sake, Jack, you didn't do anything wrong," exploded Lyn. "HE did. Don't forget there's another SHE involved, too. It takes two to tangle."

"Don't you mean tango?" said Mary.

"We know what she means!" chorused Kate and Sally.

"What a bitch!" squealed Jacky. "How could she do it? A married man with kiddies!"

Sally hung her head and bit back an instinctive defence of 'the other woman'. Lyn, however, seemed intent on forcing Sally to face the lying husband situation, holding up a metaphorical mirror to her soul. "What do you think now, Sally?"

Kate was about to come to her rescue but Sally found that Lyn's mirror was exactly what she needed to see her own life in perspective. What indeed had she been thinking, getting involved with a man who was already married? She shook her head miserably, but before she could say anything, Mary was asking Jacky what was happening to the children. That seemed to be a question much more worthy of examination at that moment.

"My babies!" wailed Jacky and was then unable to go on.

"David wants them to go to Prep school," intervened Michelle, "and then on to Public School. It's what he's always planned."

"Threatened, you mean!" erupted Jacky with a sweeping gesture of her fortunately empty glass. "He knows I don't want them sent away. It's barbaric."

"It's the education he had, darling, and he always insists that it never did him any harm."

A chorus of scoffing noises filled the room.

"I agree with Jacky," said Pru. "It's barbaric. I've never understood why the moneyed classes are so keen to send their kids into the care of strangers."

"It breeds the captains of industry, dear. The shortest cut to a highly paid job is the old school tie."

"But they're my babes," wept Jacky, holding out her glass for more while reaching for the crisps with her free hand.

"The Courts will make sure you have full access to them,

poppet. But the judge who's wearing the same old school tie will almost certainly decree that the Public School favoured by Daddy will be advantageous to their upbringing. It never did him any harm, either!" said Michelle.

They all took time to sip or gulp as they contemplated the English education system with various degrees of bitterness.

"Maybe he'll come back anyway," hiccupped Jacky.

"You surely don't want the bastard?" asked an affronted Lyn. "This is your chance to stand on your own two feet. Who needs a man who doesn't appreciate them? No, Jack, you and I are sisters on the road to self-discovery, man-less and glad of it!"

Kate glanced at Pru, both of them thinking that this said more about Lyn's present situation than her appraisal of Jacky's. Lyn clinked glasses with a doubtful Jacky and urged her to drink some more anaesthetic. Jacky did so then leaned back in her chair, murmuring that she was very tired, and promptly passed out.

"I thought this would happen," sighed Michelle. "She didn't sleep at all last night, trying to get David to pick up the phone and talk to her; and today she's had virtually no food until coming here. The wine has gone straight to her sad little head."

"It may do her good. It's an enforced sleep. We can put her to bed here and I have a feeling that she won't wake up till morning," said Pru.

"Shall we leave her where she is for now?" suggested Mary. "It seems a shame to disturb her and she won't hear anything we say anyway."

"Poor old Jacky. To think that only a week ago she thought she was the one who had the best life," sighed Sally.

"You knew something was amiss, though, didn't you, Michelle?" said Kate.

"I'm afraid so. I saw David and what's-her-face cosying

up in the office. She ticked all the boxes that Jackie left blank."

"Such as?"

"Dress sense. Social ease. Knowledge of the firm. I.Q. Sexiness."

"Yes, but apart from that?" scoffed Lyn.

"She was probably a chess grand master as well," said Kate.

"Grand mistress, in her case!"

"Poor Jacky. Her qualities of love and loyalty were dwarfed by the more obvious contents of the P.A.'s bra," said Michelle.

"Bloody men!" spat Kate.

"Except Robin," urged Sally.

"And Seb," said Pru.

"And Peter," said Michelle.

"And, I suppose, Gil," sighed Mary.

"To say nothing of my apology for a partner. And that's what I will say about him: nothing," said Lyn.

"There you are. They're not all bad."

"No, parts of them are very nice," giggled Kate.

"What shall we do about Jacky?" asked Sally solicitously.

"All we can do is to give her support when she needs it," said Michelle.

"And take her out for chocolate cake," added Lyn.

All eyes turned to her beaming face and they realised that she was actually eating rather than pushing food around her plate.

"Is this a change of heart that I see before me?" asked Pru. "I thought you and food didn't have a close relationship."

"My little stay in hospital has opened my eyes."

"And your mouth!"

"I am a new woman," Lyn said grandly. "I intend to eat sensibly and settle into my natural shape. Then I'm going to be accepted as who I am not what I am." She paused. "I don't even know if that makes sense."

"You mean you'll allow yourself to be normal, without trying to mould yourself into some skinny shape that we're told is the ideal. It may be the ideal clothes horse but it sure ain't a real woman!" said Pru.

"Here's to real women!" they chorused. "And all the real men who sail in them!"

"I wonder where we'll all be in a year's time," mused Lyn. "Will I still be looking for the real me-sized person?"

"Will my mother have regained some of her natural joie-de-vivre?" asked Michelle.

"Will I be a bit less dismissive of men?" queried Kate.

"Will I be published?" Pru wondered.

Mary ventured "Will Gil and I still be happily apart but together?"

"The only definite is that I shall be footloose and fancy free – an un-Marked woman - and we shall still be meeting each other!" finished Sally with certainty. "So here's to new horizons!"

"New horizons!"

Printed in Poland
by Amazon Fulfillment
Poland Sp. z o.o., Wrocław

51059414R00282